g st
Duke

Louise Allen

First edition 2017.

A version of the Prologue to this novel was originally published as a short story in *Love Me, Love Me Not,* an anthology by the Romantic Novelists' Association, published by MIRA (2009).

Cover design by JD Smith Design.

Requests to publish extracts from this book should be made via www.louiseallenregency.com/contact

Author's Note

Loving the Lost Duke began as a short story – *Guinea Gold* – which appeared in the Romantic Novelists' Association anthology *Loves Me, Loves Me Not* in 2009.

I am indebted to fellow author Jan Jones for the suggestion that I develop this into a full length novel featuring Sophie. The original short story, slightly edited, forms the Prologue to this new novel and the beginning of a whole new series – *Dangerous Deceptions.*

Prologue – Where An Old Love Rekindles

'Your daughter is very lovely is she not? You are to be congratulated Lady Wilmott.'

Thea looked up at the tall stranger who had strolled into the chaperones' corner. 'Why thank you, sir, but I can claim little credit, except perhaps for her colouring. Sophie must claim the praise for her sweetness and her grace.' This was no time for reticence or false modesty, not when a young lady was to be launched upon her first Season. But who was the admiring gentleman, other than an elegant sophisticate at least twice Sophie's seventeen years?

'You do not recognise me, ma'am?' He smiled and something flashed through her memory from long ago. Laughter, a tear or two, a hesitant kiss, a clumsy boy of her own age with feet and hands still to grow into.

'Perhaps...' Thea shook her head. 'You remind me of a young man from my first Season when I was just Sophie's age. Lucas Randall…' His mouth curved again into a mischievous look that sliced away the years at a stroke and she gasped. 'Why, it *is* you! And you are grown up – oh, what a foolish thing to say, of course you are, it must be all of eighteen years since we last… met.'

And how unfair it was that a gangling youth grows up to this fine maturity, to a man in his prime, with the silver at his temples lending gravitas and the lines at the corners of his eyes adding charm, when for a woman of thirty six those first betraying flags of age merely rendered them invisible.

'You joined the diplomatic service did you not?' So long ago, those unspoken messages sent in a glance, a touch. Nothing said, nothing that gave her the lie when her papa had asked, *There is no one else you have set your cap at I trust, my dear?*

'I did.' He stood beside her spindly gilt chair, relaxed, his eyes following the laughing girl down the length of the set. 'I was posted abroad and I stayed abroad – India to Spain to the West Indies and lately, Brazil. England seems the foreign country now.'

'But you are back for good?' How warm it was, the long ballroom so crowded, so noisy, so brightly lit. Her fan was little help, not for the colour in her cheeks, not for the drumming in her pulse.

'Indeed. I have been honoured with the title of Viscount Elmham, with lands marching with my own small inherited estate. It is time to settle down.'

'And to raise a family?'

'Yes. Of course, one requires a wife for that pleasant duty.'

Close to them Sophie laughed and paused in the measure, chattering to her partner while they waited for their turn to promenade. Her partner seemed dazzled.

'My father always held that a man in his thirties should marry a girl before she is twenty, that it is a very suitable age difference,' Thea remarked. *I know my duty as a mother: marry my daughter in her first Season and marry her well.*

'You followed his guidance yourself of course, Lady Wilmott.'

'Yes. Papa was always wise in matters of that kind.' *Wise and firm and always well-meaning.*

Lucas opened his dance card and glanced at it. His fingers were as brown, as long, as she remembered, but now his whole body was grown and muscled and those big hands fitted. She was staring. Thea made herself look away, stirring uneasily on the hard upholstery.

'There is a waltz shortly, I believe.'

So, he had asked. Now all that would follow was inevitable. How could he fail to be enchanted by Sophie? The next few months flashed before her eyes with the betrothal, the shopping, the planning, the wedding, the loneliness… the grandchildren. How very strange to have a son-in-law one's own age. This man of all men.

'Yes, there is.' Thea made a business of consulting the dance card. 'Sophie has been approved to waltz by two of the Patronesses.' The warm glow of maternal pride that her lovely daughter should have secured approval so easily warred with the knot of shameful chagrin twisting inside. 'But there are several dances yet, Lord Randall, and Sophie is engaged in all those up until then. Perhaps you would like to return –'

'I will wait here with you if that is acceptable, ma'am?' At her startled nod he took the chair next to her, looking incongruously masculine as he sat on its spindly frame. 'Unless you are awaiting a partner?'

'Me? Oh no, my lord, I am here *en chaperone*. I do not dance.'

'No?' He fell silent, watching as the music stopped and Sophie was claimed by yet another young man. They were falling at her feet, helpless. Thea knew she should be stricter, but memory and regret made her heart soft and her judgements indulgent. Soon enough for duty and decorum and to put dreams away in lavender.

'Were you happy?' They both spoke at once, the same words.

'You answer, my lord,' Thea insisted, fluttering her fan. 'Were you happy so far from home for so long?'

'Not at first, no,' Lucas said. 'But I would not have been so anywhere in England, so better to go away from the source of my discontent. I learnt fulfilment and satisfaction in time. I taught myself to be happy again at last.'

'Why were you unhappy here?' The noise of the room was far away now, the dancers blurred, the music a faint murmur on the edge of hearing.

'Because my heart had been broken,' he said with that smile, challenging her to take his words seriously, defying her to feel sorry for him. 'Now, your turn.'

'I was… content.' Thea chose the word with care despite the turmoil into which he had thrown her thoughts. 'Lord Wilmott was kind to me, my father was no doubt right about the benefits of an older husband. He died two years ago, of a heart condition, poor man.'

'Poor man indeed. But he had the felicity of a happy marriage and a lovely daughter. How like her mother she is.'

There was no answer to that. He had fancied himself in love with her once then, when they were hardly older than Sophie, and had believed his heart broken when she married Arthur. What had she believed? Nothing, she had convinced herself. Felt nothing, believed nothing. She had not dared to imagine what might have been, shy little innocent that she was. Not like Sophie, that bold, confident, golden girl.

And now Lucas had come back, prosperous, titled, eligible and desirable. Oh, so very desirable. And there was the image of the girl he had fancied himself in love with so long ago, ripe for his plucking. He had only to stand amongst those callow youths and hold out his hand to her. How could she resist?

Thea watched him out of the corner of her eye, saw the boy inside the man, felt the ache begin and knew the yearning had always been there, never acknowledged. Now she must put it back in that dark closet again where it had stayed so safely all these years.

'Mama!' So soon. The dances had passed as they had sat there silently together and here was Sophie. 'Oh, I think I have danced holes in my slippers!'

Sophie paused as Lucas stood up, her eyes widening

at his height, the darkly handsome looks, his air of confidence. 'Sir.' Her curtsey was everything a mother could hope for, her modestly lowered lashes a chaperone's delight.

'Sophie, this is Lord Randall.'

He bowed. Sophie blushed.

'Lord Randall is waiting to ask you for a dance.'

The orchestra struck up for the waltz. Couples began to make their way onto the floor.

'Yes, Miss Wilmott, I was hoping you could spare me a country dance a little later?'

'A country…'

He turned and held out his hand to Thea as she stammered out the words. 'Yes, when you and I return from dancing this waltz.'

'Me?' Thea stared into the hazel eyes, finding again the gold flecks, the long lashes, the humour and the tenderness as he looked at her. Her, aged thirty six. Her with the curves of a mature woman, a mother. Her, with the threads of silver in hair that would never be the gold of guineas again. Her.

'Yes, Thea. You. I have waited eighteen years for this dance.' Lucas held out his hand. 'Will you?'

The mother said *no*. The chaperone said *no*. The woman put her hand in Lucas's strong brown clasp.

'Oh yes, Lucas. Oh yes.'

Chapter One – Where A Lost Duke Reappears

'Mama is a positive menace to impressionable young ladies.' Sophie Wilmott leaned on the balcony rail and sighed. Below her the ballroom floor swirled with colour and movement and, right in the centre, a handsome middle-aged couple gazed into each other's eyes as they danced far too close for decency.

'It is romantic, their being so unfashionably in love.' Toby, her dear friend since childhood, leaned on the polished walnut balcony rail, his elbow nudging companionably against hers. 'Everyone knows the story of how Lord Elmham came back to England after eighteen years abroad and tumbled into love all over again with his childhood sweetheart.'

'They weren't childhood sweethearts. They met when Mama was making her come-out and it was all terribly proper and repressed – secret glances, heavy sighing, soulful yearnings, I imagine, from what Mama has let slip. And then she did the dutiful thing and married a man old enough to be her father and had me and never stopped loving Lucas Randall. And Step Papa did what all impoverished younger sons are supposed to do, he went abroad and made his fortune and pined for her. Then he came back with a title and wealth and found Mama was a widow and swept her off her feet and now even the starchiest old dowager whips out a handkerchief and sheds sentimental tears over them.'

'Whichever it was, they have been a bye-word for

romantic love for, what? Six years? What is so wrong with that?'

'Because they are the exception that proves the rule. Why do you think people sigh and smile over them? Because true love like that is as rare as hens' teeth. But seeing them makes every foolish girl believe that a young man who gazes deep into her eyes and whispers sweet nothings in the moonlight loves her heart and soul, when in fact all they want to do is get under their petticoats or into their trust funds.'

She had certainly fallen for that fairy tale. Head over heels into the romance woman-trap with eyes blinded by star dust, until the reality of male desire blew away every glimmer of magic. Foolish, innocent, gullible girl that she had been.

Most men wanted one thing, and one thing only. Power. They wanted money and sex too, but those were so intimately tied up with power in the male psyche it was hard to separate them, as far as she could see. Step Papa was a notable exception, a man of honour and decency. Toby, when he grew up a trifle, would be one too, she earnestly hoped.

The waltz came to an end, couples bowed and curtseyed, the floor emptied and the volume of chatter rose.

'That's pretty harsh, Sophie.' Toby straightened up and tugged down his waistcoat, the picture of wounded male feelings. 'Not all of us are rakes or fortune hunters, you know. Some of us have the purest of intentions.'

'Your intentions, my darling Toby, are very pure and very obvious – to stay as far from Parson's Mousetrap as you can get.' He grinned and settled back at the rail with her. 'You run screaming if a respectable young lady comes within five yards of you.'

'They scare the daylights out of me,' he admitted with a shudder. 'They are all done up like the prettiest of presents just begging to be unwrapped. I'm no saint, I'm tempted. But you know you mustn't so much as tug on a ribbon or you'll have compromised the chit and be leg-shackled before you can blink. And even at a respectable distance they giggle and blush and look at a fellow with those great big eyes and I haven't a clue what to *say* to them.'

'You have no trouble talking to me.' Sophie tweaked her amber silk skirts and batted her eyelashes at him. Blushing to order was beyond her and she certainly was not going to giggle, not even to tease Toby.

He grinned and bumped elbows. 'I've known you ever since you pushed me in the duck pond aged six and you don't expect me to come the pretty with you, Soph.' She could feel his eyes on her. He was about to say something typically tactless. 'But what about you? You're twenty five.' He flinched as she glared at him. 'Twenty four, then. You'll be on the shelf if you don't start doing some flirting yourself.'

'When I am good and ready. I have a system intended to save me making an idiot of myself with giggles and blushes. And it weeds out the rakes and the fortune hunters for me. I call it WWIGG.'

'Whig? You're taking an interest in *politics*? Are you set on not marrying a Tory, then?' Toby swivelled round to face her and, as always when faced with Sir Tobias Greenwich's earnest bafflement, she smiled.

'No, not the political party. It is an mnemonic to help me remember all the important characteristics of the ideal husband. W, W, I, G and G. I think about it if I find myself falling for someone with broad shoulders but no brains, or an indecent amount of charm but dubious antecedents. W and W stand for – '

'Weasely? Wobbly? Weak-minded? There's Dunsford and Pilling, they'd fit all of those, especially when Dunsford's forgotten his corset.'

'Idiot. Well-bred and well-endowed.'

'Well-endowed? You brazen hussy, you.' Toby's

grin was positively evil.

'Well-off, I mean. It's the same thing isn't it?' He was smirking. 'What is so amusing about *well-endowed*?' She had better find out, it was probably something that no-one told young ladies.

'Er, well…' Toby had gone red now. Definitely something *risqué* then. 'You know.' He made a sweeping gesture at the front of his black silk evening breeches. 'In the trouser department.'

'*What?*'

'Wedding tackle. Large. As in well-hung.'

'Wedding – ? Toby, honestly, of all the expressions! And how is a lady supposed to judge that, might I enquire?' She came over hot and cold just thinking about it. And impossible, surely, without careful inspection and that was out of the question. She hadn't even had a good look when Jonathan… *Stop it.*

'You can't. I mean, breeches are pretty tight these days, but it doesn't follow that what it's like at rest is the same as when a fellow is…' His brain appeared to catch up with his tongue and he went red. 'Oh, hell, Sophie, stop asking questions a gentleman can't possibly answer. This paragon has got to be rich and well-bred. What else?'

'I for intelligent.' She would ponder on the issue of well-endowed males later in the privacy of her own bed chamber.

'That rules me out.' Toby was unashamedly not bookish.

'So does well-off.' He had just inherited a very modest estate. 'Anyway, we don't want to get married to each other so it is academic. G for good-looking and also good-humoured, as in having a sense of humour, not being some blustering buffoon.'

'You don't want much, Sophie,' Toby observed. 'Virtually every man you will encounter socially is well-bred, but as for the rest of the list, it's a tall order to find them all in the same package.'

'I know, but it *is* very handy. I find myself becoming interested in a handsome face, or a witty or intelligent conversationalist and then I apply WWIGG and can cross the gentleman off because he doesn't meet all five criteria.' And even if he did, she would have to add the secret requirements – U for Understanding and F for Forgiving.

She thought she might have found the ideal candidate – pleasant, good-looking, a duke's grandson, intelligent company – but he seemed no more eager to advance the matter than she did. Love she did not expect or need – friendship and reliability were what were important – but *some* enthusiasm would be welcome.

'It almost sounds as though you *enjoy* crossing them all off, Soph. Don't you want a husband?' There was a screech of tuning violins. 'Oh hell's teeth they are going out for the next set and I'm promised to that Harrison beanpole. At least she's yearning after Adrian Haye, so I'm safe.' Toby fled towards the stairs and emerged just below her a minute later, running a hand through his unruly curls as he made his way to his partner.

She should go down soon herself. Lord Heaton had claimed the supper dance set and she was *almost* certain he was a WWIGG, although she had doubts about his sense of humour. But he might just be on his best behaviour which was making him somewhat solemn. But was he any better than Ralph Thorne, her exceptionally reticent leading candidate?

'Tell me, Sophie,' enquired a deep voice from the shadows behind her. '*Do* you want to cross them all off the list?'

She spun round, staggered, grasped the balcony rail. A complete stranger. A tall, dark stranger who had heard all of that. Even the well-endowed wedding-tackle part. 'Oh, my Lord.'

'Oh, Your Grace, actually,' he remarked, emerging

fully into the light cast by the great central chandelier.

'You are a duke?'

Good looking, well bred, certain to be rich. Tick, tick, tick went an out-of-control internal scorekeeper. *Pull yourself together*, her brain snapped. *You are unchaperoned in a deserted gallery with a strange man and you have just been overheard in an outrageously improper conversation. He might very well be making assumptions and intending to act on them. Which might be wickedly wonderful... Stop it, Sophie!*

'I am.'

'You can't be. I know all the dukes and you are not one of them.' He looked like dukes ought to look according to fairy tales and, disappointingly, never did. Twenty seven? Over six feet tall, broad shoulders, patrician nose, grey, beautiful eyes, exquisitely cut evening suit, flat stomach. Her gaze began to shift downwards and she wrenched it back with an effort and met an amused smile. He wasn't a mind reader, was he? 'They are all too old. Unless you are the Lost Duke.'

'I am not at all lost,' he said. 'I know exactly where I am. In the gallery at Lady Radlett's May Ball.'

Oh yes, her internal scorekeeper added, *that voice. Deep, warm, drawling. You should have added SS for Staggeringly Sexy.*

'*You* are the Duke of Calderbrook?' He nodded. 'Well, you might not be lost now, but why did you go away for so long? You've been gone for almost more years than I've been out.' Not lost exactly. Apparently he had written letters home from time to time, but all those did was track where the errant nobleman had been, never where he was going. Or what he was doing, come to that. Or why.

'Away, not lost. My nearest and... dearest knew where I was all the time. More or less.' He strolled forward until he could put his hands on the rail beside her and look down. The hooded eyes scanned the dance floor, but Sophie noticed he took care not to lean so far forward as to be seen himself. 'You've been out *that* long?'

'You have been eavesdropping.' He might at least have had the gallantry to observe that she didn't look old enough for what his calculations told him. 'And I came out when I was seventeen.' Seven years ago.

'You and your young friend intruded into my eyrie. Naturally, expecting that an amorous encounter was about to ensue, I retreated discretely into the shadows.'

'But neither closed your eyes nor put your fingers in your ears, apparently.'

'No, not that,' he admitted. 'It was potentially entertaining.' *Shameless man.* 'I congratulate you on finding this hideaway.'

'We came up from the door near the library and locked it behind us, so I suppose you used the rear corridor entrance.'

'Do you know every trysting place in every ballroom in London, Sophie?'

'As you so ungallantly reminded me, Your Grace, I have been out for years and years so yes, I know every nook and corner that rakes use to lure their victims into their webs, usually so I can take care to avoid them. And it is Miss Wilmott, if you please.'

'Gareth Thorne, Duke of Calderbrook. At your service, Miss Wilmott.' He lifted her hand in his own ungloved one and kissed her fingertips, then carefully replaced her hand on the rail. Sophie stared at the fine embroidery on the backs of her gloves and attempted to get her breathing under control.

'I am not spinning webs for innocents this evening, rest assured. No, not for innocents,' he added, almost under his breath.

Which is a good thing, under the circumstances, given that every iota of common sense I possess appears to be lying on its back, wagging its tail and asking for its tummy to be tickled. Her nostrils flared, catching a clean, faintly spicy, sharp note over the muddle of scents and smells rising in the heat from the ballroom. 'What *are* you doing, Your Grace, all alone up here? There has been no whisper of your return. Ralph… I mean, your cousin Mr Thorne, told me nothing of it and last time he mentioned you it was to say you were in the South Seas.'

His eyebrows lifted at the mention of Ralph's name, but he said nothing about him. 'I am carrying out a reconnoitre of the battlefield, Miss Wilmott.' He turned from his contemplation of the dancers and leaned back against the balcony rail to study her face. Sophie stiffened her spine and gave him back stare for stare. She was not going to blush and get into a flutter. 'You are Arthur Wilmott's daughter, are you not?'

'I am. My father died some years ago.'

'Your mother must be a beauty in that case.' He reached out and tucked a stray curl back behind her ear. His fingers were cold. 'You did not get your guinea-gold tresses from him. Or those lovely blue eyes.' He leaned closer. 'Not sapphire. No, not the hardness of a stone. A flower. Delphinium? Not quite…'

'Most gentlemen compare them to the summer sky, or forget-me-nots. It becomes rather tiresome,' she said, knowing she sounded like a spoiled beauty. But at least he moved back a trifle. She did not need to know that his eyes were a light and unsettling silver-grey with a darker ring around the iris. And she did not need to be so close to observe the indecently long eyelashes or that he had a small mole by the corner of his left eye. If, fifty years before, a beau had placed a patch there it would have been called 'the roguish', she recalled from her grandmother's tales.

'I have inherited my mother's colouring, yes.' She did have some air in her lungs after all. 'She is married to Viscount Elmham now.' The duke was still altogether too close for comfort, even though he was staring out over the ballroom again, his eyes narrowed. Then he smiled and she shivered. 'I must go down now. I am engaged for the supper dance. Welcome back to London, Your Grace.'

'Allow me to escort you to the dance floor, Miss Wilmott.'

'Thank you.' Goodness knows why she was thanking him, he obviously intended to leave the gallery anyway, because he had seen what, or who, he was looking for. She was very glad she was not his quarry. That smile had been positively wolfish. Sophie led the way to the left-hand spiral staircase and, when they were out in the corridor, locked the door and slipped the key back into its hiding place. 'This way to the ballroom.'

'I must return the key that I used.' He tucked her hand into the crook of his elbow and strolled off in the opposite direction.

Struggling was undignified. He would release her once they reached the other door, she told herself. Dukes did not abduct young ladies in the middle of balls. *Unfortunately*, said the wicked voice in her head. *Stop it!* common-sense ordered. But when he returned the key to its lock he kept walking in the same direction.

He was a duke but he had spent years living in the most uncivilised places, according to his cousin Ralph. He might have had his brain turned by the tropical sun, or have been indoctrinated into strange rites by some South Pacific tribe. Perhaps she *was* being abducted…

Sophie kept her voice steady, as much to calm her own wild imaginings as to bring him to order. 'We need to go back now. This leads only to the head of the stairs and the main entrance.' His side was hard and warm against the back of her hand. She shifted nervously and felt the silk of his coat lining slide over the silk of his waistcoat. Layers and layers over bare skin…

'Where better to enter?'

'But I have already been announced.'

'I have not.'

So how did you get in?

The receiving line had gone when they reached the famous double staircase with its gilded flambeaux holders, but a footman was still in attendance to announce the late arrivals.

'The Duke of Calderbrook,' her abductor said. 'Miss Wilmott has already been announced.'

The man threw open the double doors, Sophie gave a determined wriggle and found herself swept along regardless.

'People will think I have been outside with you,' she hissed between stiff lips.

'But you have. It is quite all right, you do not have a hair out of place and you certainly do not look as though we have been disporting in some retiring room. Don't get into a pother, Sophie.'

Disporting indeed! Was he trying to reduce her to strong hysterics? 'I am *not* in a pother.' *I am being kidnapped by a man with deliciously strong arms and swept into a scandal and if he was sweeping me anywhere else I would be delighted. Terrified, but delighted. I am obviously in the grip of a brain fever.* 'It is *Miss Wilmott* and I am exceedingly cross with you. Oh, I could hit you!' she stormed in a whisper as he took no notice whatsoever.

'Take first place in the queue, Sophie. I am certain there will be a long tail behind you wanting to do just that in a minute. Now, here we go.'

The music had stopped. The footman cleared his throat. She was going to be late for the next set.

'His Grace the Duke of Calderbrook!'

They were at the top of the sweep of steps down into the ballroom. Heads turned. There was a sudden silence, then voices began to rise. *Calderbrook. The Lost Duke? He's been gone for years. Calderbrook, Calderbrook, Calderbrook... Miss Wilmott?*

Sophie hastily tacked a faint, unconcerned, smile on her lips. The duke descended slowly, looking neither to right nor left, that devilish curve still on his lips. Under her hand his arm felt perfectly relaxed.

Sophie decided that fainting was not going to help matters, so she began to catch the eye of people as she passed, smiled, made a rueful face, lifted a brow, gave a little shrug. *I have no idea what is going on either*, she signalled. *Isn't it peculiar? What fun.*

She thought the Duke was going to simply keep going, right through the ballroom and out the other side, then he stopped in front of someone she knew, a man in late middle age and his son. He turned to her, lifted her hand and kissed her fingertips once more. 'Miss Wilmott, I thank you for escorting a poor lost soul. Perhaps I might have the pleasure of a dance later.'

'Your Grace, I would be most happy. I believe I have some free.' She dropped the slightest hint of a curtsey and stepped back into the crowd. No-one was looking at her, thank heavens. All eyes were fixed on the Duke and on the men he was facing, Lord Peter Thorne his uncle, and Ralph Thorne his cousin. Her own lukewarm suitor. They seemed stunned. Not joyful, not surprised, simply shocked.

It was not her business and it might add emphasis to her unconventional entrance if she showed interest. The violins scraped a few notes, then fell silent. The next set was forming and where was Lord Heaton?

'Miss Wilmott. Surely that was not you entering just now? And was that indeed Calderbrook?' Her partner had found her.

'Yes it was, and I believe it is.' *And put a zero in the* Intelligent *column under your name, my lord.* 'I met him just outside the door and he positively caught me up. Really quite thrilling. For a moment I thought he was going to sweep me down the stairs and abscond with me.' She produced an inane titter with worrying ease.

'Most alarming for you, Miss Wilmott.' Heaton frowned and set his jaw. 'I shall go and have a firm word with him. Duke or not, he cannot go around accosting young ladies. Are you very discommoded, Miss Wilmott? Perhaps you would prefer that I take you to your mama.'

And another zero in the Humour *column. And a tick in a new column for Pomposity. Oh dear.* Lord Heaton had been the second on her list of potential husbands. Mentally she drew a thick black line through his name. 'There is no harm done, please do not call him to account, I would be so embarrassed. Doubtless the Duke has a sense of the dramatic but I am sure the effect of dancing with you will be most calming, Lord Heaton.' She smiled and took his hand and allowed herself to be taken to join the set that was forming. Obviously the fun was over for the evening.

'Calderbrook?' His uncle stared at him as though he had descended from the ceiling in a fiery chariot. 'Cal, it really is you? Why didn't you let us know you were returning?' He was not far off gibbering.

'Yes, it is indeed I. Please, Uncle, calm yourself. This excess of joy cannot be good for you.' It looked more like shock than happiness and Ralph too was frowning, not smiling, but the frankly gaping onlookers looked equally amazed, so perhaps the lack of enthusiasm would pass unnoticed by everyone but himself. Cousin Ralph had matured into a thoroughly respectable-looking man – one who was, apparently, on first name terms with the lovely Miss Wilmott.

'Our unfriendly neighbours the French make sailing schedules a lottery, so I had no idea when I would land. Or where.' He had put his household on alert by letter but, even if he had been able to time this to the minute, he'd had no intention of alerting his relatives to his return.

Finally his uncle managed to pull himself together, took a step forward and embraced him. Cal hugged back. Despite everything it felt good. More than good. Under his hands the older man's shoulders felt thinner, he had developed a bit of a stoop. For a second his vision blurred. Stupid to feel a pang of – what? Guilt for worrying him?

The crowd gave a sentimental collective sigh and they disentangled themselves. Ralph leaned in and shook his hand. 'It is damned good to have you back, Cal, although I would hardly recognise you. When you left you were…'

'Sickly, skinny and shy?'

Ralph's mouth thinned at his mocking tone. 'You were barely convalescent from that last bout of fever. But you have flourished in seven years, that much is evident.'

'We cannot speak here – besides anything else, I must make my apologies to Lady Radlett for gate-crashing her ball. I saw the red carpet was down as I drove past and could not resist changing and coming right out again. I will call on you both tomorrow morning.'

Cal found a smile as he turned and left them to make his way towards the faintly-remembered matron who was advancing on him, plumes nodding, Roman nose twitching with well-bred curiosity. 'Lady Radlett, will you forgive me? I have barely arrived in Town and could not think of a better reintroduction to London Society than your famed May Ball.'

'My dear Duke! Enchanted and honoured.' She beamed as he lifted her hand to his lips. He had no qualms about imposing on her hospitality – the return of the Lost Duke would make her ball the talk of the Season and she would revel in every moment of the attention.

'We are all agog to hear about your travels. Dear Lord Peter and Mr Thorne have kept us all abreast of your journeyings from your wonderful letters, but that is no substitute to hearing it from your own lips. America! The Arctic wastes! New Zealand – or was it Australia? Or are those the same thing? Such a long way away… The South Seas! India! And to be gone for seven years – but it was obviously such a wise decision, for it seems to have worked wonders for your health.' Her gaze slid over his chest, his shoulders, in frank appraisal.

Cal responded automatically while he digested that piece of information. His uncle had been so very open about his wanderings, had he? Probably wise to prevent nasty rumours, the sort of gossip that might follow when a young duke leaves the country immediately after attaining his majority and release from his uncle's guardianship and control. Even more so when the duke in question had been sickly and accident-prone throughout childhood and adolescence and the uncle in question was his heir to title, power and vast estates.

'Indeed, England never seemed very healthy for me,' he agreed as guests began to crowd round to welcome him back. 'But I have been away too long and it is good to be back home again and to see my uncle and cousin in particular. I am looking forward to getting to know my family once again.'

While I work out which of them was trying to kill me.

Chapter Two – Where Sophie Damages the Duke

'I do not know whether to shake your hand or throw the fire irons at you.' His uncle paced across the rug in the centre of his drawing room, stopped and glared at Cal from under eyebrows that had grown even bushier than he remembered. 'Why the devil did you take off like that? Why have you been away so long?'

'I left you a very full letter.' Cal dropped uninvited into the nearest armchair and crossed one leg over the other. He really must get some new boots.

'Indeed you did. An elegantly composed missive of thanks for my care for your affairs, an outline of your plans and the helpful suggestion that departing like that would prevent "wearisome brangling."'

'Well, it did. If I had mentioned my plans first we would still be discussing them now,' Cal said mildly. 'I needed to stand on my own two feet. I needed to see something beyond the four walls of Calderbrook. I needed some sunshine.'

'In the *Arctic*?' Ralph demanded from the other side of the room.

'That was later. Besides, the sun shines all day and night in the summer there.' His uncle was still frowning. 'You had looked after me diligently, for so long, both as my uncle and my guardian. On my twenty first birthday you were free of the burden and I… I had never been able to rely on myself alone. I felt I was stifling under all that concern. It was invigorating to be free.'

'A fine way to thank my father for his care of you, I must say.' Ralph grumbled.

'Believe me, I know how well my uncle cared for… my estates. He could not have been a more conscientious trustee if they had been his own.' He was careful to keep his tone neutral, but the older man frowned. 'I simply felt I would be healthier, out of the country.'

There it was, the sign he had been watching for, a flickering glance between the two men, almost as if they were uneasy with each other, not only with him. Ralph glanced at his father and Peter glanced at his son. *Guilt or anxiety? Puzzlement or frustration?*

'I had brought you up to care for your great estates and the moment you have your hands on them you walk away from them.'

'I left them in the very capable hands of my carefully chosen secretary and man of affairs who was fully briefed on my wishes and plans. I have been in constant contact with him. I have not been shirking my responsibilities, believe me.'

'Prescott, that damned secretary of yours, was as mysterious as he could be.' His uncle was still not to be appeased. '*His Grace was here, His Grace was there. His Grace is travelling. His Grace is at sea. We* were at sea, I can tell you.' He stalked over to the sideboard, poured himself a glass of brandy, gestured irritably to the two younger men to help themselves, then subsided, fuming, into a chair.

'I wrote to you, every month without fail.' Cal rose, helped himself to the decanters, then poured a glass for his cousin, receiving a grudging smile when he pressed it into his hand.

'Always about where you had been, never where you were heading to.' Lord Peter was not prepared to give up his complaints. 'How the devil were we to lay hands on you?'

You were not. That was the entire point. 'I hoped to

release you to devote all your attention to your own estates, your own affairs. You had been saddled with mine for fourteen years, ever since I was seven.'

'It was my duty.' His uncle cleared his throat, glared down into his glass as though it had dared to contradict him. 'It was more than that. You were another son to me, you must know that.'

'And you were the father I never really had.' *And I believed it with every fibre of my being until I was twenty. That is what hurts, more than anything. How can I live with myself, suspecting that? How can I not?*

It had been a stifling August day and he was lying in a fever, hot, restless, with all the windows and doors to his bedchamber thrown open. The doctor in the next room had kept his voice low as he spoke to his assistant, but it had carried just enough through windows set at right-angles to each other. 'I do not pretend to understand it. That young man has suffered more unexplained fevers and internal upsets than I have ever come across. And he is accident-prone into the bargain.' The assistant had muttered something and the doctor had reacted sharply. 'Of course not! What a suggestion. Who would wish him harm?'

Who would wish me harm? No-one except... Except my heir, the man who has devoted his life to my fortune, my estates. My uncle and his son for whom none of that labour will bring the slightest benefit. Unless I die and it all becomes theirs.

And with nothing else to occupy his mind the suspicion grew until it would not leave him. Confined to bed he had all the time in the world to review those accidents. The broken girth, the sprung plank in the rowing boat, the falling masonry, the slippery step, the mysterious shot in the woods that might have been poachers. Or might not. And the succession of fevers and stomach upsets, the violent pains and cramps, the rashes and the headaches that affected no-one else, not even his closest servants.

Cui bono? Who benefits? His uncle of course, his father's only brother, and after him his cousin Ralph. No-one else had anything to gain from his death but they had everything. He logged the accidents against their frequent presence in the house and found patterns but no proof. Not one iota. Nor was there ever anything remotely suspicious in the way they were with him. But suspicion was like poison: insidious, weakening, impossible to eradicate once it had got a hold.

He was jerked back to the present by his uncle blowing his nose vehemently on a large handkerchief. 'Well, you are back now. Back with your family. But almost *seven years*, Cal.'

'Six and a half.' Most carefully not seven, the period when a death might be assumed in law. Best to be cautious, even with a trail of letters to mark the fact that he was very much alive. 'But enough of the past for now, there is much news to catch up with. Nothing dire has occurred or I would have heard of it, but my aunt is in the best of health I trust? And you, Ralph – no wife yet?'

Colour came up in his cousin's face. 'Not yet, but there is someone… that is, I have some hopes. Too soon to say yet, I am not certain. Mama is very well, I thank you.'

'Where are you staying?' Now all the awkward emotional business was out of the way his uncle had relaxed a trifle. 'Your Town house will be under wraps of course, but you are most welcome here at Mount Street.'

'Thank you, but the St James's Square house was opened up last week. I wrote from Italy.'

'We're at war.' Ralph threw back his brandy, then got up and took the decanters to refill all the glasses. 'How have you managed to travel so widely?'

'Disguise and deception added to the amusement. I must demonstrate my Swedish count and my American merchant to you some time.'

His uncle shook his head at the frivolity. His once-thick hair was thinning and almost entirely white now, although he was only in his early sixties. Guilt, worry or natural aging? 'What are your plans? Will you go to Calderbrook at once?'

'In a week or two. I must talk to my bankers, to my man of business – and Prescott has enough work for me to last a month. Then there are my tailors, bootmakers, any manner of tiresome affairs to be attended to. And I must do whatever is necessary to take my seat in the House.'

'You intend to involve yourself in politics?' Ralph leaned forward. 'The party could do with your support. Let me introduce you to – '

'Not yet.' Cal held up a hand to stay the flow. 'I have made no decision on who I support, nor on the issues, come to that. I may well sit cross-bench.'

'On the fence,' Ralph snorted.

'A place from whence I am free to follow my conscience and vote on issues as each arises. You are fiery on the subject of allegiances. Have I missed you taking your seat in the Commons, Cousin?'

'I hope to find a seat soon,' Ralph admitted. He had always been a Whig, passionate about politics, Cal remembered. Four years older than himself, he had seemed like an older brother, full of experience and ideas. It would be interesting to discover how that stood up against his own six or so years of hard-won worldly wisdom. 'I would appreciate your help.'

'Mine? I know no-one of any importance as yet.' The whole of Society, the entirety of London, come to that, was *terra incognita* to him now.

'You are a duke, Cal,' Ralph said wryly. 'You *are* someone of importance. And you have boroughs under your influence. The sitting Member for Long Fordingham is unwell and has been talking of resigning.'

Those would be rotten boroughs where bribing only a handful of electors would result in a seat in the House of

Commons. Electoral reform was certainly a cause he might become interested in. But in the meantime it was his duty to support a close relative by extending his patronage. Beside anything else it would be highly suspicious not to do so. 'Long Fordingham is yours if you want it. Just tell me what you need doing.'

Ralph's grin was almost shocking in the serious, mature face of the man who had once been his childhood friend. Cal found himself jerked back ten years or so, found himself grinning in response. He wanted to trust his cousin. Wanted to trust them both, because this suspicion was like a cancer, eating away at his memories and his childhood and what had been his certainties of love and trust.

But there was no escaping the fact that he had left Calderbrook, and his uncle's control, as a chronically sick and weak young man and within a month was well again, strong and fit and putting on inches and muscle. And he had never had the same symptoms again. Yes, he'd suffered illnesses like any traveller, but they were always easily diagnosed and they had run their course. It would be very interesting indeed to see what infections and accidents came his way now he was back in England. Time to toss another pebble into the pool and see what ripples it made.

'I wish I could stay longer.' And that, strangely, was true. He was glad to see his uncle and cousin. He had missed the two men who had once been all the family he knew, even as he had hardened his heart against them, buried the hurt and fear of betrayal behind a wall of ice. Cal shifted slightly until he could watch both their faces as he got to his feet. 'But you know what children are like. I will be a very unpopular father if I do not go home soon.'

'*Father*? You have a child?' His uncle.

'You are *married*?' Ralph. Their expressions were almost comically identical, and then there was that rapid, flickering exchange of glances again, unreadable.

'Yes, to both. But my wife died over a year ago, in India.'

'I am deeply sorry.' The enveloping bear hug stopped him reading his uncle's face, but over his shoulder he saw Ralph's expression – shock and, strangely, suspicion.

'A son?' his uncle asked.

Of course, the critical question. His answer would tell them whether there was another life between them and the title. The wealth. The power. 'A daughter, Isobel. A demanding young lady, despite being only five years old.' His uncle's face showed sympathy, interest, nothing else.

Ralph, on the other hand, was still in the grip of some other emotion. 'You will be looking for a new bride, a mother for your child,' he said tightly.

What the hell is the matter with him? 'Yes, although I must be seeking a wife in any case,' he said easily. 'Heirs, after all, are part of my duty.'

'You made a good start last night, in that case.'

For a long moment Cal was baffled, then light dawned. Miss Wilmott who was on first name terms with Ralph. Miss Wilmott, beautiful, eligible, intelligent. Desirable. He frowned in pretended confusion. 'What do you mean? Ah, my delightful blonde partner? What a very excellent suggestion, Ralph, thank you.' And if looks could kill the succession would be decided there and then. He reached out his hand, shook theirs, kept smiling. 'It is good to be back and to see you again. Will you both come to dinner tomorrow night? Yes? Excellent. Come early and meet your great-niece, Uncle.'

As he sauntered down the front steps, pulling on his gloves, he wondered whether he learned anything. No. Had he made a potential enemy of his cousin, if he wasn't one already? Almost certainly. That might be useful, because a man in a temper and under stress was far more likely to make revealing mistakes. Miss Wilmott was worth cultivating, and not only for those blue eyes and her shockingly entertaining approach to courtship.

'More flowers for Miss Wilmott, my lady.' Parrott their butler gestured a footman into the room, his arms full of fern fronds and the blue flowers of Love In a Mist.

'An unusual choice.' Her mother put down her tea cup and surveyed the bouquet. 'And rather late in the day. Who are they from, dear?'

'Is there a card, Parrott? Thank you.' All her dance partners from last night had duly sent roses that morning, except Toby who had despatched a bunch of sweet-scented pinks which he knew she loved, bless him.

She pulled the gilt-edged rectangle from its envelope. The card bore only an embossed coronet. She lifted it close to study and made out the eight stylised strawberry leaves. A duke. Ridiculously, her pulse stuttered.

Forgive my tardiness. The black writing, constrained to the small space, had an elegant masculine force. *But finding a match for your eyes challenged me. C.*

'The Duke of Calderbrook, I believe, Mama.'

'Only right and proper, considering that he could have put you severely to the blush if you were not such a poised young lady.' Her stepfather lowered his newspaper. 'I was in half a mind to have a word with him last night. That sort of behaviour leads to raised expectations.'

'Not by me, Step Papa.' Good lord, *a duke?* Calderbrook might match every one of her requirements for a husband, but she would most certainly not match his for a bride. A duke would expect a virgin.

'I do not see why not.' Mama studied the charming bouquet indulgently. 'You have the breeding, the manners, the character and the looks to make a most suitable duchess.' The dreamy smile of a loving mother who has just realised that London's most eligible possible prospect for her daughter was taking an interest transformed her expression and sent a chill down Sophie's spine.

'I promised to take Jane Arbuthnot for a drive in Green Park after luncheon, Mama. I did mention it yesterday, if you recall.' Her stepfather had presented her with a phaeton for her birthday and ever since then her friends had been begging rides in the park. It was much more dashing to be seen behind Miss Wilmott's pretty dappled mare than to drive sedately with one's mama and sisters in a barouche.

'Take a footman,' her mother cautioned as Parrott came in to announce luncheon. 'Make certain he stays with you at all times.'

'Yes, Mama.' It was Jane who would not be staying, not if her beau, a dashing cavalry officer, was at their rendezvous, but there was no need to tell Mama that and she had no intention of dispensing with a groom. She, of all people, had no intention of indulging in the slightest indiscretion.

'There he is! Captain Maxwell!'

'Don't be so eager,' Sophie murmured. 'Keep him in suspense.' But Jane was taking no notice.

The officer saluted as he came to help Jane down, then stood making polite conversation for a few moments. She had no qualms about helping the lovers, for Captain Maxwell was perfectly eligible and had patently honourable intentions. If she was Jane he would match every one of the WWIGG criteria.

It was only Jane's over-romantic sensibility that convinced her that theirs was a Doomed Love and that her father, who had simply murmured a few understandable concerns about serving officers in time of war, would refuse the captain's offer when it was made. Another example, Sophie thought crossly, of how this love nonsense clouded young women's minds.

A high-perch phaeton and pair bowled past, doubtless on its way to the more fashionable Hyde Park, and Sophie regarded it enviously. Papa had vetoed such a dangerous sporting vehicle for her, insisting on the safe, low-slung version with one well-mannered mare to draw it.

Still, she consoled herself, sending Moonstone into a brisk trot, it was a very stylish vehicle and her dapple-grey mare was a beauty. Probably this was quite fast enough, even though Thomas, perched up behind, was not making the sucking sound through his teeth that was the first indication that he thought she was speeding.

The track split and she took the branch away from the Queen's Walk towards the centre of the park, up over the slight rise, round the corner and –

'Miss!'

'*I see her*.' A toddler intent on an escaping ball scampered out from behind a bush, right into Moonstone's path. The mare shied violently, the child turned, then, disastrously, teetered back into the road. From the side someone screamed piercingly and Moonstone reared up. Sophie hauled on the reins as a figure ran out, scooped up the infant and rolled with her in his arms away from the slashing hooves to the side of the track. A tall hat spun away under the wheels and there was an unpleasant crunch as the phaeton rolled back over it.

Sophie thrust the reins at Thomas and was out of the carriage as Moonstone came to a shuddering, snorting halt. The man sat on the dusty grass with his back to her, the child between his knees, and did not look up as Sophie reached them.

'That was very exciting to be sure. Did you bump anything?' The deep voice was calm and interested.

Tousled blonde curls shook and the little girl removed her thumb from her mouth. 'Pretty horsey.'

'Very pretty,' the man agreed. 'And where is your nursemaid?'

'Miss Lucy! Oh, Miss Lucy!' A young woman in a plain blue gown and cloak and a straw bonnet ran across the track and snatched the child into her arms. The infant began to bawl.

'She was perfectly fine a moment ago,' Sophie said, relief making her sharp. 'Do not fuss her so and she will stop crying. Come and talk to the pretty horsey, Miss Lucy.'

That worked like a charm. Moonstone submitted to having her nose patted, the sobs died away and the nursemaid was able to check that her charge was not so much as bruised. She hurried her away, scolding over the renewed cries as Miss Lucy was removed from Moonstone.

'The maid might at least have said *Thank you*. If it wasn't for you that could have been dreadful.' Sophie turned back to the rescuer and found him still sitting on the grass. His back was hunched and there was something very wrong with the line of his shoulders. 'Are you all right, sir?'

He looked up as she dropped to her knees in front of him. 'You will forgive me if I do not get up for a moment. I appear to have dislocated my shoulder.' He was pale under the tan, his dark hair ruffled, his mouth set in a hard line against what must be agonising pain, but the silver eyes smiled at her. 'You drive a very dashing equipage, Miss Wilmott.'

'Your Grace.' Of course, of all the men in London to choose from, she had to run down the Lost Duke and almost achieve what seven years of perilous foreign travel had not.

Chapter Three - Where the Duke Discovers Desire

'You are in pain.' *Oh well done, Sophie. A statement of the utterly obvious. He looks as though he's in agony.*

'Dislocations tend to be uncomfortable. If you will give me your hand for a moment so I can get up without falling flat on my face again, I would be obliged.'

'I'll get my groom.' She scrambled to her feet and ran back to the phaeton. 'Give me the reins, Thomas. You help His Grace to his feet – carefully, minding his right arm. I'll drive him directly to Doctor Felbrigg.'

Toby had dislocated his arm once, hunting. He'd described it as the worst pain he had ever endured. Worse than a broken leg, worse than a shoulder full of buckshot from a pigeon-shooting accident. 'I was screaming the place down,' he'd confessed. 'Cast up my accounts, almost bit the doctor.' And now it was her fault that the Duke was suffering the same. She should never have taken that blind rise at a trot.

Dealing with the guilt at least distracted her as Thomas helped him to the phaeton and, with a lot of grunting on the groom's part and utter silence on the Duke's, got him seated. He held his right arm to his body with his left hand.

'Would a sling help?'

'No. Thank you.' He had turned a nasty shade of beige and his voice was clipped. 'Possibly a mallet to the head would. Best take me to the Park Ranger's cottage, although I am afraid it is somewhat out of your way.'

'For goodness sake,' she snapped, then got a rein on her nerves. 'As if my convenience matters. I will go direct to our doctor's house, it will be faster. He lives just off St James's Street.'

'Bossy, Miss Wilmott.'

'Sensible, Duke.'

'Call me Cal.'

Moonstone had settled into a steady walk. Sophie risked a sideways glance. 'That would be most improper.'

'And being proper is a prime consideration with you, of course, Sophie. I had noticed.'

Sarcastic beast. 'Mama would be shocked.' Thomas's ears must be flapping. She could almost feel the draught.

'Your mama, unless she is a completely unnatural parent, would be delighted to have you on terms of intimacy with a duke and we both know it.'

A suppressed snort behind them confirmed the suspicion that Thomas was following the conversation. 'Terms, possibly,' Sophie said repressively. 'Intimacy, certainly not.'

'W, W, I, G, G,' he murmured. 'With *excellent* endowments, so I have always been told.'

The gurgle of laughter escaped her before she could catch it. Brave, handsome *and* amusing. *Oh dear.* Another glance showed that his lips had relaxed into a smile, but his eyes were closed.

'We are about to turn out of the park. There may be a lurch and a bump.' They negotiated the turn to the accompaniment of a hiss of pain. 'Your hat was beyond saving, I fear.' Distraction might help.

'It was old. I need to visit my hatter, but, call me weak-willed, I am not calling in at Lock's for a new one as we pass.'

'Here we are, just turning into Park Place now. Thomas, get ready to jump down and knock.'

It seemed an age as they sat in silence waiting for

the groom to return, but he came back at last, accompanied by the doctor's man who, thankfully, seemed to know just how to extract an injured man from a phaeton with the least possible fuss.

'Stay here and walk the carriage, Thomas.' Sophie jumped down and followed the men up the steps and into the house.

'But Miss W – ' The closing door shut off the groom's protests.

'Miss Wilmott, good afternoon.' Doctor Felbrigg emerged from his study, tugging down his cuffs. 'This is a surprise. You are not unwell, I trust?'

'No, I am in perfect health, thank you. But this is the Duke of Calderbrook, Doctor. There was an accident in the park.'

'Good day to you, sir. I've put my shoulder out.' The Duke… Cal… held out his good hand to the doctor. 'Miss Wilmott assures me you are the very man to put it back.'

'Of course. Will you come through, Your Grace? Perkins, make Miss Wilmott comfortable in the drawing room and fetch her refreshments.' The study door closed firmly behind them.

It all seemed to take a very long time. Sophie sipped too-hot tea. Getting his coat off must be difficult. She nibbled at a biscuit, reducing it to crumbs, and eyed the door, listening. A swear word penetrated two layers of oak and made her blink. Then there was silence again. What horrible things was Doctor Felbrigg doing to Cal? Toby had refused to tell her what putting a shoulder joint back in place involved, but he had looked sick even thinking about it.

Voices in the hall…*Thank goodness.* The doctor opened the drawing room door and smiled. 'His Grace is back together again now, Miss Wilmott. As he resides just across St James's in the square I will send my man for his carriage. Do give my regards to Lord and Lady Elmham.'

'I am sure the sooner the Duke is back at home the better, Doctor. My carriage is outside.'

'You should not be seen driving a man about in St James's, Miss Wilmott. I thank you for your care of me, but I am quite recovered.' The Duke sauntered out of the study in his shirtsleeves, his right arm strapped to his body and supported by a sling. Otherwise he appeared perfectly restored again, the colour back in his face, the tight lines of agony gone from around his lips and eyes.

'But – '

'The relief of pain once the joint is back in the socket is miraculous. I am quite all right now.'

'Piffle.' The doctor gasped, the Duke raised one dark brow. 'You should be resting and you know it. Goodness knows why men are so stubborn, but you are all the same. And I have yet to hear that a lady, accompanied by her groom, might not drive anywhere in an open carriage in broad daylight with a respectable gentleman at her side.' Cal opened his mouth and she added sweetly, 'And you *are* respectable, Duke, aren't you?'

He huffed out a breath of laughter as the doctor's man helped him get into his coat. 'Oh, eminently, Miss Wilmott. After all, I have not been back in Town long enough to acquire a reputation for being anything else. Shall we go?'

Thomas, looking as disapproving as only an old family retainer could, walked Moonstone up to the front steps and handed the reins over to Sophie. She took them with a word of thanks, tempered by the knowledge that Thomas would tell Parrott, who would most certainly have *a word in your ear, my lord,* with Step Papa. The worst of it was, she was certain that both he, and Mama, would be delighted to think their daughter had been driving a duke about town when in fact the only reason she was doing it was out of guilt – and concern for any person who was hurt, naturally. The wicked little inner voice gave a sarcastic laugh.

'What is your address, Duke?' She crossed St James's Street at a brisk trot into Little Ryder Street and then turned right into Bury Street. Despite her bravado she did not intend to drive the direct route down St James's Street with its throngs of club-bound gentlemen and its numerous coffee houses.

'You know your way around the side streets,' Cal observed as they negotiated the left turn into King Street past Almack's assembly rooms.

'All the better to avoid the traffic in this area. Piccadilly is a dreadful crush most days.' They emerged into St James's Square and she slowed Moonstone to a walk.

'Clockwise round,' Cal said. 'The dark green front door. Thank you, Miss Wilmott. I have rarely been involved in a more entertaining traffic accident.' He got out of the phaeton, his hand lifting automatically to his missing hat. 'Now, there *is* a scandal – hatless duke in St James's. My valet will probably resign on the spot.'

'Papa!' A diminutive brunette in a green frock half ran, half tumbled down the steps and hurled herself at Cal, her arms fastening around his leg.

Papa? He is father to this – what? – five year old? No wonder he was good with that infant in the park. Then the implications hit home. A child meant a wife. And all the time the wretched man had been flirting with her.

'Isobel.' Cal scooped up the wriggling armful one-handed and was rewarded with a smacking kiss on his bruised cheek and the application of a pair of thrashing feet to his sore hip. 'Where is Nanny?'

'Lost.' Her big brown eyes, so like her mother's, widened in a mock innocence. And that had been one of Madeleine's little tricks too. The child was going to be a handful by the time she was putting her hair up and her skirts down, and he would have to buy himself a shotgun to deal with the young men.

'You mean *you* lost *her*,' he scolded. 'Now, behave properly and say good afternoon nicely to Miss Wilmott. Miss Wilmott, Lady Isobel Thorne.'

Now what was wrong? Sophie's blue gaze had all the warmth of an ice crystal, for all that she smiled at Isobel.

'Good afternoon, Lady Isobel. I am pleased to have met you, but perhaps you should not run out into the street. Your nanny will be worried about you.'

'It wasn't my fault.' The little madam quivered her lower lip and turned tragic toffee-brown eyes on Sophie. 'I'm a very good girl. Truly.'

'You are a minx,' Cal corrected absently, still watching Sophie who blushed, lost all of her poise and mumbled,

'I am very glad to hear that. Your mama must be very proud of you. Good day, Duke. I trust your arm will cease paining you very soon.' She dropped her hands and the dapple was into its stride and heading towards York Street before he could respond.

So that was what that was about: when she saw Isobel she had thought him married, believed he had been flirting with her despite it. How very flattering that it should matter to her. Cal grinned, warmed by the rush of masculine smugness. It had been a while since he had enjoyed flirting with a pretty woman and a very long time since he had encountered a well-bred young lady who had made him want to. Miss Wilmott, seen in the broad light of day and with his full attention on her and not on the confrontation with his family, was frankly beautiful. Well worth pursuing, and the suspicion that Cousin Ralph had his eye on her only added a pinch of spice.

Nanny Jenkins was standing in the open doorway, hands on hips, shaking her head at him. He had hired the fierce little Welsh widow in Calcutta in the days following Madeleine's death and she had bustled into his life, a scolding bundle of warmly-loving efficiency. Cal had been left with an infant, a guilt-inducing awareness that he was free and an almost irresistible urge to stop wandering, come back to England, see if he could finally lay his ghosts. Nanny Jenkins had taken one long, assessing, look at him and pronounced, 'The little one should be home. You'll be taking a passage as soon as you can find a ship.' It was an order and for once in his life, Cal did not demur.

'Good gracious me, what have you been doing to yourself?' she demanded now as she lifted Isobel from his arm. 'Your Grace.' It was always an afterthought, his title. 'Fighting?'

'An encounter between a phaeton and a small child in Green Park,' he admitted. 'The child is fine, I dislocated my shoulder and lost my hat.' Any proper employer would be outraged that she might suggest him capable of brawling in the middle of a Thursday afternoon. He was long since resigned to being an *improper* employer.

Prescott, his secretary, looked round the study door, studied his dusty, battered appearance and raised his eyebrows. 'There is a considerable amount of business awaiting you, sir. However it will all keep until tomorrow.' The door clicked shut behind him.

In the days before his twenty first birthday, when he had been finalising the plans for his escape, Cal had realised that he had to leave behind him a confidential secretary of the utmost respectability, intelligence and probity. If he could not, then there was no way he could square his conscience about abandoning his estates to be administered at arms' length. George Prescott, the third son of Lord Warnley, a neighbour, was the soberest, most hard-working and conscientious man Cal had ever encountered, despite George's youth. He had left university with honours and was choosing between the various flattering offers of work he had received, which included posts with a bishop, two lords and a leading member of the House of Commons, when Cal poached him.

He was one of only three men in whom he had confided his suspicions about his uncle and cousin. The second was Jared Hunt, originally employed as his fencing master, a taciturn man of lethal fighting ability whose past was a mystery. He was a year older than Cal, had presented himself in answer to an advertisement and appeared to have no background whatsoever, only excellent references from two French émigré sword masters.

His loyalty became apparent when he had taken Cal to one side a month before he put his plan of escape into action and warned him that he was suspicious about the accidents and ill-health that had plagued him. The relief at finding someone with whom he could discuss it, and the knowledge that he wasn't losing his mind, had given him the strength he need to break free.

He left George behind him as his confidential secretary with powers of attorney, the only man who knew where he was going in advance and who received letters and orders from wherever Cal went. Jared travelled with him, at first while he was still weak from the last bout of illness, as his bodyguard. Then, as his health returned, as his friend and companion.

The third man in his confidence was his valet, Michael Flynn, a young Irishman whom Cal had rescued when he was being beaten up by a gang of toughs on a New York street. He had got the battered youth back to his dingy lodging room, tended his wounds and thought nothing of it until Flynn had turned up the next morning at the hotel, his smart appearance marred by two magnificent black eyes, and announced that Mr Thorne – as he was calling himself – needed a valet and that he was his man.

Cal had noticed his clean nails, his sharp shave, despite the bruises, his well-chosen clothes and agreed.

'You know what I am,' Flynn had blurted out. 'You know why they were having a go at me?'

'Because you're a molly,' Jared had growled as he squinted down the length of the fencing foil he was polishing.

'You don't mind?'

'Lay one finger on my knee, lad, and you're a spit roast,' Jared drawled. 'Otherwise you can be romancing the kitchen cat for all I care. But it's not up to me, I'm not the one you'll be helping into his small-clothes.'

In his innocence Cal had puzzled over how Jared had known. As far as he knew he'd never met a man who preferred to lie with his own sex, but he suspected he probably had and that it was his own inexperience showing. His uncle was intemperate on the subject, which seemed a good enough reason to take the opposite view. 'You're hired on a month's trial,' he said, waving towards the heap of portmanteaux that held his crumpled and unvaleted clothing. 'See what you can do with that lot, and Mr Hunt's while you're at it.'

After a month Cal could not imagine how he had managed without Flynn. The valet moved from body servant to confidential servant to friend and Cal revealed his true identity, though not the reason for his travels. But Flynn was sharp, with an inbuilt level of wariness that a hard life had taught him. 'What's the danger in England then, sir?' he'd asked one day when he was heaving off Cal's boots. Cal told him and Flynn shrugged. 'Bloody hell. Still, I suppose if you need a motive for murder, getting a dukedom is a pretty tempting one.' In Cal's opinion that summed things up nicely.

Now he trudged upstairs to find Flynn and a change of clothing, leaving Isobel telling Nanny all about the nice lady who had driven Papa home. Flynn, emerged from the dressing room and pursed his lips at the sight of Cal's battered person.

'Fighting, sir? Or courting?'

‘Impudent devil. I shudder to think what goes on in your imagination if you think I could get into this state courting.’ Although come to think of it, the afternoon had certainly advanced his relationship with Sophie Wilmott.

‘A jealous rival?’ The valet circled him. ‘Tsk. How did you get out of your coat?’

‘Painfully. I dislocated the shoulder joint and the doctor wanted to cut my clothes off.’

‘He might as well have done,’ Flynn said as he tossed the coat aside and held up Cal’s boots to study the scuffed leather. ‘This lot is fit for the rag and bone man. I’ll send for hot water, you’ll want to bathe before those bruises get any worse and you seize up completely.’ He paused with one hand on the bell pull. ‘And is the lady who brought you home unhurt herself?’

‘The lady almost ran me down,’ Cal said with a straight face, provoking a whistle of surprise.

‘And I thought Naples was dangerous.’

Ah yes, Naples. That had been fun. Dirty, dangerous, violent and full of dark-eyed, voluptuous women, most of whom came with knife-wielding brothers or husbands. He had been a married man of course, but even so, flirting had been almost obligatory. And Jared had been bedding one married beauty and he suspected that Flynn had been up to something with her younger brother… that evening the three of them, swords drawn, had only just managed to escape alive.

Good times – ‘*Damn it!*’ Having the strapping removed was almost as painful as having it applied and certainly an antidote to reminiscence.

Finally the large copper bath was filled and Cal sank into it with a wince, wondering if it was going to take a block and tackle to haul him out. But this was too good to worry about that now. He closed his eyes, inhaled lemon verbena-scented steam and contemplated courting Sophie Wilmott in earnest and not simply as a means to needle Ralph.

What was his equivalent of Sophie's WWIGG list? W for well-bred – this theoretical woman was going to be a duchess, when all was said and done. I for Intelligent, definitely, or he'd be bored in a week. F for Faithful. He had no tolerance for infidelity. Beautiful? Not necessarily. What was inside was more important. Elegant was more like it. Beyond that he wasn't fussy. Preferably not a brunette again, definitely not a vapid giggler and hopefully without irritating baggage in the shape of strange or impecunious relatives.

What did that make? W.I.F.E., of course. He'd take that as a good omen that he should proceed with courting *someone.* So, think about Sophie. Blonde, elegant in a lively kind of way. Intelligent. Good family. And beautiful. Very beautiful. That guinea-gold hair, those blue eyes, that slender, curved figure, those long fingers caressing the reins, closing round the whip handle…

'Sweet dreams?'

Cal woke up with a painful jolt, slid beneath the water and came up spluttering to glare at Jared Hunt who lounged against the wall at the foot of the bath regarding him with an evil grin.

'What?'

Hunt pointed at the bath. 'I was expecting to find you battered, bruised and nursing your injuries, not daydreaming with an impressive cock-stand breaking the surface. Who is she?'

Cal looked down. *Ah.* Yes, probably another sign that he should be courting Miss Sophie Wilmott.

Chapter Four - Where Sophie Becomes Uncertain

'I am not bandying a lady's name about over the bathwater.' Cal lobbed a wet sponge at Hunt who ducked, swearing.

He stayed bent over the bath studying Cal's damaged body with the detachment of a fencing master assessing the fitness of his pupil, his long, tightly-plaited queue sliding over his shoulder. 'Strange that you can journey round the world with scarcely a scratch and the moment you are back in England you end up battered and bruised.'

'This was definitely an accident.' Cal sat up and began to soap himself one-handed. 'But I am contemplating some provocative action that should produce a reaction if anyone does have an eye on my title.'

'Marriage would certainly do that, if that's what's preoccupying you,' Hunt agreed. He hefted a jug of clean water and poured it over Cal's head.

He came up spluttering. 'And the lady in question may well be of interest to my cousin. Give me a hand to get out, will you?'

Hunt hauled him to his feet, passed him a towel and listened while Cal explained about Sophie and Cousin Ralph's apparent interest in her. 'It's a complicating factor. If he does nothing to counter you then he is lacking in backbone but we're no further forward as regards his private feelings about you. If he does react strongly we won't know whether it is to protect his position with the lady or because he is using that as an opportunity to damage you.'

'Now *that* would be a scandal, to inherit a dukedom by killing your predecessor in a dual over the future duchess.' Cal gave up on drying himself with one hand and shrugged damply into his silk banyan. 'Ralph's not a hot-head, nor is he reckless. Damn it, Jared, I could almost think this is all my imagination now that I am back in the country and I've met my uncle and cousin again. It seems such a gothic tale.'

'And yet?' Hunt followed him through into the bedchamber where Flynn was laying out clothes. 'You said *almost*.'

'And yet. I told them I had a child and they exchanged such looks. Or, rather, they looked *at* each other. It was not an exchange, it was as though each was startled and was checking for the other's reaction. Very odd. I caught them doing the same thing in the ballroom last night.'

'It is one of them who is plotting and the other suspects them,' Flynn stated.

'That is how I read it. But how to establish which it is, I don't know yet.' He sighed and ran his hand through his wet hair. 'Damn it, I had hoped to come home and realise that it was all in my imagination. That I had been sick and brain-fevered and had it out of proportion. Now I fear I was right all along.'

'So, what is to be done?' Hunt picked up a fencing foil from the rack in the corner and lunged with it, a straight, killing strike that plucked a flower from the vase on the dresser.

'Court a bride, watch my relatives and guard my back while I expose it as temptingly as I can.'

'You marry and you have another life to guard. You get your bride with child and you have two,' Hunt observed as he shredded a second blameless bloom.

That had occurred to Cal as well. He plucked another flower from the vase and tossed it up for Hunt to skewer in mid-air. 'The lady would be safe enough until I married her. So I must get to the bottom of this before then, mustn't I?'

'And when you do and discover that your uncle or your cousin truly is guilty, what will you do then?' Hunt's dark, sardonic face showed nothing but mild curiosity.

Break my heart. 'I'll think of something.'

Ralph Thorne *might* be the one. Sophie passed him a cup of tea and watched covertly while she served the other guests who had called that afternoon. Mama's At Home days were Tuesday and Friday and there were four ladies gossiping over the Oolong while the three gentlemen who had come in their wake made inroads into the macarons and tried not to look as though they wished they were at their clubs.

Ralph was the fourth, and the only unmarried, man present and he had made it subtly apparent that he was there to see her and not as part of the polite social round. He smiled, a slight curving of his lips, as she turned back to him from the tea tray. He matched every one of her criteria. He was well-bred and even Mama, who rather hoped for a title for her, had no objections to the grandson of a duke. He was certainly comfortably off, intelligent, good-humoured and good-looking, even if he was a paler copy of his cousin Calderbrook.

And, while her heart could not even manage the smallest flutter when she was with him, civilised indifference was definitely a safer basis for a lasting marriage than foolish passion which could only fade with time or be killed with sudden, vicious disillusion. Mr Thorne certainly showed no sign of succumbing to any variety of passion in her presence but he did look as though he might be understanding and forgiving, something a duke could not be when considering marriage.

Yes, she could like Ralph Thorne very well and she could make him a good wife she was certain. She really must stop thinking about dukes and certainly in the same breath as marriage. He, the singular duke in question, *was* married of course, for she did not believe for a moment that he was openly acknowledging a love-child by raising her in his London house. Gentlemen simply did not do such things.

And besides, even if he had been a bachelor, he was not for her, however much those silver eyes seemed to speak to her of shared knowledge, of shared awareness. It did not matter that she had seen him exhibit courage and physical prowess and the grace to smile and comfort a small child when he was in great pain. And she most certainly should not be thinking about those long legs and broad shoulders and muscled thighs, not when she was talking to a gentleman who, though no weakling, was not such an impressive physical specimen.

It made her just as bad as those men who chatted at a reception while keeping one eye open for someone of more interest. *Superficial, rude, unladylike*, Sophie chided herself. She must not become hard and cynical and calculating because one man had taught her that love could not be trusted. She smiled more warmly at Mr Thorne and reminded herself that the Duke had flirted with her, which under the circumstances was quite beyond the pale.

'I do hope your cousin is somewhat recovered today,' she said, then almost bit her tongue. What was she doing? She'd had no intention of mentioning him at all.

'Calderbrook?' Ralph said. The tea slopped into the saucer. He muttered something under his breath and put down the cup on a side table. 'He is unwell?' That was very sharp indeed.

'He rescued a little girl from being trampled in the park yesterday. She ran in front of my horse and he dived to save her. He dislocated his shoulder, I fear.'

Ralph winced. 'Painful. Did you… It was an accident you say?'

'Why yes, of course. How could it be anything else? I was driving my phaeton up that rise in Green Park rather too fast, the child ran out and the Duke snatched her up safely.' His face was unreadable now, a polite blank. 'Why should it not be an accident?'

'No reason at all,' he said, with a smile and a shrug. 'I am doubtless too protective. My cousin comes back to us after years abroad, safe and sound and twice the man he was and it would be a tragedy if he met with some danger here.'

It would have been a tragedy anywhere. What an odd thing to say. And danger*?* A prickle of apprehension touched the nape of her neck. 'It must have been very difficult, him being away for so long.' Now they were launched on the theme she could not seem to let it go. Dare she ask about his wife? Where had she been at the ball the other night? Resting, perhaps while her husband prowled about agitating young ladies.

'Difficult? Yes it was certainly that. Oh, my cousin left the estate properly looked after and he kept in constant contact with his secretary and man of affairs. And he kept us fully informed about where he had been, as you know. I could never fault him for neglecting his duties. And we knew he was well – at least, that he was at the moment he had sealed the most recent letter, which was sometimes months before.'

'Rather like having a family member in the navy or the East India Company or perhaps running estates in the West Indies?' she suggested. Ralph's reaction did seem rather extreme, more like that of a sensitive sister than an adult male cousin.

'Yes, of course. We were not alone in having that sort of concern always at the back of – ' He broke off, staring at the door.

'His Grace the Duke of Calderbrook, my lady.' The footman stood back for Cal who went directly to his hostess.

'Lady Elmham.' He was in immaculate biscuit-coloured pantaloons, Hessians with silver tassels, dark blue swallowtail coat and crisp white linen, a stark contrast against the black sling that supported his right arm.

Sophie had told her mother about the accident and how she had taken Cal to the doctor and then home. Even if she had been alone and without a groom to witness everything, she did not deceive her parents, not any longer.

'Good afternoon, Your Grace.' Her mother rose and shook hands without revealing for a moment that she had noticed the sling, let alone that she knew the circumstances of the injury. 'Who may I make known to you? Lord and Lady Philpott. Mr and Mrs Wigton and Miss Wigton. Mr Parsloe. Lady Penelope Harrington.' There was a round of handshaking before the duke took a chair beside Sophie. 'And of course your cousin and my daughter you know. Sophie dear, a cup of tea for the Duke.'

'Of course. Good afternoon, Your Grace. Milk or lemon?'

'Good afternoon, Miss Wilmott, Cousin. Lemon, if you please.'

She passed the cup, waited while he stirred the tea and returned the spoon to the saucer and the other guests had recalled themselves and resumed their conversations. In for a penny, in for a pound. It was ridiculous to edge around the subject, speculating. 'The Duchess does not accompany you?' Sophie enquired. On her other side Ralph drew in a sharp breath.

'I am a widower,' Cal replied.

'Oh.' *Oh, good. Oh... how truly* awful *of me.* 'I do apologise.' Were her quite dreadful thoughts written right across her face?

'For leaping to conclusions? Did you think me a wicked rake?'

From the corner of her eye Sophie saw Ralph draw himself up in his chair as though to spring to her defence. 'Of course,' she said with a laugh. 'A quite outrageous flirt, Duke.' As she hoped, Ralph relaxed a trifle as though believing that this was merely a jest. 'Do you plan a long stay in London, or are you *en route* for Calderbrook?'

'I thought to finish the Season here, outfit myself, and then go to Calderbrook in July.'

'I would have thought that after all this time you would not be able to keep away,' Ralph said. Was it her imagination or was his tone judgmental?

'I can restrain my desire to walk my ancestral acres quite easily,' Cal said, taking a macaron from the plate Sophie offered. She had the ridiculous sensation that she was flinging herself between the two men when, really, not a word had been said out of place. 'After all, they do not hold the same charms of familiarity for me as they do for you, Cousin.' He bit down on the sweetmeat and she gave a little shiver.

Ralph put down his empty tea cup with a snap.

'Some more tea, Mr Thorne?' Try as she might, her voice sounded strained to her own ears. It would be Ralph's third cup and he was already ten minutes past the half-hour's stay that, by custom, morning calls were limited to. Across the room the Wigtons, who had arrived after him, were getting to their feet and making their farewells.

'Thank you, but I must take my leave. Miss Wilmott.' Ralph rose and bowed slightly, making eye contact with pointed emphasis. 'Cousin.' She watched him as he made his way across to her mother, exchanging a word with the remaining guests as he went. Surely he was not put out because Cal had joined them? That would imply that he was jealous – and that he had something to be jealous about. Or a right to the emotion, come to that, given that he had not said a word that might be construed as intended to fix her interest.

Now she was being unfair. She had considered Ralph Thorne as a potential husband very seriously, so she had no right to feel he was being presumptuous in taking an interest in her and her relationship with other men. And she had encouraged him, gone driving with him, browsed and chatted in the bookshop when they met there, strolled with him in the park. Danced two sets with him at every ball this Season.

The man might very reasonably feel he had some claim on her attention after that, even if he was playing his own cards very close to his chest.

'Miss Wilmott?'

She started in her seat and turned back to the Duke. 'Your Grace?'

'The weather seems settled fair. Will you do me the pleasure of driving with me tomorrow?'

Would she? Ralph usually asked her to drive with him when he came to take tea, but today he had not. Even so, she had absolutely no excuse for driving with the Duke. Or having anything to do with him, come to that.

'I bought a matched pair of bays for my new high-perch curricle at Tattersalls' this morning. Will you adorn it when I show them off for the first time?'

The temptation was strong and, of course, it was the prospect of driving in a sporting vehicle and pair, not by the prospect of his company, that lured her. Sophie winced at her own attempts at self-delusion. 'Should you be driving with an injured arm, Duke?'

'It is my whip hand so I find I can manage well enough. In fact I am only wearing this sling to convince my secretary that I cannot tackle the pile of paperwork he has deposited on my desk.'

She did not believe that for a moment. 'Or perhaps

you wear it to attract the ladies by appearing to be a wounded hero. Which, of course, you are,' she added, contrite. 'I shudder to think what might have happened to that poor child, or, to be utterly selfish, how I would be feeling now, if I had hurt her.'

'I have not noticed any hero-worship so far. Lots of meaningful gazes because I am a duke, of course. It is very flattening to one's self-esteem to know one's title is the main attraction.'

'As opposed to your beautiful soul or your great mind or your fine profile?' Sophie enquired wickedly.

'Ah, some hero worship at last. You had noticed those?' The deep voice sank to a seductive murmur and his enigmatic eyes gazed into hers, keeping their secrets.

'No, I cannot say that I have. You, Duke, are a wicked man.' She knew he seen the twitch of her lips that she simply could not control.

'Despite that, will you drive with me?'

It was very tempting to say *yes*. Was it always wrong to give in to temptation? Yes, she was going to drive with him. It was a foregone conclusion from the moment he asked her, and she knew it. There was only so much will-power a woman could exert. He was gorgeous, he made her laugh, he was dangerously seductive. Not that she would ever allow herself to be seduced again.

'Yes, I will, thank you.'

'At three if that is convenient?'

The other guests were rising to leave and the Duke rose with them, made his farewells with the maximum of grace and the minimum of fuss. Sophie watched him listening to Lady Philpott's chatter as she preceded him into the hallway, answering her nonsense with grave courtesy. Oh dear, she could come to like the wretched man entirely too well.

'A note for you, Miss Wilmott.' Parrot stood beside her, proffering a salver with one folded sheet of paper on it. 'Mr Thorne realised he had forgotten to ask you something and did not feel he should intrude again.'

The note was unsealed. *Forgive me, but I neglected to ask whether our usual drive would please you tomorrow. I very much look forward to it, as I do to all our time together. RT.*

And she had just agreed to drive with Cal tomorrow. *Our usual drive... our time together...* Ralph Thorne sounded proprietary, all of a sudden. She suspected that the Duke's flirting had nettled him and provoked this change of tone. She had made a mull of this because she had not been paying attention to her own feelings, let alone his. She had encouraged him, she knew she had, and now she was going to hurt his pride because, compared to his cousin, Ralph seemed to fade into the background as he was probably all too well aware.

She only hoped for his sake that it would only be hurt pride if he asked for her hand and she hesitated, because, suddenly, all her certainty that she could make a loveless, but amiable, marriage was shaken. Yes, she did pray that Ralph did not hold deeper, passionate feelings for her that he was concealing. And she had an uneasy feeling that he would not make a good enemy. She had no wish to be the cause of trouble between him and his cousin.

Chapter Five - Where the Duke is Provoking

By half past one the next day Sophie had written a careful note to Ralph thanking him for his invitation but pleading an earlier, unspecified, engagement; had resisted her mother's attempts to rig her out in her very newest walking dress and bonnet and had wrestled with the tricky question of how one indicated to a gentleman that, while he had done nothing to offend you, you did not wish to be courted by him. Which was made even trickier because it would be truly, hideously, embarrassing if the Duke was doing no such thing and it was all in her imagination.

The Duke of Calderbrook appeared to feel they shared a secret intimacy because he had overheard her conversation with Toby. She supposed, in way, they did, for no gentleman should have such an insight into the mind of a well-bred young lady on such a sensitive subject as marriage. Certainly she felt he understood her in a way that no man, including her stepfather and Toby, did. Ralph Thorne never showed any awareness of her emotions, although he was usually sensitive enough to her mood.

She dithered over which pair of gloves to wear. Tan? No, hideous with the blue of her walking dress. Black? No, that looked as though she was in mourning. *Oh, for goodness sake!* She seized a pair of blue ones which were just the wrong shade to match, ignored her maid's protest at the contrast, and jerked them on. The Duke was not courting her, she was most certainly not trying to attract him and the shade of her dratted gloves was the kind of trivial, brainless detail that empty-headed girls spent hours worrying about.

'There's the knocker, Miss Wilmott.' Mary was edging closer as though to make a grab for the unsatisfactory gloves.

'Yes.' Sophie closed her fingers firmly around her reticule and escaped.

The Duke was making polite conversation with Mama in the drawing room. At least Step Papa had the tact not to appear too. That would have made it all too obvious that the pair of them were assessing a potential suitor.

'Miss Wilmott.' He was on his feet fast, smoothly, without any indication that his shoulder was handicapping him.

She bobbed a curtsy, saw Mama cast a startled glance at the gloves, which in the brighter light of the drawing room were most certainly the wrong shade, and smiled. 'Good afternoon, Your Grace. I am quite ready, I wouldn't want to keep your horses standing.'

'You are thoughtful, thank you.' He said nothing further until they were out on the front steps, then he asked, 'What do you think of them?'

A gentleman soliciting her opinion on his horses? Unheard of. Most men assumed their judgement was perfect in such matters and that she would be admiring whether the beasts were knock-kneed, spavined or sway-backed. 'I think they look magnificent from here.' Sophie went down to the pavement and across to look at their heads, then their backs and quarters. 'Perfect confirmation, kind eyes and they seem very steady as they stand there. What are they like in traffic?'

'Steady there too. I would not be taking you out if they weren't. Excitement is one thing, recklessness when I have one useful arm, quite another.' Cal came to help her up into the high seat, then went round to the other side to climb in before he adjusted the carriage rug over her knees. 'I thought you would prove to have a good eye.'

Ridiculous to be flattered. Foolish to feel a skip of her heart when he mentioned excitement. 'Why should you think so?'

'Your dapple mare. Stand away from their heads, Ben.' The tiger scuttled round to the back and swung himself up onto his tiny perch.

'She was a present from my stepfather.' Sophie resisted the instinct to clutch at the side rail of the phaeton as it moved away from the kerb. On its long springs the motion of the carriage was like being suspended in a swing.

'Who bought her without consulting you?' Cal sent her a sliding, sideways look that made her laugh.

'No, *after* consulting me.'

He eased the reins and the pair stepped out, black tails swishing, glossy rumps gleaming. 'No, *walk*. And you have seen a lamp post before, and a dog, you air-headed creature.' He touched the right-hand horse lightly with the whip and glanced at her again when she laughed. 'That's the dim one. His brother got all the brains.' He eased the reins again and they began to trot, perfectly balanced.

Good horses or very assured driving? She suspected both. 'Where are you taking me, Duke?'

'I was waiting to see what you were wearing. That isn't a new outfit, so I assume you are not eager to show it off along Rotten Row. Green Park is rather – What?'

'How do you know this is not new?' Sophie demanded. 'It is a perfectly nice walking outfit.'

'I never said it was not, although I would have said *charming* rather than nice, if you had asked. But you wouldn't have been so careless over your choice of gloves if it had been brand spanking new.'

'I was... distracted. And then my maid so obviously wanted to make a fuss about them that I was stubborn.' It was her turn to send a sideways glance. Cal's eyes were firmly forward, watching the road, but the corner of his mouth twitched. 'Don't laugh at me.'

'I would not dream of it. I think the northern end of Hyde Park and then perhaps Gunther's for an ice if this sunshine stays with us?'

'That would be delightful.' And a route over the hillocks and dips of that end of the park which would be *interesting* in this vehicle. Ralph always drove her sedately around Green Park, or along Rotten Row if it was the fashionable time to be seen there.

'Shall we see what they can do?' Cal asked as they turned in through the Uxbridge Road gate. Almost on her nod the bays broke into a controlled canter. 'All right? Hold on to my arm if we're swaying too much for you.'

It was tempting and would probably be far more comfortable than clenching her fingers around the thin side rail, which is what she had been about to do. Sophie slid her fingers under Cal's arm and curled them into the crook of his elbow. He was warm and solid and she could feel the movement of his muscles as he controlled the pair with small movements of his fingers.

'They are behaving beautifully.' *And you drive like a dream.* Which was very attractive, she acknowledged. A man performing something physical with skill was bound to be so. Her imagination slid treacherously towards what other physical skills he might have.

Stop it, she told herself. This outing was doing nothing for her acceptance that the Duke really could never be more than an acquaintance. *You are not what he will be looking for. Dukes want pure, well-bred brides. With the emphasis on pure, which I am not.* Which was ridiculous, but then Society and men made the rules, not the young women caught up in them.

'Would you like to take them?' Cal reined in the pair who dropped from their canter down to a walk and then to a halt.

'Drive them? Me?'

'You have got good hands,' he said, as though she assumed he'd be nervous that she was cow-handed. It not did appear to have occurred to him that she might be terrified of driving this swaying, fragile vehicle and two unknown blood horses.

And that, of course, was an unspoken challenge that could not go unanswered. 'If you are sure, then thank you, Cal, I would love to drive.'

She took the reins, letting the pair settle and get used to the pressure coming from a slightly different angle. Cal handed her the whip and she eased the reins, clicking her tongue in encouragement as they moved off. 'It is easier to balance when I have the reins,' she said, surprised.

'You know what is happening, so your body is ready for the movement,' he said, cheerfully ignoring the fact that he had just referred to a lady's *body*. Mama would have kittens, Sophie found it refreshing. It was also rather… stimulating that he was thinking about it, even in the context of driving.

Her hands must have done something on that thought and the bays began to trot.

'All right?' Cal sounded perfectly unconcerned at the increased speed.

'Wonderful!' She would like to canter, but that would be foolish, this first time. She had just caught the thought, was telling herself firmly that there wouldn't *be* a second time, when a rider on a chestnut gelding, who was crossing at right angles, reined in abruptly, then trotted down the track towards them until the gelding was almost nose to nose with Cal's pair. Faced with the options of running him off the track or stopping, Sophie stopped, fuming.

Beside her Cal straightened in the seat. 'Cousin. What in Hades do you think you are doing?'

'What am *I* doing?' It was Ralph Thorne, she realised. 'What are you thinking of, giving the reins of that lethal equipage to Miss Wilmott? That is no vehicle for a lady – and a *pair*, for Heaven's sake. I would never dream of handing the reins of my carriage to her.'

'Then she probably finds driving with you a dead bore,' Cal drawled. 'Which is no doubt why she is driving with me and not you.' The air was suddenly crackling with the unspoken threat of violence.

Sophie clenched her teeth on the questions she knew she must not ask. Had Cal known she regularly drove with Ralph and that was why he asked her? But why, unless he wanted to make his cousin jealous – and why would he want to do that? *Men…* she could knock both of their heads together just now.

'I happen to be sitting right here and I am quite capable of answering for myself, thank you, gentlemen.' They both looked at her as though she was a juicy bone they had begun to fight over and then, engrossed in their antipathy, had forgotten was actually there. Sophie stifled a mad urge to giggle. 'If I had received your invitation first, Mr Thorne, I would have been delighted to accept it as I always find our drives together most entertaining.' She resisted the temptation to jab Cal in the ribs with her elbow, just in case he hadn't caught that. 'As it was, the Duke asked me before I received your note and I am equally delighted to be driving with him and most flattered that he should allow me to take the reins of his very well-behaved pair.'

Cal bit the inside of his lower lip to stop the smile that would, doubtless, have Ralph off his horse and at his throat, thinking it was directed at him. *Touché*, Miss Wilmott. 'Both a gracious lady and a diplomat,' he observed.

Beside him there was a low growl. Well, yes, he was being patronising and he probably deserved that reaction, but it was Ralph he wanted to inflame, not her. At least, not in this way. The thought of Sophie inflamed with another kind of passion altogether had him hard with wanting in a flash of heat. *Hell.*

'If you will excuse us, Mr Thorne, I really do not want to keep the horses standing,' Sophie said crisply. At least she was annoyed with both of them.

Ralph touched his whip to the brim of his hat and turned the chestnut off the track, cantering away without a backwards glance.

Sophie let the pair walk on, a rather less tidy manoeuvre this time as her tension communicated itself to the horses. 'Are you – '

'Is he – No, you go first, Sophie,' Cal murmured.

'Are you deliberately trying to pick a quarrel with your cousin, Duke?'

So, they were back to titles, were they. 'Certainly not,' he lied. 'But he is acting like a pompous ass.'

'You both were,' she said snappishly. 'Or, rather, like boys.'

Cal let that go, it was too near the truth to counter convincingly. 'Tell me, is he courting you?'

'No. Yes... Perhaps.' Sophie let the pair trot and reined them back. 'He hasn't said anything either to me or to Step Papa. He doesn't... that is, he has not...'

'Tried to kiss you?' If Ralph had tried anything more he'd have his balls.

'Yes, I mean, no, he hasn't.'

'So how long has *perhaps* been going on?'

'About three months. We are almost at the Serpentine, which way should I go?'

'Follow the road round and we will go back north up the eastern edge of the park,' Cal said with a vague wave of his hand that sent a stab of pain through his sore shoulder. 'Three months? And he has made no declaration, not tried to make love to you? What the devil's the matter with him? Does he snarl at any other men who take you about or ask you to dance?'

'Only you,' she admitted. 'I suppose it is very

gentlemanly to be so, um, well-behaved, but…'

'You rather wish he would get on with it?'

'If you put it like that, yes.' The smile was back in her voice now.

He fell silent, watching the horses as she negotiated the stretch of road alongside the water. He didn't want a sudden flight of duck to spook them and unnerve her. Once they were safely past the danger he said, 'And what will you answer when he does, finally, summon up the courage to put the question?'

'That is none of your affair, Duke.' She reined in. 'Will you take them now, I am becoming tired.'

'Yes, of course.' Cal took the reins, adjusted his grip on the whip without actually wincing and sent the pair into a collected canter. 'I will drive you home directly.' He wanted to ask her more, never mind that it was already a most improper conversation and she had very firmly, and properly, snubbed him. But Ben was up behind and, discreet as he was, he had already overheard too much.

He half expected to be treated to affronted silence for the half hour it took them to reach her front door, but he should have realised that Miss Wilmott was far too well-mannered for a fit of the sulks. She remarked upon the weather, other carriages they passed, the gait of his horses, the latest plays and the crowded streets, all in the most pleasant of conversational tones. By the time they drew up at the Wimpole Street house Cal was wishing for either stony silence or a tongue-lashing. If she was auditioning for the role of duchess she could not have performed better.

Ben jumped down and ran to the horses' heads. Cal dismounted with rather more caution, cursing his stiff shoulder and very much aware that he was smarting at not being able to vault down. To be fretting about it was almost as humiliating as feeling twenty years older than he was.

Sophie allowed him to help her alight. 'Thank you.

That was most… instructive. I did appreciate being able to drive such a dashing vehicle, Duke.'

'I would be honoured to take you out again, Miss Wilmott. We never made it to that ice cream, did we? Perhaps another time.'

'I do not think that would be a good idea, do you, Duke?' She did not wait for his answer before she mounted the steps with a smile for the butler who had flung the door wide for her.

Cal drove off down Wimpole Street very conscious of his tiger's crashing silence behind him. He had known Hooper, Ben's grandfather and the stable master at Calderbrook, since he was a child. On hearing of his impending return Prescott had sent to his long-unvisited estate for grooms and a coachman and young Ben had come too.

In a few days Cal had discovered that, besides being a magician with horses, the lad had an almost irrepressible urge to comment on everything. He was also vocal about how pleased everyone was that His Grace was home and how his 'granfer' had given him a lecture on the importance of a tiger. 'He said I was a confidential servant, 'cos of what I see and overhear when I'm out with my gentleman,' he had reported, swelling with pride.

'He did?' Cal had asked, managing to keep his mouth from twitching into a smile.

He must have looked sceptical because the boy said fiercely, 'I can keep me trap shut. Gossip's for girls. And Granfer said I would be a bodyguard too.'

'A *what?'* What did old Hooper know if he thought Cal needed a bodyguard?

'I'm to throw myself between you and highwaymen with shooters and make sure you get's home when you're top heavy,' Ben had announced with total confidence. Cal had refrained from pointing out that the boy's skinny little body would hardly stop a bullet and that he was not in the habit of driving himself when too drunk to cope, but he *had* believed in the lad's loyalty and guts.

'Well?' he enquired when the heavy breathing became intolerable.

'You made a right pig's ear of that, Your Grace, iffen you don't mind me saying so.'

'Would it make any difference if I did? No, don't answer that. I made a pig's ear of it, as you so tactfully put it, only if I was actually courting the lady. I am not.' He was not ready to commit himself. Not yet.

'You wuz winding up Mr Thorne then. So 'e's not a friend, even though he's your coz? I likes to know, see, so I knows who's on our side and who isn't.'

'Side?' Cal probed, keeping his voice casual.

'Granfer says that's important for a confidential servant like me to know who the Master trusts and who he don't.' The tiger relapsed into thoughtful silence then added, 'She's got nice 'ands, the lady.'

She's got very nice everything, Cal mused as he drew up at his own front door and handed over the reins to Ben. It was very tempting to let himself daydream about getting *his* hands on her.

He trudged up the steps, shoulder and back aching, half-regretting he'd taken Sophie out that afternoon and not let his shoulder heal for a few more days. But damn it, he wasn't an invalid any longer, hadn't been for years, and he was tough enough to get fit again without mollycoddling himself.

'Your Grace.' Benson, his town butler, took hat and gloves.

'Have a hot bath drawn will you? I'll be in my study.'

'Your Grace, there's – '

'Later, Benson.' Cal scooped up the letters from the salver on the side table and walked down the hall as he studied the envelopes. The study door was ajar and he went in, elbowing it shut behind him, head still bent over the post as he broke the seal on the thickest letter. A sound made him glance up, just in time for a clenched fist to connect solidly with the point of his jaw.

Cal went down, banging his head against the door panels, then his bad shoulder for good measure. His right hand slid the knife from his boot even as the damaged shoulder joint screamed for mercy.

Then he saw who had hit him.

'Ralph. What the hell was that for?' *As though I don't know*. He kept his fingers around the hilt of the knife hidden against his leg, but made no attempt to get up. It would be interesting to see what followed. Because if this was intended to be a murder, then he knew just how he would do it if he was in Ralph's shoes.

Chapter Six - Where Sophie Plays Cupid

Cal stayed where he was and waited for Ralph to make his move. His cousin stood there, silent, cradling bruised knuckles and breathing heavily, then reached out a hand.

Here we go. Haul me to my feet while I'm still groggy, swing me round and one hard shove against the edge of the fireplace and there goes my skull. A terrible accident while we were fighting over a woman. You only meant to hit me, never to kill me, but…

'Get up, for God's sake.' Ralph bent, clasped Cal's uninjured arm and heaved. Cal came up, apparently off-balance, the knife still by his side, waiting, waiting… as his cousin gave him an ungentle shove into the big chair behind the desk. 'I didn't hit you that hard.'

'Hard enough.' Cal slid the knife back into his boot and cradled his right arm against his side. 'Hit my bad shoulder on the door.'

'Well you should not have been out driving a lady with it if it is that bad,' Ralph snapped. 'You should be resting.'

'I have spent too much of my life in bed, resting.'

His cousin shot him a look, as though not certain whether there was a *double entendre* in the statement. 'What are your intentions towards Miss Wilmott?'

Cal sat up straighter and put both hands on the desk. Ralph, on the far side, shifted uncomfortably, put into the subordinate position. 'Are you betrothed to Miss Wilmott or have any kind of understanding with her?'

'No.' His cousin set his jaw, the embarrassed, angry colour coming up in unflattering blotches over his cheeks.

'Nor are you any relative of the lady. As far as I am aware, and I took pains to find out, Miss Wilmott is unattached. So, by what right are you asking my intentions? Or punching me in the jaw in my own house, come to that.'

'I am courting her. I have been for weeks.'

'Not according to Miss Wilmott who is, it seems, rather confused by your intentions, given your lack of ardour.'

'My *what?*' Both of Ralph's fists thudded down on the desk and three pens fell off the standish with a clatter. 'What the devil has she been saying?'

'Nothing at all to the matter. However, if you have been courting her for weeks and she is unaware of the fact, then I would suggest that a certain passion might be lacking.'

This is the point where he goes for my throat.

Ralph slumped into the chair on the other side of the desk and dragged his fingers through his hair. 'I thought we were friends. I have never come across a woman I can talk to like that. It's not that I'm in love with her, but I ought to marry and I was wondering if we would suit.' He looked far more fraught about it than his words suggested. 'And then you came along.'

'And you got an attack of dog-in-the-manger?' Hell, now he was feeling sympathetic. He should be goading Ralph and yet he could not do it. Damn it, this was the man who had helped him through his first blundering, confusing encounters with girls with cheerfully frank good advice from his own hard-won experience.

'It doesn't occur to you that you never had any trouble before with thinking about beautiful, blonde, blue-eyed women in all manner of ways that do not involve friendship and that therefore a friend must be just what

Sophie is to you?'

'Sophie?' It came out as a growl.

'In my thoughts,' Cal said smoothly. Sympathy would only stretch so far. He had no intention of discussing his exact relationship with Sophie Wilmott. Especially when he hadn't worked it out for himself. Other than to find himself permanently aroused when he was around her. Or thought about her, come to that. 'Have a drink.' Either Ralph was the world's most inept murderer or he had lost the ability to improvise. *Or he is innocent.*

'Thanks.' His cousin stayed slumped in the chair.

'You can pour. The decanters are over there. I am going to stay here nursing my dislocated shoulder, broken jaw, cracked skull and bruised arse, three of which you are responsible for.'

Ralph heaved himself to his feet, a spark of his old spirit in his eyes as he narrowed them at Cal. 'If your jaw was broken you couldn't speak, your head is too hard to crack and I am not even going to contemplate your bruised backside.'

He poured brandy into two glasses with a heavy hand and dumped them on the desk before he sank back into the chair again. 'Are you going to marry her?'

'Can't tell you, not yet. I don't know what I want to do, let alone what she does. But she is eligible and I need a wife, someone to be a mother to Isobel. Someone to do all the things a duchess does.'

'Like give you an heir.'

'I have heirs. Two of them.' This was getting too close to the knuckle. Suddenly he didn't want to confront this, not yet and not now with Ralph slumped in the chair opposite looking tired and depressed and with his own head aching and apparently incapable of rational thought.

'Two heirs presumptive, not an heir apparent,' Ralph said. He took a deep swallow of the spirit then slammed down the glass, suddenly angry. 'I don't want your bloody title and you have years to get an heir in.' Had there been an emphasis on the *I*? 'Marry Sophie Wilmott, why don't you? Raise a brood of sons, trail about in ermine and a coronet. The sooner the better. I am sick of living in the shadow of your bloody dukedom, of it being all my father ever thinks about.'

He was on his feet and out of the door before Cal could stand. There was the sound of voices in the hall, then the front door closing.

Jared came in without troubling to knock. 'What in Hades was that about? And what has happened to you now?' He clenched his fist and tapped it against the side of his own chin.

'My dear cousin landed me a particularly fine right hook for interesting myself in the lady he has been courting. Or not courting. He doesn't seem too sure which it is. However, he passed up a perfect opportunity to beat my brains out and make it look like an accident and has informed me that I should marry and sire an heir because he is, and I quote, sick of living in the shadow of my bloody dukedom.'

'How come you let him flatten you?' Jared took another glass and a finger of brandy, took the seat Ralph had used and rolled the glass between his long, swordsman's fingers while he looked over the rim at Cal, dark gaze assessing.

'He took me by surprise. And yes, that should not have happened and yes, I will take more care with him in future. But it at least proved that he isn't thinking of leaping on any opportunity to finish me off. He thought he had stunned me. He could have thumped my skull onto any sharp surface in this room and made it look like the chance result of a fair fight over a lady, a tragic accident. He wasn't to know I had a knife drawn on him that he could not see.'

'Or he is slower on the uptake than either of us and can't grasp an opportunity when it's under his nose,'

Jared mused. 'Tell me about the lady.'

'Bugger off,' Cal said amiably. Jared grinned and they sat savouring their drinks in silence. There was something about the way that his friend lounged there that made him uneasy, but he couldn't put a finger on it until the other man turned sideways, propped his elbow casually on the edge of the desk and crossed his legs at the ankles with a sigh of contentment.

'What was the matter with him?' Cal wondered aloud. Jared cocked one brow in question. 'My cousin. Yes, he was in a state over Soph – over the woman. Yes, he had thumped me and then found himself being, apparently, forgiven. Before I left England he was the big brother, the dominant one. Now he ends up on the visitor's side of the desk with a glass of my best brandy, having an amiable conversation, and yet he was as uneasy as a thieving servant hauled in here and trying to lie his way out of trouble. Look at you – sitting in the same place, doing the same thing, and you are as relaxed as an old pair of kid gloves.' Although Jared usually was relaxed, up to the point when he became a lethal predator.

'He is worried about something,' Jared mused. 'Something beyond a rivalry over a woman. The only question is whether he is worried for himself, or for his father, or for the pair of them.' When Cal simply grunted the other man lounged to his feet, finished the brandy in one swallow and stood there looking down at him.

'Now what? I've seen butchers eyeing a side of beef with less intent.'

'Come upstairs, let me check your head and your shoulder. I'd feel happier if you had two functioning arms and one of them your sword arm. An absence of concussion might be a good idea as well.'

'In a while.' Jared was right. He had neglected that shoulder and he had almost let himself be knocked out when he needed all the brain and all the muscle he could muster. It was not like him to ignore his fitness, or to let himself be distracted. Life was too dangerous for either. But first he needed to work out why his focus was so off. It wasn't hard to find the answer, not when he was honest with himself. Sophie Wilmott.

'Mr Thorne!' Bother the man. Lady Pettigrew's masquerade ball was a noisy, and to be frank, sweaty, crush. People shrieked to be heard above the babble of conversation, the musicians struggled even to be noticed and the windows were flung wide onto the humid summer air, giving the costumed, crowded, revellers as much relief as hot wet towels applied to their perspiring faces. It was, of course, a huge success, a magnificent squeeze destined to be written up at length in the Society columns of tomorrow's *Morning Post.*

It was also an exceedingly difficult occasion at which to firstly identify a masked gentleman in fancy dress and then haul him off to a corner secluded enough to hold a delicate conversation in.

Ralph Thorne was tall, which helped, and not given to flamboyant displays, which meant she could eliminate a pirate king (shirt open to the waist and bare feet), both Chinese Emperors (too much *macquillage* and false hair), the Egyptian mummy (hardly moving in a tangle of bandages and a vast *papier-maché* mask) and Louis XIV (too fat). That left about a hundred and fifty men.

And then she spotted him. Trust Ralph to choose something as simple as a highwayman, just like last year. He was wearing plain riding dress, a black cloak, a cocked hat, red-spotted neckerchief and a simple black mask.

'Mr Thorne!' Sophie gathered up her trailing skirts of shredded blue silk in a myriad of shades and began to wriggle through the crowd until she was right behind him. '*Ralph.*'

He turned and peered at her mask of aquamarine silk encrusted with pearls and shells. 'Madam? You know me… I mean, you think you know me?'

'It's Sophie,' she hissed. Really, she was not vain, but no-one in London Society had hair quite the shade of guinea-gold of hers. The man had spent hours in her company and he still could not recognise her and her water nymph costume was not *that* concealing.

'Oh. Good evening, Miss Wilmott.'

They were standing right in the path to the refreshment room. Sophie winced as Neptune's trident prodded her in the ribs. 'I need to talk to you.' She tugged at Ralph's arm.

'This isn't really the place for a conversation.' He looked decidedly harassed.

'As you have been avoiding me for a week it will have to do.' She linked arms with him and began to work her way towards the terrace windows. At least he was too well-mannered to stick his heels in and refuse to move.

'Phew.' She fanned herself vigorously with her free hand once they reached the terrace. Mama had said she would need a fan, but she hadn't been able to find anything that went with her costume and now she was regretting it.

'Miss Wilmott, would Lady Elmham approve? We do not have a chaperone, would you not rather go back inside and I will fetch you a drink?'

'No, thank you.' She as beginning to wish for Neptune's trident herself. 'The terrace is brightly lit, there are people all over the place and I only want to go as far as this balustrade. See? Perfectly respectable.' She turned and faced him, 'Ralph, why have you been avoiding me for the past week?'

'I have not,' he began.

'Even with that mask on you look shifty. Are you angry with me for going driving with Calderbrook? Because I did receive his invitation before yours. Honestly, I had no intention of snubbing you. I really do not want to lose a friend over something as foolish as this.'

'Is that how you see me? As a friend?' He shifted so he was closer, trying to search her expression behind the mask.

'Yes, of course.'

'I was concerned that I had – Oh, the devil.' He took a hasty pace away and then back. 'I was concerned that I had perhaps raised expectations that I had not intended to raise. At least, not yet. I mean I might – But I thought that I ought to – ' He broke off and tried to run his hand through his hair, realised that he was wearing a hat and stopped with a muttered curse.

His behaviour had been so possessive when they had encountered him in the park that she thought she would have every reason for assuming just that. Men were such idiots sometimes. 'You had not,' she said. 'If, perhaps, I had a *tendre* for you, then I might have assumed... something. More from your frequent invitations than anything else.'

'But you haven't?' he asked, anxious, seeming a good ten years younger than his age. When she shook her head he sighed, once more the sober adult male she had come to know.

'You are not making a lot of sense, Ralph.'

'I know. I told Cal that he ought to marry you.'

'You did *what*?'

'You would make an excellent duchess. That's why I – He is attracted to you.'

'How do you know that?' She ought to wave it aside, laugh it off, but she couldn't. 'Has he said so?' she demanded sharply. Along the terrace a few heads turned. Sophie made herself laugh, shifted so she was looking out from the balustrade across the gardens with their lantern-lit walks. The cousins had been discussing her.

Ralph moved to stand beside her. 'I have eyes in my head. He is attracted and you have the breeding, the looks, the intelligence and the upbringing.'

'Do you think he will consult the stud book, want to look at my teeth, calculate how many good breeding years I have left in me?' she enquired sweetly. 'I do have nice strong fetlocks.'

'Sophie!'

She had shocked him with her frankness. Well, good. She *had* begun to have expectations and she strongly suspected that he hadn't known his own mind, had been testing the waters for both of them. Now that his cousin had come along, a man who outranked him, was infinitely more wealthy and rather better-looking, he had decided she was not worth fighting for.

It occurred to her, rather guiltily, that she was as bad as he was, that she had been thinking seriously about Ralph as a potential husband, had been trying him out in many ways, before the Duke of Calderbrook had come on the scene.

'I do not look for a duke as a husband,' she said with perfect honesty and leaned a little against Ralph's shoulder. No duke would consider her a suitable vessel to bear his precious heirs, not when she confessed her past, as she would have to. There were ways of feigning virginity, apparently, but she felt revolted at such deception. What a sordid way to begin a marriage.

The truly wretched thing about it was that she did not think herself ineligible. She had made a mistake, been too trusting and romantic and she had suffered for it. Now she had a secret to keep. None of that made her poor duchess-material. She was older now, wiser. But a man would dismiss her out of hand for that one slip. Hypocrites, the lot of them.

But Ralph was still puzzling her. 'Tell me why you were seeing me, inviting me out driving, partnering me so often at dances if you were not serious.' A sudden explanation came to her. 'It isn't because you wanted me as camouflage because you are not, er…' Oh Lord, she had blundered into quicksand now. Best to say it quickly and then sink with embarrassment afterwards. 'Not, um, *interested* in women?'

Ralph's expression was answer enough. 'No! That is *not* it. You shouldn't even *know* about things like that, Sophie.' He took a few agitated paces along the terrace away from her and then back. 'Lord, I do not know when I have been more put out of countenance.'

'Why, when you are not that way inclined?' she demanded. 'You owe me an explanation, Ralph. If I was to complain to Step Papa that you had been raising false expectations then there would be the devil to pay.' It was blackmail, but she was determined to get to the bottom of this now.

'Can you keep a confidence, Sophie?' He leaned on the balustrade, his mouth set.

'Of course.' Now it was her turn to be affronted.

'I am heir presumptive to the dukedom, after my father.'

'That is no secret.'

'No, but with Calderbrook abroad for so long, in such remote, dangerous places, my father wanted me to marry, and marry well.'

'And produce another in the line of heirs in the event of Cal's death? That is... calculating.' She found that she was shocked.

'He would say it was prudent. My father *is* a very prudent man, careful, with an eye to securing the future as well as the present. He has served the dukedom for almost my entire life. It is not any desire for personal gain, you must believe that. It is simply...'

'Prudent. Yes, I see.' She must not judge, she had no responsibility for an ancient title and name, for vast estates that must have the security of a master and an heir after him. 'But why, if you set out to find yourself a wife, did you not look for someone for whom you could feel more definite about than me?'

'Because I am already in love,' Ralph said bleakly.

'And if I cannot marry her, then better to find someone with whom I can be friends, for whom I have a liking.'

Sophie swallowed a number of heated, hurt, words and waited until she had her voice under control before she spoke. 'I think I am exceedingly angry with you, Ralph Thorne. To be courted in that lukewarm way and then for you to consider marrying me even though you harboured such feelings for another woman – Why, that is downright deception.'

'But most aristocratic marriages are not love matches,' he protested.

'No, they are not, but they start with basic honesty and, I hope, without one partner yearning for someone else.' *I would have been honest with you about my past.* 'Who is she, that she is so unsuitable? An actress?'

'No, nothing so very shocking. Eva is the daughter of Calderbrook's tenant at the Home Farm. She is intelligent, educated, warm, lovely. And she is of honest yeoman stock without a drop of blue blood in her veins.'

'Does she love you?' Not that he deserved it. Poor woman. Another victim to the ideal of love above everything in a relationship.

'Yes,' Ralph said bleakly. 'But she understands that it is my duty to marry well.'

'Poppycock. Calderbrook is home now. He is fit, well and looks perfectly capable of siring a regiment of sons once he marries. The succession is his affair, not your responsibility.' She gave his arm an exasperated tug. 'We can't talk about this here, come down to the garden.' Ralph allowed himself to be guided down the steps and onto one of the gravel walks. 'You are a grown man, for goodness sake,' Sophie lectured as they walked. 'Tell your father that you will marry who you please. Besides anything else, a dash of good solid yeoman blood could only improve any blood line, I would say. Look, here's a seat.'

Ralph slumped next to her, slapped his hat down on

the stone and dragged off his mask. 'You are right. I've been an idiot. But… But if I wed Eva I don't know what my father will do.'

Chapter Seven - Where the Duke Experiences Fireworks

Sophie was here somewhere. Cal had located her mother who, like most of the more mature ladies, was only lightly disguised, and wheedled a description of Sophie's costume from her. It was obvious from her raised eyebrows and the little smile on her lips, even as she scolded him for asking, that she was pleased he was paying her daughter such marked attention.

The masquerade was becoming noisier, hotter, and was probably as crowded as it could get without people being lifted off their feet by the press of bodies. Locating one slender water nymph in all this was going to be no easy matter, even with the famous guinea-gold hair to look for.

He had almost given up on forcing his way through the mass of revellers and was turning to try the refreshment room when he caught a glimpse of sea-green draperies fluttering on the edge of the terrace. By the time he reached the same spot she had disappeared, only the flicker of a hem vanishing down one of the paths betraying where she had gone.

A masquerade ball was not the occasion for a stroll in the gardens, not if one was an unmarried lady. Cal set off in pursuit, telling himself it was only his duty to rescue her from whatever compromising indiscretion she had got herself into. The fact that he knew far too much about the kind of indiscretions one could commit in the dark corners of moonlit gardens only added to his sense of urgency.

Low-pitched voices, one male and gruff, one female, emphatic and recognisably Sophie's, drifted back to him from behind a dense bank of shrubs. Cal approached, soft-footed. At least if they were talking she hadn't fallen into the clutches of the sort of man who would take instant advantage of her innocence. He stopped and listened, the stiff leaves of the plant prickling his legs through his thin silk evening breeches.

'For goodness sake,' Sophie said in an unmistakeably *pull yourself together* tone of voice. 'You are what? Thirty two? Stand up to him – it is about time you made your own life. He can choose to be tied up in what he sees as his duty, but I cannot for the life of me see why you should be.'

Whatever he had stumbled upon, it was not passionate love-making. The unseen man muttered something. 'Excellent,' Sophie said briskly. 'So, when will the wedding be?'

Cal, who had half-turned away, froze. Not passionate loving making, indeed. No, this was practical Miss Wilmott applying her sensible approach to finding a marriage partner. Ludicrous. Someone had to stop it.

Exactly why a respectable marriage – to a well-bred, well-off, intelligent husband – needed stopping, or why, if it did, he was the one who should be doing so, Cal did not stop to ask himself. He rounded the corner as the man, a highwayman, stood up and smiled down at the water nymph. 'I will be certain to send you an invitation.'

As he straightened Cal saw his unmasked face. Ralph. He stepped back silently into the shadow before he was seen. What in Hades was going on? His cousin would hardly be sending his own betrothed a wedding invitation, which meant that Ralph was marrying someone else and that Miss Logic herself was promoting the match. That was very fast work on Ralph's part if he had been half-heartedly courting Sophie for weeks. Presumably love at first sight, which seemed unlikely. He waited, hoping for another crumb of information.

'We should go back,' his cousin urged.

'It is so hot and so noisy. You go. I'll sit here for a few moments longer.'

'I should not leave you alone out here.'

'Nonsense, you must be wanting to go home and pack ready to leave tomorrow. You are going to go to your Eva tomorrow, aren't you?'

Even in the moonlight Ralph's blush was visible. *Good Lord, the man must be completely smitten.*

'Even so – '

'I am armed,' Sophie announced in much the same way as she might have remarked that she had a fan. 'There is a knife strapped to my thigh. Should anyone become a nuisance a prod with that will see him off.'

Dear God. The images that *knife, thigh* and *Sophie* combined conjured up had him rock hard in a second and were so distracting that Cal missed Ralph's words of farewell. When he came round the bush again Sophie was alone, her face tipped up to the moonlight as though to bathe in its rays.

The moment he appeared she was on her feet. 'I wish to be alone, sir. Please leave me.'

It took Cal a moment to remember that he was masked and that she could not know him. Had that boast about the knife simply been a way of reassuring Ralph that she was safe to leave or was she really armed? And, if so, why? He took one step nearer. One more and he would unmask, he had no intention of terrifying her.

'Very well, if you insist on intruding I must show you some discouragement.' Her hand went to her skirts and slid the fluttering silks up her right leg to the knee.

Discouragement? Cal could not have dragged his eyes away if she'd had the knife actually at his throat. He stopped dead and held up one hand in surrender. He might be all kinds of rake, but she was exposing enough flesh to ruin her if anyone came around the corner.

When Sophie released her skirts and took three steps forward so that they were toe to toe it took him so much by surprise that the palm of his raised hand was a fraction from her breast. It seemed strangely reluctant to move, even when she leaned forward and peered into his masked face. Somehow, with more willpower than he knew he had, he pulled his hand back.

'Cal,' she stated. 'I thought it was you. You have a most regrettable tendency to lurk about eavesdropping on my private conversations with other men.'

'How the he– how did you know it was me?' He had thought his disguise perfect. Black breeches, shirt, neckcloth and stockings and a masterpiece of a coat from the last century that he had picked up in Venice, unable to resist the sheer glamour of it. It was of black velvet embroidered thickly with silver, with whale-boned skirts that flared from his hips and a matching waistcoat. He had scraped back his hair under a white powdered wig from the same period and wore a black Venetian mask of pressed leather traced with silver. It covered his face from brow to just above his mouth. Impenetrable. He would have wagered on it.

'The way you move.' Sophie tipped her head to one side, as she studied his masked face. 'Your eyes, now I am near to you. I do not know anyone else with eyes of that silver-grey.'

She was so close that he could smell her scent, light and teasing, something with citrus and spice to it. And warm woman, still flushed from the heat of the ballroom. His body, already hard and primed, became harder. There was a trace of wine on her breath and beneath that the innocence of toothpowder. Her costume, with its flirty skirts and swooping draperies looked almost naughty, but it was cut cleverly to preserve her modesty, showing only a maidenly swell of white breasts and shoulder, bare arms adorned with fine kid gloves and a tangle of aquamarine bangles. But he had seen that length of slender stockinged leg, glimpsed the beginning of her white thighs above her garter and every sense was attuned to the naked woman beneath the draperies.

His palm was still towards her, the back of his hand to his chest. He only had to relax his wrist and his fingers could caress those smooth white curves, slip under the loose layers of silk to find her nipple. *Lean towards me, take the guilt away from me. Kiss me. Touch me.*

'Who is Ralph marrying?' he asked, his voice harsh with the effort of not saying all those other things, the words he wanted to whisper to her as he pulled her down with him to the wide stone bench.

'That is Ralph's secret.'

'I am the head of the family,' he said, wincing at the sound of his own pomposity. On the other hand, pompous heads of families did not ravish young ladies in the shrubbery…

'I am sure he will tell you when he is ready. He has to ask her first.' Sophie was still looking into his eyes, hers like tiny pools of deep ocean waters behind the mask. They narrowed as she smiled. 'He is in love, Cal.'

'Then what the blazes has he been doing hanging around you?' he demanded.

'He thought she was… lost to him,' Sophie said. That was not the truth, or, at least, not all of it. He was coming to know her and she was hiding something, or, rather, simply not saying it. 'He had resolved to make a marriage of convenience.'

That made sense of a sort. It certainly explained Ralph's half-hearted attempts at courtship. 'You have been matchmaking.'

She made a little humming noise that might have been agreement, might have been amusement. 'I know I think it is foolish to marry for love, or what one deludes oneself is love, but I had to make it up to him after I told him I was beginning to think that his interests did not lie with the female sex.'

'You hussy.' He grinned at her. 'What does an innocent like you know about such things?'

'I am not as sheltered as you seem to think, Your Grace.' The laughter had gone from her eyes even as her mouth continued to curve in her enchanting half-smile.

Kiss her. Just kiss her and stop fantasising about it. She is more than capable of boxing your ears if she doesn't like it.

'What are you smiling about?' Sophie was suspicious now, her eyes narrowed not in laughter, but in mistrust.

'A voice in my head.'

'You hear voices?' Now she was all concern. 'You must have hit your head the other day and not realised.' She stepped back, caught his hands in hers and tugged him towards the seat. 'You shouldn't be in this noisy place drinking alcohol. Rest a moment and then get a footman to call your carriage. You should see your physician in the morning. Or perhaps tonight.'

'No, Sophie – ' *On the other hand...* Cal kept hold of her hands as he sat and she perched close beside him, anxiously scrutinising as much of his face as she could see.

'Take your mask off, that cannot be helping.'

Obediently he untied the strings and put it down beside him. 'Perhaps I have a fever.'

'Oh, yes, you have. You are very warm.' Her hand, cool and gentle touched his forehead, heated by the mask he had been wearing for over an hour. Her fingers trailed down his temple, under his jaw and rested lightly at his throat. 'And your pulse is beating very strongly. Yes, that's right, close your eyes, Cal, rest a little. Perhaps we should loosen your neckcloth.'

Bliss. Her fingers worked at the knot and she pulled the ends loose. Cal could feel her body pressing against his as she worked, the warmth of her breath against his cheek, the cool of the night air as the fabric came free, the scent of her… The choking sensation as the ends of his neckcloth were drawn sharply together, strangling him.

'Sophie!' Cal hooked his fingers into the tightening fabric and pulled enough to get some air into his lungs.

'You, Your Grace,' she said, giving the ends a little jerk with each word by way of emphasis, 'are a rake and a flirt and I know exactly what that voice in your head was talking about to produce that smirk.' She released the ends of the neckcloth and treated him to a smug smile of her own.

'You baggage,' he said. *Clever, clever baggage.* 'I do take *no* for an answer, you have only to say if you do not want me to kiss you.'

'But I do want you to kiss me,' she said demurely. 'I just wanted to make it clear that I am not one of those silly girls who let themselves be lured into the shrubbery and cannot deal with the results.' That ended up sounding rather grim, he thought. Perhaps a friend of hers had experienced… results.

'Just a kiss?' Cal enquired, setting his hands around her waist. There were no stays under the shifting, slippery layers of silk. Just warm, curving female flesh. 'You have made an excellent beginning on undressing me that it seems a pity to waste that effort.'

She went deliciously pink. 'Just a kiss. One kiss.'

One kiss can last a long, long time, Cal told himself as he settled Sophie against him. She was pliant, responsive, not at all tense. *She has done this before*, he thought as he bent to her lips, his tongue sweeping along the lower curve to taste. She opened to him at once, her mouth sweet and soft, her tongue making a small, but confident, sweep over his in return. She tasted of the strawberries and champagne from the buffet and something tart, perhaps lemon, and she tasted of Sophie, just as he had imagined she would taste.

Cal smiled against her lips as she made a little

purring sound and wriggled closer. *I'm doing this to your satisfaction am I, Madam?* Yes, she had been kissed before, but there was still an innocence, a freshness, about this caress. She was tasting him, just as he was tasting her. She was exploring the man, he sensed, not simply wanting sensual satisfaction. And when he slid his hands up until his thumbs brushed against the underside of her breasts, she pulled back a little. No wanton, Sophie.

He took the hint, slid his hands down again, focussed on making love to her mouth and enjoying her increasingly bold responses. His body nagged at him for more, but he ignored the pulsing, building pressure, the insistent thrust of his erection beneath the thin knitted silk of his breeches.

A kiss, one kiss, could last all evening. The resulting arousal could last a week at this rate, but he would worry about that, take care of that, later. Cal sucked on her lower lip, nipped, laved the tiny bite with his tongue, and was not surprised when she nipped in return, then slid her lips across his cheek to nibble his earlobe.

Perhaps this couldn't last all evening after all. Much more of this and he would either spend like a randy youth or have to go and throw himself into whatever water feature was tinkling on the far side of the garden. A wicked, pointed tongue ran around the curve of his ear, then her teeth found the lobe again.

And the world exploded.

For a second Cal thought it was the most violent orgasm he had ever experienced. Then Sophie's teeth closed painfully on the tender flesh of his ear and she jerked free with a startled yelp.

Cal found himself on his feet, Sophie pressed to him protectively, his hand reaching for where his sword would have been if he had been wearing one, and the sky above crackled and banged and trails of stars cascaded across the darkness.

'Oh, fireworks!' She was laughing in his arms, the

minx, shaking with amusement.

'It is all right for you,' Cal grumbled in to her hair, taking the opportunity to lash his arms even more tightly about her. 'I may never recover from the shock. I will probably become impotent and end my days in a monastery.'

Sophie gave a little wriggle, sending fireworks of their own through the relevant organs. 'I do not think that is going to be a problem, Your Grace.' She came up on tiptoe, pressed a fleeting kiss to his lips and stepped back. 'Don't forget your neckcloth. And your wig is crooked. I must go back to Mama.' Then she was gone into the shadows.

'Baggage.' Cal collapsed onto the bench and made a business of retying his neckcloth, straightening his wig and retying his mask in the hope that the visible effects of that little interlude would subside before he went back into the light.

That had been a revelation, he thought as he took his time strolling back along the winding paths to the terrace to join the crowd still exclaiming over the fireworks. Not that he hadn't expected to enjoy kissing Sophie Wilmott, or that he hadn't expected that she might be willing to kiss him. No, it was the effect it had on him, the wanting to do it again, as soon as possible, for as long as possible and the almost contrary realisation that there was no impatience to move things on faster than Sophie was willing to be wooed.

Wooed? Hell's teeth, had he actually decided to woo the woman for herself and not simply to provoke Ralph? He supposed he must have. That was an interesting revelation. Cal strode through the ballroom, now far less crowded with the pyrotechnics still in progress, and took a glass of arrack punch from the buffet, knocked it back in one and almost choked. Lord, but Lady Pettigrew's butler did not stint on the alcohol. At this rate he was going to be hung-over, blue-balled *and* a suitor come the morning.

He picked up another glass and sipped with more caution. Sophie certainly met his requirements for a wife and, having heard her give a very full explanation of her desiderata for a husband, he was confident he matched them all. After this evening she was even in a very good position to judge whether he might be considered well-endowed. Now all he had to do was to consider tactics, although he could not imagine her mother and step-father turning down a duke for their daughter.

As he strolled back out to the terrace it occurred to him that Isobel might have a view on acquiring a stepmother, but she had seemed to like Sophie. And then there was the question of Sophie's safety. Surely she would not be a target until she became pregnant? He took off his mask and scrubbed one hand over his face, actually *thinking*, it seemed, for the first time since his mouth had met Sophie's.

'Evening, Duke.' Lord Wortham, similarly unmasked, strolled past. 'All right? You look as though you've just been jabbed with a pin!' He went on his way, roaring with laughter.

Jabbed with a pin? Knocked on the head, was more like it. When Madeleine had announced that she was expecting his child he had still been too angry at having been trapped into marriage to care – until the baby was born. At which point it was love at first sight. But Sophie… his children… This was different and he was not at all sure he liked the way it made him feel. Terrified.

Chapter Eight - Where Sophie Confesses

It was difficult, not thinking about the Duke of Calderbrook. In fact it was impossible. And that sinister Jared Hunt hadn't helped matters. Sophie threaded some green silk floss onto her needle and tried to feel some enthusiasm for the bell pull she was embroidering.

Last night had been magical and exiting and decidedly agitating, but not as agitating as walking slap into Mr Hunt, unmasked and looking exceptionally dangerous in plain black. He wore his hair unfashionably long, tightly braided and tied back with a strip of leather, usually. Now it was loose, flowing around his shoulders, and he looked like some Renaissance Italian searching for an arras to hide behind before stabbing someone with a stiletto.

She had curtseyed, one hand to her mask to be certain it was securely back in place and he, bother him, had bowed and said, 'Good evening, Miss Wilmott.'

Then, when she would have passed him by without any further conversation, he had put out one hand to detain her. 'Miss Wilmott, a word of warning.' She had been so taken aback that she had simply stared at him as he added smoothly, 'I suggest that toying with the Duke's affections might not be a good idea, not if there is another man in the equation.'

'I… There is… Have you been spying on us?'

'I watch his back, not what he does. His Grace takes his honour very seriously, and, of course, that of the women in his life. He has killed his man before now in a duel and I really would recommend that you take care.'

'Killed?'

'In America. Someone who tried to lure his wife into an entanglement. He was a dangerous opponent, a man with a reputation, but the Duke did not hesitate to challenge him.' He bowed once more and strolled off leaving her shaken and apprehensive, staring after him.

Sophie came back to the present with a start and found herself back in the drawing room. 'The Duke of Calderbrook, Miss Wilmott.' Parrott was managing to look both smug – which went with being a superior butler – and indulgent, a fairly nauseating combination.

Sophie jabbed her needle into her thumb, said something regrettable under her breath and tossed aside the embroidery frame with its new blood spot to add to the misshapen flowers. Sewing was one of her skills, but her concentration had been completely absent these past few days. 'Thank you, Parrott. Please send Mary down.'

'I could just leave the door open, Miss Wilmott.' She could have sworn the butler's left eyelid drooped into something perilously close to a wink. 'I will be right outside.'

'Very well.' Parrott being obvious was probably less embarrassing than having a witness in the room as she dealt with last night's impetuous kiss in the cold light of day. Her heart was pounding and she felt decidedly light-headed which was embarrassment of course, and nothing whatsoever to do with wanting to see the man again.

'His Grace the Duke of Calderbrook.' Parrott opened the door onto a vast bouquet of flowers which appeared to have legs of its own. Legs clad in exquisite Hessian boots and exceedingly tight biscuit-coloured pantaloons.

'Your Grace.' She stood up and curtseyed to the bouquet which sank to reveal Cal behind it. 'Are you entertaining tonight and carrying the flowers home yourself? There are enough there to deck three rooms, I should imagine.'

'Miss Wilmott. Having presented these I will just hand them to Parrott who is so *conveniently* placed to take them.' Cal turned and thrust the flowers through the open door, presumably into Parrott's arms, then strolled in and took her hand. And kept hold of it. 'I thought that it seemed an appropriate bouquet for courtship.'

'Courtship?' Sophie sat down with a bump, dragging Cal down beside her. Fortunately they both found the sofa. 'But it was just a kiss,' she hissed. Now what had she done? It had been an impulse, an irresistible moment of yielding to desire and attraction. 'Surely you cannot take seriously anything that happens at a masquerade. Not anything so harmless.' *Although your henchman seemed to take it seriously enough.*

'Harmless?' Cal still held her hand, his thumb tracing lazy circles in the palm. 'I didn't get a wink of sleep all night, you have afflicted me with, er... insomnia.' His face was perfectly serious but his eyes, those haunting silver eyes, were alight with laughter.

'Do not laugh at me, please. It really is not funny.' Sophie bit her lower lip as though the sharp little pain would steady her voice.

'No, of course not.' Cal was instantly serious. 'Sophie, what is wrong? Has anyone threatened you, told you not to marry me?'

She shook her head. 'No. Who on earth would do that?' The grip on her hand that had tightened, relaxed again. 'No, I just cannot. And no-one saw us. There is absolutely no need to fear I have been compromised.'

He was frowning now. 'Sophie, you do not dislike me, I know that – you are too honest to pretend simply because of my rank. You are not frightened of me, not after the way you let me kiss you. And, forgive me if this seems arrogant, but surely I match most of your little list of desirable attributes in a husband.'

'You match all of them as you perfectly well know. But I cannot match your equivalent list.'

'You most certainly do, which should be obvious to you. Is it because I have been married before, have a child?'

'No. No, of course not. Your daughter is enchanting.'

'Then I can only assume I have offended you in some way.'

'*No.*' She was going to have to tell him. 'I will tell you, but not here. We can go into the garden, out of earshot of the house.'

She led him out, past the butler who apparently thought he was being tactful, instead of looking ridiculous, inadequately concealed being the bouquet. 'Parrott, we are going into the garden. Please see that we are not disturbed.'

'Certainly, Miss Wilmott. Some tea perhaps?'

'Nothing, thank you.' The horrors of having to deal with tea cups and dainty biscuits on top of this tightened her voice to a snap.

Cal said nothing, holding the door, offering his arm down the short flight of brick steps to the tiny circle of lawn, dusting the seat of the garden bench with his pocket handkerchief. Even when she sat he remained silent as he stood before her, watching her face.

'You are very quiet,' she managed after a long minute.

'I am wondering if you need reassuring that whatever it is you are summoning the will to tell me about, no word of it would ever pass my lips.'

'No, I need no reassurance about your honour, Your Grace. The problem, you see, lies with mine.'

'Go on.'

'I am not a virgin.'

'Do you still love him?' She could tell nothing from

Cal's tone, nor, when she glanced at his face, his expression. He looked, and sounded, serious and concerned. Not, thank goodness, murderous.

'*No*. And thank you for assuming that I would not have… Would not have acted without deep feeling. After my bold behaviour last night, you would have every reason for labelling me fast.'

'You would not have kissed me if there had not been some feeling between us, Sophie. I do not, for one moment, believe you wanton or wicked. Would I know him?'

'No.' No, thank goodness. Jonathan Ransome had vanished from Society after that night without leaving a ripple. He was a younger son on the fringes of the fashionable world and if his friends were puzzled over his absence she never heard a whisper of it. Perhaps she had humiliated him so comprehensively that he did not dare show his face again. That had certainly been her intention. 'I was mistaken in him. We parted the same night. Not amicably. No-one knows. Not my parents, not my maid. He left London.'

'And there were no consequences?' Her face must have betrayed something for Cal dropped to one knee beside her and took her hand. 'Is there a child for me to add to the family, I mean. I know there must have been consequences to your feelings.'

'No, no child. But, you cannot still seriously wish to press your suit? Not after this.'

Cal shifted to sit next to her. 'I cannot pretend I do not wish that had not happened to you, Sophie. You have been hurt, your feelings about marriage must, inevitably, have been compromised. I cannot tell you I do not want to kill the man who hurt you, because I do. Badly. It was a while ago? And this is why you carry that knife?'

'Yes, it was. Just after Mama remarried. And yes, I carry that knife because before I had no way of defending myself, not at first. I never want to be in that position again.'

His face darkened, then he smiled and said, 'And you were young and foolish and romantic, which is why you said your mother and stepfather are a bad influence. I thought you were jesting, but you were not, were you?'

She shook her head. 'Cal, we cannot forget this.'

'No, of course not. But if you were a widow and had been married to a man you adored, just think how hard I would have to fight to keep from jealousy. Now I can dislike this former love of yours with a clear conscience.'

'You do not love me. I do not love you, and yet you would be jealous?' *Am I seriously considering this? Marriage to this man? A future as a duchess? Yes, I suppose I am.* If only she did not feel mildly queasy with nerves and some sense of impending disaster. That was no way to feel when the most eligible man in London proposed to you, perhaps it was simply the ominous fencing master's dark warnings nagging at the back of her mind.

'I am possessive, Sophie. What I have, I hold. If this man comes back and tries to claim you then he will be facing me at dawn in some meadow, whether or not you find you have any feelings left for him.'

That should have been terrifying, instead, strangely, the admission was reassuring. Sophie's spirits began to lift. 'Tell me something.' She turned her hand so his was palm up and began to trace the strong lines in his palm. 'Is that sauce for the goose as well as the gander? May I expect fidelity from my husband?'

'If you are faithful to me, Sophie, I will be faithful to you.' There was a subtle threat in that she did not want to think through. Of course if she married Cal she would be faithful, anything else was out of the question.

'Then you still wish to marry me?'

'I do. We will do this in form, I think. I will call with all due ceremony on your stepfather, present my credentials, speak solemnly of settlements, ask his permission to address you. When will I find him at home?'

'He will be in this afternoon. I do not believe he is expecting any visitors.'

'Then I will go home now and send a very proper note.'

'And Mama will be thrown into ecstasies and I will spend a dreadful few hours while she rakes though my entire wardrobe, has my maid try out at least three different ways of putting my hair up and bursts into happy tears every few moments.'

'Then I am happy to make her happy. And to see your smile come back. I am sorry you had to relive that, Sophie, but I am glad you were so honest with me.' Cal hesitated, looking down at their joined hands. 'Honesty is very important to me. Honesty, trust, loyalty. Sophie, you are level-headed, aren't you?'

'I hope so. Why, do you fear my head will be turned at the prospect of such an elevation?'

'No. I fear that you may become a target of sorts. Once it is known that you are important to me, of value to me, then others might seek to attack me through you. I do not want to frighten you, only to put you on your guard.'

Sophie had not realised how warm and happy and *safe* she had felt a moment ago. She had told Cal her secret and he still wanted to marry her. She was going to be a duchess, married to a man she liked and desired – and now it was as though she had taken a step and found a pit beneath her feet.

'Cal, has someone been sending you threats?'

'No, nothing of the kind.' She was not certain that she believed his reassuring smile. 'Perhaps I have become so used to travelling in dangerous parts of the world that I have come to expect perils around every corner. There is nothing to worry about, but I would not have you doing anything incautious.'

'Of course.' And why did she not believe him for a

moment? And yet, despite the cold sinking feeling in her stomach she realised that she still felt safe with Cal. He would look after her and she would look after him, Sophie resolved. Someone needed to do something about that darkness he hid so well, and who better than a wife?

Cal ran down the front steps, jammed his hat on his head and strode off down Wimpole Street. *Damn and hell and...* He exhausted an extensive repertoire before he turned towards Cavendish Square and was forced to slow by the crowds on the pavement. Had he let his true feelings show? He thought not, hoped not, because he did not want to hurt Sophie and it was his problem, not hers, that he felt so bitterly the fact that she was not a virgin, that he would not be her first lover.

It was illogical, emotional and downright unjust to feel like that. *He* was not a virgin, for God's sake, hadn't been when he had married Madeleine, hadn't stayed celibate after her death, so why did he feel like this about Sophie? It was not as though she was playing fast and loose, taking lovers, here there and everywhere. She had fallen in love with this man, whoever the bastard was, found she was mistaken in him and had been regretting it ever since. And, however it had played out, it had been bad enough for her to feel safer carrying a weapon now.

He went back over what he had said to her. Yes, he had managed to keep the disappointment, the irrational anger with her that he knew was unjust and unfair, out of his voice, out of what he had said, otherwise he was certain she would have refused to marry him.

So, he was starting this marriage with a mountain of lies. He was angry and disappointed that she'd had a lover. He was not telling her that he thought his life might be in danger and was marrying her anyway. She had told him frankly about her past and he had carefully not revealed anything of his first marriage.

'Cal? Didn't expect to see you around here.' Jared

stood directly in front of him, a rock in the river of passers-by who muttered and frowned and flowed around him on either side. No-one would jostle him of course, not after one look. 'You have a face like thunder. Coffee might help.'

Cal shrugged as Hunt took his arm and steered him through the door of a nearby coffee house, grunted when offered coffee then sat and drummed his fingers on the scarred table top until his friend slapped his own hand down to still the noise.

'Stop that, you are driving me mad. What's wrong?'

'I took a good hard look in a mental mirror and didn't much like what I saw.'

Hunt waited until the coffee came, then pushed one cup towards Cal. 'Drink it, then confess these dark sins that cloud your soul and I will shrive you.' When Cal scowled at him he shrugged, grinned and lounged back in his chair, fingers curled around his drink.

'I asked Sophie Wilmott to marry me.' Cal swallowed the coffee in one gulp, wincing at its bitterness.

'And she refused you?' Jared was gratifyingly amazed.

'She accepted me. I didn't tell her about our suspicions, I didn't tell her about Madeleine and I was… reticent about my feelings over something she confided in me. Not a very admirable start to a marriage.'

'You stumbled into the last one like an innocent lamb to the slaughter,' Hunt remarked with brutal honesty. 'Perhaps you are due your secrets this time.'

'Damn it, should I have told her why I left England? Should I even be thinking about taking a wife, starting a family, with this unresolved?'

'What if it never is? Do you wait until your uncle and cousin predecease you before you risk it?'

'No, of course not.' Cal snapped his fingers at the waiter for more coffee. That revelation about Sophie's lover had plunged him in to a fit of the blue devils and he needed to haul himself out of it. Fast. 'I marry her, as soon as possible. If there is a long engagement then she is vulnerable. Married, I can protect her. And I go to Calderbrook, start making my presence felt, start acting the duke. Either that will provoke them and I deal with it, or they will have accepted it and given up, or we were mistaken all along.'

'You will tell her what we suspect?'

'No. I could be wrong. I pray that I am wrong. I told her to be cautious because my rank might make me a target. She'll be careful. Sophie's not some air-headed little miss.'

'I am sure you are right.' With the cup to his lips it was impossible to read Hunt's expression.

'I had better be.' Cal flexed his sword hand. 'I protect what is mine, Jared. My title, my estate, my child. And now, my wife.'

The other man just nodded. Jared did not say, as Cal believed he had every right to say, that he had not protected Madeleine. Could he have kept her safe in the face of the disease that struck down so many Europeans in India? Probably not. Had he secretly wished that she was gone? Not dead, just *gone.* Yes, of course he had and had that made him less observant, less careful of her headaches and megrims? Perhaps. But Sophie would be different.

'I can't sit here all morning.' He got to his feet, tossed coins on the table. 'I have to go home and compose a respectful note to the man I wish to be my father-in-law in the hope he will grant me an audience and give me permission to court his stepdaughter.'

'You are a duke.' Hunt got to his feet slowly, exuding a subtle menace that had every man in the place eyeing him askance. 'No-one refuses you anything.'

Chapter Nine - Where Sophie Anticipates Delicious Danger

'Sophie is a gem, I can only be gratified that you noticed the fact, Your Grace.' Lord Elmham got to his feet and tugged on the bell pull that hung beside the desk in his study.

'Call me Cal, please, sir. You are giving me your permission to address Miss Wilmott?'

'Her mother would rend me limb from limb if I did not and besides, that accords perfectly with my inclination.' The door opened behind Cal. 'Please ask my stepdaughter if she would be good enough to receive His Grace in the drawing room in half an hour, Tomkins.'

'My lord.' The door closed again.

'Time for a brandy, I think, while the ladies decide on the perfect *toilette* to wear to receive a ducal proposal.' The viscount turned from the side table with two glasses in his hand. 'I assume Sophie will not be taken entirely by surprise?'

'I believe not. I have not tried to hide my admiration from her.'

'Good. You never know which way she'll jump, Sophie. She's a mind of her own and she's been devilish picky these past few years. Says her mother and I set a bad example by being in love and that a sensible girl doesn't look for it. What do you say?'

'That liking, respect and desire are admirable foundations for marriage. Love may follow.' Whatever love was. But a man on the cusp of marriage was supposed to use the word.

'Desire?' The viscount's brows drew together sharply.

'Desire. It always seems to me to be a foolish thing for a couple to marry when there is no desire. Leads to all kinds of… wandering. I do not intend to wander, my lord.'

'She is a good girl, Sophie.' Her stepfather was still frowning.

'Nothing in her behaviour towards me has given me any reason to think otherwise,' Cal said with perfect truth and considerable hauteur. Kisses in the shrubbery, however delicious, were not an indication of wantonness, whatever chaperones might say.

'Yes. Yes, of course.' Now he had flustered his future father-in-law. Cal recalled Sophie talking to her young friend on the balcony and telling him that when Elmham and her mother had first fallen in love nothing was exchanged beyond a few lingering glances, heavy sighs. Had the man gone off and lived like a monk for almost twenty years? He rather doubted it: he most certainly would not have done so. On the other hand, once married, that was that, so far as he was concerned. 'I do not wish for a prolonged betrothal. A special licence, a private ceremony in, say, a month's time.'

'A month? Isn't that rather hasty? People will talk.'

'Not if they have any sense of self-preservation, they won't,' Cal said with a smile that showed his teeth. Ralph had reminded him of who he was, what he was. Not the wary, frightened youth he had left home as, not the hardened traveller he had become, but a duke. A power in the land. 'It will be as Sophie wishes, naturally.'

Elmham brightened. Doubtless he was thinking that any young lady would want months of shopping to amass her trousseau. Cal felt his smile softening into something more genuine. Perhaps when Isobel reached marriageable age he would be on that side of the desk, haggling with *her* chosen man, trying to hold on to his little girl for as long as possible.

He almost said as much, then thought better of it. Just at the moment Elmham the romantic did not need reminding that Cal had been married before, that Sophie would acquire a stepdaughter of her own. 'You will wish to see my man of business, study the settlements I propose to make.'

'Thank you, yes. You will be living chiefly on your estate at Calderbrook, I imagine?'

'Certainly. There are other houses, but that will be our home, assuming that Sophie does not take it in strong dislike.'

'But you have not visited it since your return to England?' Elmham was obviously seeking a tactful way of enquiring whether the house was neglected and unfit for his stepdaughter.

'No. Under the circumstances perhaps a house party would be in order.' The restlessness to be out of London, to be at Calderbrook, had been gripping him for days. It was only Sophie who had been keeping him in London after the first few days, not all his careful, rational plans, he realised. He had thought to let Isobel settle after all the traveling, equip himself properly, get back into London Society and watch his uncle and cousin. But that had meant ignoring the tug at his heartstrings to go home. Now he could let himself follow his heart not his head and return to Calderbrook.

The clock on the mantle struck and both men glanced up. 'I should not keep a lady waiting and more than twenty minutes have passed.'

Elmham stood up and extended his hand across the desk. 'Good luck.'

Would he need luck? He was a duke after all, as was all too apparent from the way the butler escorted him across the hallway to the drawing room. He was not quite rolling out a red carpet before Cal's booted feet, but his demeanour suggested one could be produced for him at twitch of the ducal finger.

But he found he did not want Sophie to agree because of his rank and status. He wanted her to agree because she thought it would be pleasant to be married to him, that she liked him, that she found the prospect of bearing his children attractive.

It was tempting to go to the over-mantle mirror and twitch at his neckcloth, run his hand through his hair, both actions likely to wreck Flynn's exertions to turn him out as the ideal suitor. It was equally tempting to pace up and down. Neither was dignified, both showed a lack of control and of self-confidence. Where was she? A full half hour had elapsed since her step-father sent the message and she had known he was coming which should have given her more than enough time to choose a gown and fiddle with her hair.

Cal took up a stance in front of the window, hands behind his back as he watched the passing traffic. This was really extraordinarily nerve-wracking, even though he knew she was going to say *yes*. How did men cope when the outcome was in question? How did you school your face and keep your dignity in the event of a rejection?

His first marriage had been, almost literarily, a shotgun affair. He had gone to the bed of a woman he had every reason to suppose was interested only in pleasure as he was and had then been confronted by her indignant father, apparently a most respectable Boston merchant. Cal had seduced his innocent flower, he had worked his wiles on a young woman unused to the ways of wicked English gentlemen. He was a vile seducer.

Caught hook, line and sinker. The only mercy was that he had never revealed his title to his father-in-law and had managed to keep it a secret even from Madeleine until she was dying in Calcutta. He had been travelling incognito, but using his real names because Thorne was a common-enough surname, and had told anyone who enquired that he was from country gentry, travelling in search of adventure. What he had not hidden well enough was that he had the money to travel as he liked, even if he was happy to rough it when necessary. That was what had attracted Madelaine's father. It had been another hard lesson in how trust can be utterly mistaken. But Sophie –

The click of the door latch brought him round. *Ah yes, Sophie.*

She stood in the middle of the floor, the door firmly closed behind her, and dropped into an elegant curtsey. 'Your Grace.'

'Miss Wilmott.'

This time he was going to do things properly, with a flourish. Cal took two long strides across the floor, held out his hand and when Sophie, blushing delightfully he was pleased to see, took it, he dropped to one knee, kissed her fingers and looked up. 'Miss Wilmott. Sophie. Will you do me the honour of becoming my wife? I admire you and I desire you more than I can say.'

The blush deepened when he said *desire,* but she was smiling. Sophie gave his hand a little tug, so he stood, still holding her hand and waited for her answer. Her blush, her smile, the frisson of anticipation were all curiously pleasant.

Yes. Oh yes. The words stayed inside her head as Cal stood looking down at her, patient, assured. Waiting. *Admiration and desire.* He had the sensitivity not to make protestations of love, which he knew she did not want, did not expect. Of course she didn't and, it was quite clear, neither did he. And yet she must be infected with Mama's romance after all, because part of her, an irrational, foolish part, yearned to hear him say, *I love you.* It yearned, even if she knew the words would not be true, even as she winced away from the memories. She had heard those words often enough from Jonathan – and look where that had led.

This was a man she liked, trusted, found interesting – and desirable – and he was offering her a marriage beyond her wildest dreams. She would be foolish indeed to hesitate for a moment.

'Yes, Cal. I would be honoured to be your wife.'

Sophie had expected to be seized in a passionate embrace and fiercely kissed. She had fantasised about it all afternoon until her toes had curled in her satin slippers and her mother had repeated a question about pearls three times without an coherent answer.

In the shrubbery at the masquerade Cal had been passionate, exciting, tender, with the thrilling edge of a man only just in control of himself. Now he no longer needed that control. She was his. *Well, almost.* Sophie was not entirely certain she wanted what came after the kissing. That had been uncomfortable, embarrassing, painful and messy. It was inevitable, of course, and necessary, but kissing was wonderful. Being kissed by Cal was bliss.

'What are you thinking about? Your eyes have gone all misty.' His breath was warm on her lips and she blinked and found herself drawn very close to him, both her hands caged in his as he bent over her.

'You kissing me,' she confessed.

And, finally, he did. It was respectful, almost chaste. Disappointing. Sophie pressed closer, ran her hands up his arms, encouraging. In a moment it would be a demand.

Cal lifted his head. 'I would give it about thirty seconds before your parents come through that door. Call me lily-livered if you like, but I have no desire to be lectured by your mama for unleashing my unbridled lusts in her drawing room.'

Sophie was still in his arms, still laughing, when the door opened, just as he had predicted. Mama looked bemused, as though laughter was not what she had expected. Step Papa seemed relieved. Had he thought she might have refused Cal? She knew she had been a worry to him with her steady refusals to accept perfectly eligible suitors and her rejection of romance.

Kisses and hugs for her. A handshake for Cal and, to his barely concealed alarm, a kiss from her mother.

'Now.' Mama settled in a swirl of skirts and beamed at them. 'We need to fix a date.'

'A month's time,' Cal said, clashing with Step Papa's, 'Six weeks at least.'

'Two months,' Mama pronounced, her smile steely.

Cal's eyes narrowed and Sophie thought of protesting that she was of age and that she could marry when she liked, then bit back the protest. Two months and then start her married life in perfect amity with the parents she loved or begin it in a squabble that would inevitably sour their feelings for Cal. 'Very well, Mama, if you feel that would be best.' She met his gaze with a rueful smile and saw he understood. He wasn't happy though. *Unbridled lusts…*

'And the church.' Mama was happily working down a mental list. 'St George's Hanover Square? Or would you prefer to be married from Long Hampton?'

'That is Step Papa's country estate,' Sophie explained. 'It would be the village church because the house does not have its own chapel.' She hesitated, not wanting to hurt Step Papa's feelings by saying that the house was rather small for the number of guests a ducal wedding would demand. 'I do find the vicar rather dour.'

'Yes, he is, poor man,' Mama agreed. 'He is capable of making any ceremony gloomy, which is perfect for funerals, but otherwise… not.'

'With a special licence we may marry where we choose,' Cal said. 'Calderbrook has its own chapel. But you would want to see it before deciding. In fact I have no doubt you would like to see the house and meet the staff in advance of arriving as the duchess.'

'That sounds perfect,' Sophie said hastily over

Mama's faint murmurings about St George's.

'Then I will organise a house party for, shall we say, ten days' time? That will give you the opportunity to start on your shopping, place orders with your *modiste* and make whatever mysterious preparations a trousseau involves.' He waited for their agreement. 'Why not invite your bridesmaids? We will make a party of, say, twenty for a week or ten days? That will give you the opportunity to see how the house functions and we can decide over the wedding arrangements.' He smiled at her parents, then sent her a look that she had no difficulty interpreting. There would be more than enough opportunities for deliciously unbridled lusts at Calderbrook.

'I would like that very much.' She swept on before Mama could find any reason why that was not a wonderful idea. 'Shall we make a guest list for the house party now? Then we can send out invitations immediately.'

'I... very well. We will leave you to do just that. You are very thoughtful, Your Grace.' Mama got to her feet, hesitated as though uncertain whether or not to embrace Cal again and eventually went out, her husband at her heels. The door stayed open halfway this time. Mama presumably knew all about the temptations of proximity.

She felt suddenly shy. 'Thank you for not pressing the issue about the date. I would not want to spoil my last days here with any dissention.'

Cal seemed to have caught her formality. 'You are quite right, and it is your decision. I must confess to impatience.'

'Yes,' Sophie murmured as she seated herself at the little table in the corner that served as the ladies' writing desk.

Cal picked up a chair, set it beside hers and bent to take her lips in a hard, fleeting kiss. 'That must suffice for now. Pick up that pen before my resolve weakens. You and me, your parents, my uncle and his wife, Ralph. That is seven. I would add Jared Hunt. Eight. Your bridesmaids?'

'There are three unmarried friends I would like to have, and one who is married, so that would add five with her husband. May I ask Toby?'

'Of course. That makes thirteen which leaves us seven more to find. Who else?'

It took them half an hour to finalise the list, adding some of Cal's re-found friends and another married couple to reassure the mothers of the single girls. 'If anyone we ask would like to suggest a friend, we can expand on the twenty,' he said as Sophie copied the list out again for him to send his half of the invitations. 'It is a big house.'

'How big?' Her stomach gave a little swoop. *Duchess, big house... It is going to be vast and so is everything to do with this marriage. Vast numbers of servants, of tenants, of ancestors, of responsibilities. I have not just agreed to marry a man but a small nation state.*

'About twenty principal bedchambers as I recall.' Cal was frowning with the effort to remember and did not appear to notice her convulsive grip on the table edge. Best not to ask how many minor bedchambers. 'Not that I took much notice before. I wasn't very well for a lot of the time I was growing up and housekeeping details just passed me by.'

'What was wrong with you?' She had rarely seen a healthier specimen of manhood and it was hard to imagine Cal laid low by anything for long.

'Some childhood ailment, I suppose.' He shrugged. 'The doctors never came up with a diagnosis, but it cleared up after I went abroad.'

What aren't you telling me? He was just too casual about it, too glib. The temptation to ask Ralph was strong, but that would be disloyal. Probably Cal was embarrassed by a perceived weakness and would tell her all about it when they knew each other a little better.

Men require managing, Mama always said, although Sophie recognised that she managed Step Papa far less than she had Papa, which was interesting. Papa had not regarded women as anything but decorative accessories. To be loved and cherished, certainly, but if anyone had suggested that a female had a brain capable of reasoning and decision-making beyond the menu for the week or the choice of a bonnet, he would have thought they were mad. But Step Papa not only loved her mother, he admired her, asked her opinion, shared decisions.

'Do you think me merely a decorative accessory?' she asked before she had time to think about it.

Cal paused in the process of tucking the invitation list into his breast pocket. 'Why do I sense a trap in that question? Decorative, yes. An accessory, certainly not, except possibly before or after some criminal act.'

'Me? A criminal?' Sophie protested. She tried to establish his true feelings and he insulted her?

'No, an incitement to crime.' Cal moved close. Very close. 'To holding you to ransom for a million kisses, to kidnap so I can tempt you to all kinds of wickedness on some desert island. I want to make love to you in every public park in London, I want to tear the petals off every rose bush I encounter to strew over your naked body. I want to corrupt you utterly, my lovely Sophie.'

Oh. My. Goodness. She had thought to find a respectable, tame, marriage. One that was safe, comfortable. Suitable. And now she was betrothed to a barbarian, a tiger. A man who would consume her. *Deliciously. Dangerously.*

'You may try, Your Grace.' She went to the door, dropped a very proper curtsy and batted her eyelashes, making him laugh. 'But I am determined to be the very model of a most proper duchess. Good day, Your Grace.'

The glimpse of his smile vanishing as she closed the

door was very gratifying. Two could tease.

Chapter Ten - Where Sophie's Past Comes Back to Haunt Her

Word of the betrothal spread through Society as fast as gossip could flow, even before the invitations to the house party were out and long before the wedding invitations were written. Within a day Cal was being congratulated wherever he went and Sophie was mobbed by her friends, gazed at enviously by her few enemies and pointed out as An Example by ambitious mamas to their daughters, regardless of protests that there were no more eligible dukes to ensnare.

'I hadn't told anyone, and even if all the people we invited to the house party have told their friends, it is still incredible how news spreads,' she whispered to her mother one evening a week later. Yet another green-eyed matron had just congratulated Lady Elmham on her triumph before turning back into the throng at Mrs Wissonsett's musicale.

'Servants,' Mama whispered back as they made their way to one of the sofas arranged around the string quartet. 'It only takes one scullery maid to tell the footman next door and it is all over Town before you can say *trousseau.*' She sat in a rustle of aubergine silk. 'Good evening, Lady Horton.'

The dowager on her other side nodded and peered round to fix Sophie with a beady gaze. 'And where is your young man, hmm? Vanished again, has he?'

'The Duke had a previous engagement, Lady Horton.'

'Fiddle-faddle. He can't stand hearing catgut tortured and that's the truth.' The old lady nodded briskly. 'Sensible man.'

Fortunately the ensemble began to play, leaving Sophie in peace to contemplate her new life married to the *sensible* duke. The wicked, passionate duke. The duke with dark secrets and hidden depths. Her duke.

She was still lost in a happy daydream of being the perfect duchess by day and the perfectly wicked one by night when the music came to a halt amidst a smattering of applause.

'There is Cousin Harriet.' Her mother stood up and waved across the room. 'Keep my place, dear, I must ask after Cousin Wallace's gout.'

For a moment she was free of curious well-wishers. Many of the ladies were discreetly making for the retiring room in case the next piece proved to be a long one and gentlemen were hurrying to the buffet to collect drinks for their partners. Sophie amused herself watching the whispered argument between the viola player and the cellist over a piece of sheet music and then froze, breathless. For a second she could not understand what had seized her with such apprehension, then a tall figure passed behind the platform, walking diagonally from a side door to the buffet.

Blond hair, an attractively elegant profile, a winning smile, just now directed at a blushing young lady in his path. Jonathan Ransome. Her past come back to haunt her.

Her instinct was to get up and run, leave the room before he turned his head and saw her. Sophie tightened her grip on her fan and made herself stay where she was. If he was back in Town she would have to face him and deal with him sooner or later – and better sooner, before he encountered Cal. But she was *damned* if she would go to him.

Sophie put up her chin, unfurled her fan and smiled

as the mother of one of her chosen bridesmaids bore down on her, plumes fluttering.

Apparently she was sounding perfectly rational, because Mrs Gilbert kept up a cheerful flow of conversation, expressed delight at the house party invitation and admired Sophie's gown.

Mama would be back in a minute, surely? Then Mrs Gilbert moved away and Jonathan Ransome, the man she had been in love with, the man who had ravished and betrayed her, was standing there, a glass of champagne in each hand, smiling down at her as he had that first time when she had tumbled head over heels in love with him. *The deceiving toad.*

'Miss Wilmott. Such a pleasure after all this time.' He handed her the glass which she took. It was that or throw it in his face.

Beside her the sofa was empty. Lady Horton was across the room chatting to an acquaintance and there was nothing to stop him sitting down beside her, which he did with a flick of his coat tails, taking up all the remaining space.

'Mr Ransome.' Sophie maintained her smile, somehow. 'Why, you haven't changed at all since I last saw you.'

As she had left him drunk and tied to the frame of a sagging bed in an inn, dressed in a highly compromising manner, that was intended to infuriate. It appeared to have succeeded. Jonathan's beautiful blue eyes darkened and his smile vanished.

'Yes, I do owe you a debt for that, Sophie darling.'

'Think nothing of it. After all, I was only taking something in return for what you took from me, Mr Ransome. I do hope I provided some entertainment for your so charming, so boisterous friends.' The same drunken louts in the taproom he had threatened to share her with unless she yielded to him.

'Have you missed me?'

'Not at all.'

'I went home to Cornwall to look after my father's estates,' he said, the smile back in place, just as if she had enquired where he had been.

'Such a nice long way away from anyone laughing at you,' Sophie said sweetly.

'And while I was away you lingered on the shelf. Pining, were you, Sophie?'

'Rather less than I do for my dentist.' She laughed and fluttered her fan in case anyone was watching them.

'But sitting on the shelf gathering dust paid off, I hear. A duke, no less. Clever Sophie.'

So, now they were coming to the point of all this. What did he want in payment for his humiliation? 'Aren't I just?' she agreed.

'And what will His Grace say when he discovers that his bride is no virgin?'

'He knows. Naturally I was honest with him.' That was a blow to Jonathan, she could tell. 'If he had wanted some virginal little chit just out then he would have proposed to one.'

'I doubt that he wants a woman who was whored round the taproom of the Black Bull at Hounslow though.'

'So, now we come to it. A lying blackmailer as well as a rapist. I cannot imagine how you can face your own reflection in the glass of a morning.' How she was keeping her voice soft and low and a smile on her lips she had no idea, not when her stomach was cramping and her body aching with the effort not to tremble. 'What exactly do you want, Jonathan?'

'Vengeance, sweet Sophie. And money. Lots and lots of money. Every drop I can squeeze from you.'

'Then do have a few drops to be getting on with.' She stood up, tipped her full glass sideways into his crotch, then dropped the glass onto the sofa beside him. 'Oh, Mr Ransome! You appear to have wet your breeches.' She whisked her skirts aside with a *moue* of distaste. Heads were turning, quizzing glasses raised.

Jonathan blundered to his feet, a dark stain spreading embarrassingly across the falls of his biscuit-coloured knee breeches. He hissed a word at her that fortunately she could not make out, then stormed from the room, hands clamped to his groin.

Her mother hurried over. 'Sophie dear, are you all right? Wasn't that young Randolph or Ruskin or whatever his name is? The one who used to hang around you?'

'Ransome, Mama.' She lowered her voice a little, but not so far that those around could not hear. 'I think he had been drinking and, er, lost control of himself. So embarrassing.'

'Tsk!' Footmen hastened across and lifted the sofa away. 'Ale house manners. Your stepfather and I never liked him.'

'You didn't? I used to think him quite pleasant.'

'I know you did, dear. But we thought his manner encroaching and there were rumours. Vague, but unsavoury. I had intended having a quiet word with you if his attentions became any more pronounced, but then he just seemed to vanish from Society, so that was all right. Now, let us find a new seat over near Cousin Harriet. I think they are about to begin playing again.'

Sophie sat on the hearthrug before the banked fire in her bedchamber and contemplated her options. Paying Jonathan a penny was insupportable and besides, she was certain that once he discovered she would pay he would never stop bleeding her. She had confessed to Cal that she'd had a lover, but not the circumstances. She could tell him everything and she had no fears that he would not believe her, but the trouble was, she knew he would be furious, not with her, but with Jonathan.

Which would not be too bad, because she wouldn't tell him who the man concerned was. But if Jonathan carried out his threats and spread the story, then Cal would hunt him down and kill him, she was quite certain of that.

The scandal would be enormous. She would be ruined, Cal would have to flee the country, or at the very least, face court. She supposed a duke might have a good chance of evading the death penalty for a killing in the course of a duel, but she would not want to wager on it.

Her parents had heard unsavoury rumours about Jonathan before, so perhaps he had seduced, or ravished other young women. If she could discover something criminal about him, something that would not bring shame on anyone else, then she would have a lever against him.

So, how did one go about finding an enquiry agent? Toby, of course. He would help.

Sophie penned the note asking him to call, then went to bed and lay awake wondering what to tell her old friend. Not the truth, that was for sure, because Toby would be after Jonathan the moment he heard and he was equally inept with both pistols and rapier. She couldn't live with herself if Toby was hurt, or worse, helping her.

'*Oh what tangled webs we weave, when first we practice to deceive,*' she murmured, wriggling down under the covers. This had begun because she was a romantic, an innocent, had become worse because she had discovered an unexpected talent for revenge and now she was hiding her ex-lover's name from her husband-to-be, her blackmailer's name from her best friend and concocting an elaborate lie to get him to help her find an enquiry agent. And when she had found one, then she had to visit him without letting Mama guess anything was wrong in the slightest.

And pay him. Somehow. This was becoming hideously complicated.

'You want a *what*?' Toby stared, open-mouthed. 'I

honestly do not think that's a good idea. I mean, the fellow has hardly been back in Town a few weeks. Surely he hasn't had time to set up a little ladybird, too busy. And even if he has, best not to know about things like that, my Mama always says.'

'Toby, darling, what on earth are you talking about?'

'Calderbrook's mistresses.'

'Mistresses? He has got more than one?' *He has* any?

'As far as I know he hasn't got a mistress, that's what I am trying to say. Don't get into a tizzy and snap at me, Sophie. I haven't got one either.'

'I don't care about your mistresses, Toby, other to hope that you find a nice one. And I certainly do not want to track down Calderbrook's light of love, if he has one. This is about a friend of mine who is falling for a man, but she is worried about rumours she's heard and wants to find out if they are true.'

'Well, so long as you don't want me interfering in Calderbrook's private life.' Toby gave an exaggerated shudder and flung himself into the nearest armchair. 'He'd run me though if he found out, although I suspect he would tear my head off first or set that sinister swordmaster of his on me. So what's the name of this shady cove? I'll find out about him for you.'

'I can't tell you that. If he is perfectly innocent and marries my friend, then you will know who she is and I am sworn to secrecy.'

'Ah, good point.' Toby frowned and lapsed into silence, brooding. Sophie curbed her impatience and waited. He was not a great thinker and it was usually best to leave the cogs to grind slowly round in their own time.

'I know.' He sat up abruptly. 'Finchingfield was convinced someone was cheating at cards and set this man on him. Sure enough, tracked him back to York and found he'd been run out of town for running crooked games. Now what was his name? Frogmore, that's it.'

'The agent?'

'No, the card sharp.'

'I need the *agent's* name and direction, Toby.' *Patience. You can't strangle him now, you need him.*

'Ah. Right. I'll go and find Finchingfield, he's bound to be at White's. Won't be long.' He went out, then put his head back round the door. 'Has your cook got any of those macarons, do you think? The almond ones?'

'I'll get her to make some.' Sophie lobbed a cushion at him. 'Now, go!'

Cal stood on the pavement outside 32, Ludgate Hill and studied the items displayed in the window of Rundell, Bridge and Rundell. *Jewellers and Goldsmiths to Their Majesties*, it said above the door under the array of royal crests, which should be good enough for a duchess.

The strong boxes at the bank were stuffed with gems and jewellery that would be Sophie's for her lifetime as soon as the knot was tied, but he wanted to buy her something chosen for her, not anything like the ponderous stuff he recalled from all the family portraits.

He could go in and as soon as they realised who he was they would be prostrating themselves in their eagerness to lay things out for him, but he wanted to have some ideas about what Sophie would like best before he entered. Sapphires would suit her, of course, and in his pocket he had a packet of uncut Burmese stones that he'd bought in India that he wanted to consult the jewellers about, but aquamarines would be prettier, lighter. Perhaps something in aquamarines and pearls, for day wear?

He found he liked the bustle of the City. People had purpose and the juxtaposition of the great cathedral of St Paul's, just up the hill from where he stood, made a dramatic contrast with the lowering presence of the Newgate and Fleet prisons and the Old Bailey. Distantly there were sounds from the river to add to the mix and he would walk down to it past the Bridewell when he had completed his business and didn't have a small fortune of gemstones in his pocket.

He was turning to the door when a flicker of golden hair made him stop and stare up the hill at the slender figure walking away from him. He caught the glimpse of a veil as she turned her head to speak to the woman beside her, a maid from her clothing, but the back of her hair showed under her hat, guinea-gold in the sunlight. Surely not Sophie, on foot, in the City? No lady walked there in the heart of the business district.

Cal set off after her, cursing under his breath as slower pedestrians got in his way. She crossed the road, continued up, then stopped and seem to consult a paper in her hand. Then she turned left and vanished. He broke through into a gap in the throng, took the turn into a quieter street and glanced up. Ave Maria Lane.

And there was Sophie, studying her piece of paper again, unmistakeable now he was close.

'Sophie! Miss Wilmott.'

She spun round then took a step back. 'Your Grace.'

A few passers-by stared. The maid curtseyed. Cal doffed his hat. 'Sophie, what on earth are you doing here?'

He couldn't see her face properly behind the fine black net, but he heard the 'Um…' perfectly clearly.

'Does you mama know you are walking about in the City?'

'Er… No.'

'Then what are you doing?'

'I don't want to tell you,' she said with disarming frankness.

'That is perfectly obvious.' He should probably be annoyed, he was certainly suspicious, although quite what of, he wasn't sure. 'But I think you had better.'

'I need to buy you a wedding present,' she stated with an abrupt wave of her hand towards the shop they were standing outside.

Cal stepped across and looked in the window at an array of canes, walking sticks, riding crops and assorted leather goods. 'Ah. That is very thoughtful of you. But you should not be out on the street in this area. Surely there are suitable shops in St James and Mayfair?'

'Yes, but I was told that the things here are as good, but not so expensive, so I thought I could find you something nicer than if I was shopping there,' she explained earnestly.

Damn, I've embarrassed her. He was so used to having enough money for whatever he wanted that it hadn't occurred to him that his betrothed might want to buy him a gift and not be able to afford something she thought would be fit for a duke.

'You do not have to spend money on me. Look, Sophie, let me find a hackney to take you back.'

'No, thank you.' Now he had hurt her feelings. *Double damn.* 'I will go in this shop and when I have finished in this street then I promise we will take a cab straight home.' She lifted her veil and gave him a dazzling smile. 'And you can't come in too because that will spoil the surprise.' Sophie paused on the threshold of the shop, kissed her fingers to him and disappeared inside.

Minx. He was going to enjoy being married to Sophie. Cal considered waiting for her, making certain she found a hackney quickly, then shook his head and went back down Ludgate Hill. She had her maid with her and she was not fresh from the schoolroom. He doubted she'd appreciate him hanging about as though he didn't trust her.

Cal pushed open the door to Rundell, Bridge and Rundell. That was one thing he could be certain of with this wife. He could trust Sophie. He was certain. *Almost certain.*

Chapter Eleven - Where The Duke Has His Suspicions

Cal vanished from sight and Sophie let out a *woosh* of breath. What on earth would she have done if the shop had proved to be a wig maker's or a ladies *corsetiere,* or even a seller of dubious prints?

'May I help you, madam?' The assistant emerged from behind the counter and brought forward a chair for Sophie.

'Thank you, no. I was actually… Yes. Yes, you may help me. I need a present for a gentleman, one who can afford whatever he likes, so it must be something original, rather than simply expensive, if you understand.' If she bought Cal a gift here it would mean she was not a liar and it would give him time to get clear. Unless he was lurking, not trusting her to do as she promised. 'Mary, please go and see if the gentleman has gone. Discreetly now. This is a surprise,' she explained to the assistant who was looking at her somewhat askance.

'Of course, madam. Might I suggest a walking cane? We have some newly arrived with the most interesting heads. You may choose one and be certain it will be unique. I always say a gentleman cannot have too many canes.' He tittered. 'Just like a lady and reticules.'

'Quite. Yes, show me some please.'

By the time Mary had returned to say the coast was clear and Sophie had been through virtually every cane in the shop in revenge for the reticule comment, had made a selection and arranged for it to be delivered, a good half hour had passed. She felt secure enough, with her veil resumed, to knock on the green door two houses along from the shop. *Josiah Tanner, Confidential Agent* the discreet brass plaque read. It all seemed respectable enough and the soberly-garbed man who opened the door to her inspired the sort of confidence that a solicitor did.

'Please come in, madam. Do you have an appointment?'

'No. I did not want to put anything in writing. I can wait if it is not immediately convenient to see me.' Anything rather than run the risk of bumping into someone she knew again.

'As it happens I am free for an hour, madam. Will you come through?'

The office was like a solicitor's too, which was calming. Sophie left Mary sitting in the hallway and kept her veil in place. 'I am being harassed by a man to whom I was once unofficially engaged. When we broke it off he vanished from London, and my life. I am now betrothed to another gentleman. Meanwhile the first man has returned to Town and is attempting to extract money from me with threats of plausible lies told to my fiancé.'

Mr Tanner merely nodded encouragingly. Presumably he was used to hearing this sort of tale day in, day out.

'I have no intention of paying him and have heard recently that there were rumours in the past of rather shady dealings on his part, although I have no idea what they concerned.'

'No, people do not tell young ladies such things,' he murmured. 'A pity. If they did a lot of unpleasantness might be avoided.'

'I thought that if I could establish the facts about this past history it might be possible to… deal with him.'

'Apply counter-pressure. Quite. We have a name for the gentleman?'

Sophie opened her reticule and handed over the notes she had made. 'His name, where he was living when he was in London before, a description. He said he has been rusticating in Cornwall on his father's estate, but I have no details of exactly where it might be or whether that is the truth.'

'This is an excellent. I must congratulate you, ma'am, on your organised approach. It is always so easy to panic under these circumstances. Now, how much time do we have?'

'I think I can stall him until the wedding, and perhaps a little beyond if he thinks I have no access to money yet. Two months, I suppose. But sooner if at all possible.'

'Of course, one does not want such unpleasantness to persist for a moment longer than necessary. Now, do not worry. I do not know of this gentleman but I will put an investigation in hand immediately.' He drummed his fingertips on the sheet of notes. 'Even if there is nothing in his past, it may be possible for one of my *larger* associates to have a quiet word with him.'

'Violence? Oh no, I couldn't agree to that.'

'No, no. Just the suggestion that someone is taking an interest, shall we say, is usually quite enough for a man of this stamp to decide there are easier pickings elsewhere,' he said soothingly.

'And your fee?'

'Let me see.' Mr Tanner jotted some figures down, added them up and passed the paper to Sophie. 'Unless we become involved in excessive travel costs that should cover it. With a ten percent advance if that is possible?'

'Yes, of course.' It was better than she had feared. 'I brought some cash with me.' She handed it over, received a receipt and then saw the flaw in her careful anonymity. 'How do you report to me?'

'Do you have access to *The Morning Post*?' Sophie nodded. Mama read it and virtually every household she knew took it along with *The Times* for its more relaxed style and coverage of social events. 'If there is something to report I will place an advertisement signed Green Door and addressed to Miss X. If you are in Town you can visit me, or if not, write with instructions on where I may send a report, or a representative if that would be safer.'

It all seemed so organised and ordinary, Sophie thought, as she and Mary climbed into a hackney carriage and drove back towards the Strand. She had experienced more embarrassing interviews with her doctor. Then she shifted uncomfortably on the lumpy seat as a cold trickle seemed to track down her spine. This was nothing like a visit to Doctor Felbrigg – he never suggested sending a "large associate" round to deal with a rash or an earache.

'Sir?'

Cal focused on the man who stood before him, his expression decidedly nervous. Had he been frowning? He made himself smile and saw the assistant relax too. 'I am Calderbrook.'

The assistant snapped to attention. 'Your Grace.' Another man appeared with a chair which he set reverentially next to the counter before effacing himself. 'How may we assist you?'

'A present for a lady. A betrothal gift.' He had no difficulty interpreting the beatific smile on the man's face. A duke, a duke about to marry, a duke about to spend a lot of money. Jeweller's Heaven.

Cal sat and discussed his ideas and looked at one piece after another while the wary, suspicious, instinct that had kept him alive as he circled the globe kept nudging for his attention. Sophie close up, deliciously flustered, earnestly explaining about buying him a present on a budget, had disarmed the immediate flare of mistrust. Now he wondered just how well he knew the woman who was about to become his wife in a few weeks. She was clever, he knew that. Clever enough to throw him off the scent if she was up to something. Her story about finding a present at a good price was plausible, yet there was something in the way she had reacted in the second that she recognised him… For a moment, veiled as she was, he thought her recoil was one of fear.

The days before the house party passed with uncanny speed and smoothness. Responses flooded back, several people took up the offer to add another guest and two bridesmaids would be accompanied by their sisters, while Cal invited another three gentlemen. 'We'll be about thirty, I imagine,' he said casually. 'Jared's gone down to make sure everything is in order.'

Sophie was not sure she liked the silent Mr Hunt with his unfathomable brown eyes and swordsman's grace. He saw too much and he looked as though he had a short, sharp method of dealing with problems. Given that the advertising columns of *The Morning Post* remained stubbornly free of notices from Green Door she could only hope that *she* was not going to prove a problem for him to deal with.

Lady Christabel Faversham, her best friend, and the only married lady amongst her bridesmaids, slipped onto the bench next to her beside the Serpentine two days before the departure for Calderbrook. 'I thought it was you, Sophie darling. What are you doing here? I thought you would be locked up with dressmakers until the last minute.'

Sophie turned to kiss the proffered cheek. She could hardly tell the truth, that looking at dabbling ducks was soothing and she hoped it would enable her to present a calm and tranquil façade to the world, even if her mind was paddling in circles as fast as the ducks' feet beneath the surface.

'I escaped. Even Mama has to stop writing lists sometime and I think – *hope* – that the moment has come. Although as I came out for this walk I had to pretend not to hear a faint cry of *bedroom slippers* from upstairs.'

'How are you?' Crista tipped her head on one side to study Sophie. 'Happy and harassed or panicking? He is very gorgeous, your duke.'

'Um,' Sophie agreed. He was. Utterly gorgeous. And very intelligent and, she suspected, ruthless.

'Scared? You know, if your mama hasn't explained things, I am more than willing to. There is nothing to be worried about. Actually, there's a lot to look forward to.' Her smile was cat-with-the-cream smug.

I hope so, it couldn't be worse than the first time. And Cal is... 'Goodness no, I am not at all worried or nervous about *that.*' Eager, yes. Terrified, yes. 'It is just, oh…' She flapped her hands, trying to catch the elusive comparison. 'You know when we were children and made ice slides in winter? You run and jump on and you slide and slide and it is wonderful until you realise you don't know how you are going to stop at the other end?'

'Ye…ss,' Crista said dubiously. 'I think so.' She was probably far too well-behaved to have ever done anything of the kind.

'Well, I feel like that. I am sliding along at great speed and everyone tells me how wonderful it all is, and Cal is kind,' *I think, I hope,* 'Only I hardly see him and when I do he is rigorously proper and Mama is always there too. And I am hurtling towards the wedding day with a man I hardly know and then…. What? A lovely soft snowdrift or an icy gravel path?'

'You will be a duchess, that is the *what*. And your Cal will be there all the time for you to get to know and he will be gloriously *im*proper and everything will be wonderful.'

No, Sophie thought, *nothing is ever* wonderful, *not once the bloom is off innocence and trust. With that gone* very good *and* exceedingly pleasant *are the best to be hoped for*. After all, that was why she had drawn up her careful list of characteristics of the ideal husband, the realistic qualities, not the fantasy qualities that daydreams spoke of.

'That's better,' Crista said as they kissed goodbye. 'You are smiling now. And don't forget to send samples of your wedding gown fabric today so I can wave it at Madame Prunel and make sure we do not clash horribly. And I will see you at Calderbrook in three days time. I cannot wait!'

Sophie walked home, her maid at her heels, and tried to make herself believe that before the end of the week she would be in the house that would become her new home, with the man who would be her husband. Cal had told her airily that she had no need to worry about a thing. His aunt would act as hostess, of course, as it would be most improper for her, an unmarried lady, to preside, so she could relax and become familiar with the house and staff at her leisure.

'*Men*,' she snapped at Toby who wandered in an hour later, casual as ever in the household in which he had run tame since boyhood.

'What have I done now?' He perched on the edge of her writing desk and began to play with the strips of blue silk and blonde lace that lay beside the notepaper.

'You? Nothing, or at least, provided you don't get ink on those, you will not have done. Let me have them so I can wrap them up with this note for Crista. But tell me, do *you* think I will have nothing to worry about and can relax and enjoy myself at this house party?'

'You have nothing to do except look lovely, smile a lot and try and look modest about catching a duke.' He folded the scraps and slid them into the folded paper she held out.

'I take it back. You are as dense as Cal and Step Papa. I have never been to the house before, the servants will all be weighing me up and finding me wanting, Cal will turn into a horrible stuffy duke the moment he sets foot on his ancestral acres again and I will commit some hideous *faux pas* which will demonstrate how unfit I am to be a duchess.'

Toby looked at her. 'Idiot.'

'I am, aren't I?' Suddenly it was funny and they were both laughing and the tension and exaggerated terrors fled.

'And I will be there, so if you do commit some outrageous crime, like goosing a handsome footman or drinking out of your fingerbowl, I will distract attention in a dramatic manner and no-one will notice.'

'How?' Sophie, found her handkerchief and mopped her eyes.

'I'll goose a footman too, or thrown my fingerbowl over my dinner partner – we've always scraped through disasters, Sophie, we'll survive this. And once you are a duchess no-one can judge you, short of the royals, and possibly an archbishop.'

'Or my duke,' she murmured, sobered again.

'Calderbrook is in love with you, you will be able to twist him round your little finger.' Toby shifted off the desk and went to sprawl on the sofa.

'He is not.'

'Then why is he marrying you?'

'Because he has come back from a very unconventional life and he wants someone acceptable, with whom he gets on, but who isn't just out of the schoolroom. He matches all the criteria on my shopping list for a husband and I, apparently, match his for a wife.'

'Love you or not, he can't expect you to know how to be a duchess right from the first, not unless your father had been a duke and you had learned at your mother's knee. Besides, he's setting the *ton* on its heels himself, so you could be goosing an entire flock of footmen and no-one would notice.'

'Is he?' Sophie paused halfway through sticking a row of wafers on her little package of material to seal it.

'What has he done?'

'Just being mysterious is enough. First there was all the speculation about his daughter, lots of old pussies hissing about that. Then it turns out that he married her mother with the utmost respectability in Boston, in America. So now they are gossiping about whatever nameless sins he has committed that meant he had to stay away for so long.'

'If they were nameless they will have a hard time naming them,' Sophie snapped. 'At least no-one is claiming that Cal is an imposter.'

'They'd try that because it would be a delicious scandal – if it wasn't for the fact that his uncle and cousin acknowledge him,' Toby admitted. 'But the Thornes have the most to lose and they accepted him from the first, so that juicy bone isn't for chewing.'

'He needs to marry and settle down and become respectable before his daughter is old enough to hear any of this nonsense,' Sophie mused. 'She seems very bright and little pitchers have big ears.'

'You see? It will be easy. You are respectable, everyone likes you, so you can save your duke from scandal and he will fall madly in love with you,' Toby said and grinned evilly. 'You will present him with a brood of little dukelets and become a byword for conjugal bliss. Ow!'

Sophie's engagement diary hit him squarely in the midriff, but she found, even as she threw it, that she was laughing again. Whatever else went wrong in her life, Toby was the rock she could depend upon. *Dukelets, indeed.*

'Say something, Sophie.' Step Papa was smiling, almost laughing at her.

'I… It is large, isn't it?' The length of Calderbrook's south front rose like a cliff along the far side of the lake. Hundreds of windows glinted in the sun, columns topped by a pediment rose all four floors at the centre, crisp white stone seemed to reflect back heat, even at the distance of half a mile.

They were arriving at Calderbrook the day before the rest of the guests so that Sophie could relax, Cal had said. *Relax?* She searched for something less gauche to say as the carriage wheeled left on to the bridge across the lake. 'It is exceedingly handsome, but not as large as Longleat or Blenheim. Which makes it more…' Home-like was *not* the phrase she was searching for. 'More approachable. I like it already.'

They were watched for, of course. Four be-wigged and liveried footmen appeared before the carriage had come to a halt and Cal followed behind them, running down the sweep of front steps then striding towards the coach.

He was looking every inch the duke, Sophie saw. His new wardrobe must have arrived – and thank goodness she had taken great care with her *toilette* that morning. He would have nothing to blush for when his staff set eyes on their new mistress for the first time.

A footman positioned himself at the carriage door as it came to a halt, swung it open and bent for the step, but Cal was before him at the opening, both hands held out to Sophie. 'Welcome to Calderbrook, Miss Wilmott.'

All she saw was his smile and the warmth in his eyes and how handsome he looked. What a relief it was to be received like this when she had been so nervous! Sophie got to her feet and held out her hands to meet his. 'Thank you, Your Grace.'

Her new, tight, elegant, little shoe caught in the hem of her equally new walking dress with its unfamiliar quilted hem and she tripped, stumbled and fell out of the carriage, into Cal's arms, bonnet and reticule flying.

He caught her, of course. It was like crashing into a door, albeit one that took two steps backwards on impact. He felt solid and strong and safe and, as her fingers gripped broadcloth and silk, expensive. Ducal. He even smelt ducally expensive in a subtle kind of way. And she had just made a complete spectacle of herself in front of a platoon of footmen and, she saw over his shoulder as they clung together, the entire staff, trooping down to line the steps.

Chapter Twelve - Where Sophie Reviews the Troops

Cal set her back firmly on her feet, took the reticule and bonnet from the expressionless footman who had retrieved them, and handed them to her. 'Are you unhurt?'

Sophie nodded, words failing her. She managed to set her bonnet on her head and tie the ribbons in a passable bow.

'That desire to kiss the soil of your new home is very flattering, my dear.' *Oh, thank goodness, he is smiling still.* 'Or was it me?' he whispered in her ear. 'Now that *is* flattering.'

And the smile was still there in his eyes and his hand stayed on her arm as he waited for her mother to be helped down by the footman. He kissed her hand, shook Step Papa's. 'Welcome to Calderbrook. I hope you will regard this as your second home from now on.' He set her hand on his arm and turned to face the front of the house. 'Time to review the troops, Sophie.'

'How many are there?' she whispered as they walked across the gravel.

'It is the full set, inside and out, right down to the mole catcher and the boot boy, so a hundred, more or less,' he murmured back. 'Don't worry, I'm still learning names myself, there won't be a written examination before dinner.'

He had her laughing by the time they reached the staff and suddenly it was easy to smile and exchange a few words with Renshaw the butler, Mrs Fairfax the housekeeper, Mr Oakes the Steward and Monsieur Colbert the chef. Sophie stopped halfway up the steps and addressed the blur of faces looking down at her. 'Thank you all very much for making me feel so welcome. I cannot pretend that I will learn everyone's name immediately, so you must forgive me if I have to ask once or twice.'

That was greeted by a murmur, then someone down on the gravel beside the steps threw a battered hat in the air. 'Three cheers for our new duchess!'

'That was well done,' Cal murmured as they finished the climb, cheers ringing in their ears. 'You are obviously a natural.'

Footmen overtook them on either side, threw open the doors, and Sophie stepped over the threshold.

'I cannot carry you, not this time, or I might just keep going up the staircase – '

Whatever improper thing Cal was about to murmur in her ear was drowned out by the clatter of small feet running across the marble floor.

'*Papa*!'

'Isobel, slow down.' Cal stooped to pick her up but the child swerved to a halt, her bottom lip stuck out as she glowered up at Sophie.

'It's you.'

'Yes. I am very pleased to meet you again, Isobel,' Sophie said warily, with as much warmth as she could muster. She didn't know much about small children, but this looked like a tantrum in the making

'I'm not pleased to meet you.' Dark eyes flashed. 'Papa said I was getting a new mama, but I don't want one. And I don't want *you*.' And with a stamp of her foot she had whirled around and was running back towards the shadows under the stairs.

'Isobel! Come back here this minute,' Cal bellowed, then, when there was no response he swore softly under his breath. 'I apologise for that. Perhaps I should not have told her yet, but I thought it would make things easier.'

'She is very young and she is jealous, I expect,' Sophie said calmly. *And I thought I only had to learn to be a wife and a duchess. I thought the child would be the easy part.*

'Her mother's child,' Cal said with an edge to his voice. 'She should apologise to you, of course, but this might not be the moment.'

'No, no I do not want her to apologise. We will pretend that did not happen and she and I will begin again next time we meet.'

'As you wish. We can discuss this later.' Cal moved into the hall allowing in a knot of footmen, followed by the butler, steward and the housekeeper ushering in her parents. Everyone else, she assumed, had made their way to entrances at the side or back. At least only two footmen had witnessed that little scene, although doubtless it would be all over the house come dinner time.

'Mrs Fairfax?' The housekeeper came forward, bobbed a curtsey. 'Please be so good as to show Lord and Lady Elmham to their suite. I will look after Miss Wilmott.' He turned to her mother. 'We have an hour until luncheon, I hope that is sufficient for you to relax a little after your journey. A footman will come and escort you to the dining room when it is time.'

In the face of such smiling firmness her parents allowed themselves to be carried off by the housekeeper, her mother sending her a look that combined delight, warning and mild alarm all in one lift of the eyebrows and a faint shrug.

'Miss Wilmott?' Cal offered her his arm and strolled towards the foot of the stairs. 'I should, of course, be taking you to a guest room next to your mother's. I am, however, going to install you in the duchess's suite now so you can tell me if there are any changes you want making before the rooms become yours. Very shocking, of course.'

'It is?' It was certainly a surprise.

'Wait and see.' Cal led her up the staircase, along a broad corridor to the other side of the house and opened a door in front of them into another passageway running at right angles. 'These are our private rooms.' He waved a hand at the row of doors, walked to almost to the end of the left hand branch of the passage and opened one. 'Your bedchamber.'

Cal stood back to allow her to walk in and Sophie went immediately to the window. 'Oh, how lovely.' Spread out before her was parkland and clumps of trees, a herd of fallow deer grazing and the sparkle of water, half-concealed by the swell of the land. She turned, running one hand down jade green silk curtains and then turned a slow circle on the great rug spread out in the centre of the room – all pinks and greens and faded gold. 'I love it.' She perched on the end of the bed and leaned back on her hands to admire the plasterwork of the ceiling, then the panelled walls. Her favourite painting would go *there*, her Chinese silk shawl would be perfect draped over *that* chair…

Cal strolled in, closing the door behind him and propped one shoulder against the delicate carved bedpost. 'I see it has you approval.'

'Oh yes. I may be marrying you simply for my bedchamber, Your Grace. But why is it shocking?'

'Connecting doors, inside as well as those outside. Although actually it is more of a series. That is the door to your dressing room, but that, on the other side, is to your sitting room, which leads to my sitting room and then my bedchamber. Of course, it is such a walk that I am thinking of installing refreshment tables at intervals otherwise I may be too weak to do more than fall at your feet when I get here.'

'So my virtue can be safeguarded by two doors to lock and the fact that you will be in a fainting condition even if you should breach them?' Sophie enquired, wondering why she wasn't as pink as a peony. Was Cal actually asking her permission to come through those doors tonight?

'Exactly. And the fact that I believe I can rely upon you to tell me exactly what you do, and do not, want, Sophie. We have not dealt so far in false emotions and coy euphemisms but in facts and in trust.' There was the faintest emphasis on the last word. Or was it her guilty conscience making her over-sensitive? 'And one of those facts is that there is a certain attraction between us.'

Yes, her cheeks were definitely pink now, she could feel them warming, just as she could feel other parts of her body heating and softening. She managed to nod, not breaking contact with Cal's heavy-lidded gaze.

'So, given that we are going to be married very soon, what is there to prevent us acting on that attraction now? Unless that makes you uncomfortable, or it spoils how you want your wedding day to be.'

'No. Under the circumstances I am not harbouring romantic dreams of my wedding nights.'

'You mean after the man to whom you were *unofficially engaged*?' Cal's mouth twitched slightly at what she supposed he would describe as a coy euphemism for her lover, but his face was serious, even when she shook her head. 'There is something, isn't there? Am I being insensitive?' He seemed to be asking himself the question more than her. 'We have been practical and sensible and frank and now I am setting out to strip all the magic out of it. And there should be some magic, shouldn't there, Sophie? Some sprinkle of star dust, some gesture to Venus and not simply a ceremony and a social event. A commercial transaction.'

Cal pushed away from the post and wandered towards the window. It looked casual, the action of a man strolling about his possessions, looking at the view, but Sophie sensed that from another man that jerk upright might have been an ornament thrown into the hearth or a fist thudding against the wall.

'Was that what it was, your first marriage? A commercial transaction?'

'If only it had been.' His snort of amusement might even have been genuine, but she couldn't see his face. 'I thought I was getting into a monetary exchange, that I was setting up a mistress, that Madeleine was one of the sisterhood who did not expect marriage, more a solid financial recompense for their favours. I was young, and more than that, sheltered from spending so much time at home... ill. I had *some* experience, of course, I thought I knew my way around and perhaps I did, but not enough to recognise a respectably-raised young lady from a merchant family who was a good enough actress to counterfeit a high-class courtesan.'

'And then her father appeared on the scene with a shotgun, I suppose.'

'Indeed he did, just as I was about to finally claim the very expensive reward I had paid for over several weeks of negotiations. I wasn't so green as to yield instantly. I had the family investigated and yes, they were solid Boston merchants, wealthy, well-respected. Madeleine wasn't carrying another man's child, she had not so much as a smudge on her character.'

'They had discovered who you were, that you were a duke.'

'No. They had not. No-one knew and I never told them. Madeleine had no idea that she was a duchess until she was dying. I told her then to reassure her about Isobel's prospects. If they had known, then I think I would have walked away from it and to hell with honourable behaviour.'

'Why didn't you? The fact that they had no idea who you were does not make their behaviour right.'

'Because apparently she had fallen in love with me.' He shrugged, still looking out of the window. 'We were introduced at some reception or another, not that I can recall it. I had made acquaintances in good Boston society soon enough. I was obviously an English gentleman of some means, so very acceptable, even though everyone thought I was Mr Thorne of nowhere in particular. I was invited to all kinds of events. Apparently I snubbed her. I'm not aware of it, it certainly wasn't deliberate, but they were merchants and I was fresh from the London *ton.*'

'And we do not mingle with cits,' Sophie said ruefully.

'Exactly. So she decided to make me take notice. I think she assumed that once we had made love, once I had properly got to know her, I would want to marry her. But her father wasn't so hopeful, so he precipitated matters.'

'She must have felt dreadful.'

'I have no idea. I wasn't feeling too wonderful myself. I was cold and I was angry and I made it quite clear that I was a gentleman – hence my agreeing to marry her – but they were inferior, as demonstrated by their behaviour.'

Cal paced back from the window and resumed his position propped against the bedpost. 'Jared tried to talk me out of it, said we should just walk away, catch the next boat to Buenos Aires, but I was on my high horse by then. I would show these colonials how an English gentleman behaved and so on and so forth and so idiotic.'

'If you had not married her you would not have Isobel,' Sophie suggested tentatively.

Cal smiled, a quizzical twist of the lips. 'Very true. And it wasn't all rows and sulks and frosty silences, as Isobel is evidence. We learned to co-exist and she had courage. She thought she had caught a well-off Englishman visiting America and that I would take her back home and she would live in the lap of luxury. In fact she ended up travelling the globe in luxury one week, in extreme discomfort and some danger the next.'

And the whole experience has left you with no

sympathy for girlish dreams of romantic wedding days, or blushing brides and their wedding nights. But he does seem to value honesty. Sophie took a deep breath. 'I would like to make our wedding night the first time, for us.'

Cal shifted to sit beside her on the end of the bed, took her lightly by the shoulders and turned her towards him. 'I like that you are honest with me, Sophie. That you tell me what you want, what you think is right, not what you imagine will please me.'

'It would please me to make love with you now,' she admitted. 'But I think I would always regret it, just a little.'

His smile was rueful. 'I am not certain that I like the results of all this frankness though. Would a kiss be a cause for regret?'

She had been at arms' length when he had begun speaking, now, by some magic, she was against him, both of them twisting to face each other where they sat. It would not take much to fall back onto the bed, to twine themselves together, to find themselves at the point of no return. 'Not a kiss, no,' she said, as much to herself as to Cal.

He was holding himself back with an effort that was palpable, now she was coming to know him. His body where she pressed awkwardly against him was tense, the body of a fit man, a horseman, a swordsman. His hands, one splayed on her back, one in her hair, betrayed his urgency and his desire by their very stillness as much as his mouth on hers by its heat.

Even though her experience with Jonathan had been unpleasant it had been an education and her body knew what was happening, knew what it wanted from his. And, heaven help her, so did she and if she knew that if she yielded, if she leaned into him, let her hands stray from his shoulders down his chest, down to his waist, his hips, then they would both lose control of this.

Sophie freed her mouth, let her head drop to rest on his shoulder and finally allowed herself to encircle as much of his torso as she could. Cal gathered her tight against himself, his lips moving in her hair.

Finally he released her, set her on her feet between his knees. 'I want you.'

'I know. I want you too.'

'Don't look so grim about it, we will remedy the situation soon enough. Your hair is coming down.'

It broke the spell as it was doubtless meant to. Sophie went to the dressing table and managed to restore some order. At least when she rang for her maid it wouldn't look as though she had been embracing a duke on the bed.

This new duchess of his would do well. Very well. Cal lounged against the bedpost, willing his over-interested parts to shut up and calm down. He liked her honesty, even if it was leaving him decidedly uncomfortable. He liked the way she moved and the way she looked and the way she had dealt with his staff. Modest, honest with them too, and yet quite clearly in control. She might be inexperienced at running a household, let alone one this size, but she would not allow herself to be taken advantage of or duped by the servants.

And Sophie had dealt with Isobel's tantrum with a calmness that surprised him. He suspected it was going to surprise Isobel too, once she experienced more of the steel spine that he fancied Sophie's curves and femininity concealed.

She tamed a wayward curl with a determined jab of a hairpin and swivelled round on the stool.

'Will you show me the rest – my other rooms, yours?'

'Very well.' He led her across to the door to the dressing room which had a bath with moulded swans' heads and necks for taps set half way along its length.

'Hot running water?' She was into the room, trailing her fingers over the taps. 'What luxury. I will never get out of it.'

'You will have to take turns with me. They haven't finished mine yet. I swore that after washing in everything from glacial melt-water streams to a bucket on a ship that I was going to have running water in my houses.'

'And you did my bath first?' Sophie whirled round, came up on her toes and kissed him, a swift, lightening-strike on the mouth, then she was off exploring the clothes presses.

'Of course.' Cal considered running a cold bath there and then. 'Obviously, I didn't know it would be for you, exactly, I just sent orders for a start to be made here.'

Did he detect a slight stiffening in her shoulders at that tactless reminder that he had wanted a duchess, right away, and she just happened to fit the bill? His imagination, surely? She had wanted a husband without emotional strings attached, she had been clear about that.

But all Sophie said was, 'And what is in here?' She opened a door. 'Oh, my. It actually flushes with water?'

'It does. Come and see your sitting room.'

She slid her hand under his elbow and he thought again that she was just the right height for him. Madeleine had been a pocket Venus, gorgeous to look at, lush, feminine, but she had never felt quite right on his arm. Or in them, come to that. Sophie seemed to… fit. Ah well, he was a duke, he could afford to order made-to-measure.

'What are you smiling about?' She looked up, head tipped to see his face properly.

'A whimsical thought. Now, is the colour to your taste?' he asked as he led her through to the sitting room. This was newly decorated too, on his orders when he reached London. He had left it to his senior staff to chose exactly what was done and he wished now he had taken a more personal interest.

'I love the colour, that old rose and the soft gilt and

ivory.' She walked around, touched the desk, bounced on a chair. 'I might change the furniture around.'

'Whatever you like,' Cal agreed, distracted by the thought of how there was room in that chair for both of them and what an interesting height it was.

'Now you are frowning.'

'Was I?' *Wondering just why I am crazy with desire for you, that is all.* Yes, Sophie was very beautiful, yes she was refreshingly open and obviously intelligent, but he had seen any number of beautiful, intelligent, interesting women over the past years without becoming obsessed with the idea of getting them into bed. And that had nothing to do with the fact that he had been married and inconveniently inclined to honour his wedding vows.

Sophie was in motion again, circling the room, touching things as if nothing was quite real unless her fingers stroked it. Lord, there went his imagination again. 'Through here is my sitting room. I don't know how much I will use it.' Cal opened the door and followed Sophie in. 'I've got a study downstairs.' He strode across the Aubusson carpet and opened his bedchamber door, unable to cope with the sight of Sophie caressing any more objects. 'And this is as far as we are going today.'

Chapter Thirteen - Where Sophie and the Duke Survey a Bed

Sophie's eyes were wide as she stood on the threshold and studied the bed which was, he had to agree, quite indecently large and ornate. 'It is very…'

'I'll have it moved into the State Bedchamber and get something simpler. That chamber never did get a bed. It was all done up for George II and he went and died before he got here, which saved the family a great deal of money, I suspect.'

'State bedchamber,' Sophie said faintly.

'There's an entire suite of state rooms. Wonderful for entertaining visitors on wet days and for children playing hide and seek. We will probably lose Isobel in there for weeks at a time.'

'I hope not. Did you have to sleep in that as a child? It must have given you nightmares.'

'No, I was spared that. I was ill, or laid up after one accident or another half the time, so much that I had a suite in the West Wing. Much more straightforward furnishings.' He eyed the monstrosity. 'In fact this is too short for me. Apparently in those days people slept sitting more or less upright. You will have to help me choose another bed, there must be enough in this place for us to find one the right size for us.'

The blue eyes turned to give him a look which said very clearly that she knew exactly what he was hoping might happen on a tour of bedchambers combined with the close study of beds. 'You promised.'

'I know. And I did not for a moment believe you would actually help me chose a bed.'

'I cannot imagine what Mama would say.'

'I can. Come along, Sophie, back to your bedchamber. You may lock all the doors after you, ring for the maid and play with the plumbing. They should have brought you some tea up by now.'

'Cal.' She stopped in the middle of her sitting room, stood in front of him and looked steadily into his face, all the laughter gone. 'What do you want of me? I realise I don't know you, not at all. We kiss, and we make jokes and… I do not know you.'

'I want whatever you can give me, Sophie. Nothing more. What do you want of me?'

'I don't know that either.' She said it abruptly, as though the admission had been forced out of her. 'I really do not know.' Then she was gone, a whirl of blue skirts and flying ribbons, and the door shut and there was a soft click as the key turned.

Whatever had that been about? What had impelled her to ask such a question? The answer should be obvious. Cal wanted a lady of breeding who could act as an hostess, who could manage large households, who would give him children and raise his daughter. And yet she had been compelled to ask and he had thrown the question back and she hadn't been able to answer him.

A faint sound made her start before she saw it was a maid who was setting out tea things on a small table in the window embrasure. 'Miss Wilmott, I've brought you tea.' It looked more like a comprehensive meal. 'Is there anything else you would like? Different cake, perhaps?'

'No, this looks excellent, thank you – ?'

'Betty, ma'am.' A bob of a curtsey.

'Could you ask someone to fetch… to run my bath in twenty minutes? And send my maid up to help me dress.'

'Mary's unpacking your things now, Miss Wilmott. I'll just tell her when you want your bath for.'

Betty, Mrs Fairfax the housekeeper. Only about ninety eight more names to learn. Sophie poured herself a cup of tea, selected a watercress sandwich and gave herself a brisk talking-to while she ate. It took another sandwich, ham that time, and a scone with blackberry jelly, but she had talked herself into something approaching calm confidence by the time Mary appeared to announce that her bath was ready.

Sophie Anne Mathilda Thorne, Her Grace the Duchess of Calderbrook. Yes, this is what I want.

The positive mood lasted into the evening, despite Mama worrying at their unconventional arrival. 'I was not at all happy with the Duke sweeping you off like that.' She eyed Sophie with what looked like apprehension as they sat in the drawing room waiting for Cal and Lord Elmham to come in from the hall where they were deep in conversation about, of all things, the weaponry of the South Pacific islanders. 'He is very forceful in a quiet way. Were you at all… flustered?'

What a marvellous euphemism. Yes, Mama, we were both very flustered. 'Not at all, Mama. The Duchess's suite of rooms has just been refurbished and Cal asked me to use them so I could identify any changes that I wanted for after the wedding. I did go as far as his sitting room, which apparently he isn't likely to use, but that is all.' Her mother looked relieved. Presumably she'd had nightmare visions of Sophie being pursued round the bedchamber by an amorous Duke attempting to anticipate the wedding. 'The plumbing is amazing, Mama. All the latest innovations. You must come and try the bath for yourself.'

They were discussing how Step Papa might be induced to fit modern pipework into the London house when the men walked in, Step Papa carrying a strange green blade that seemed to be made of some kind of stone and Cal charmingly apologetic for neglecting them. After that, it seemed to Sophie, Cal seduced her parents with as much ease as he had almost seduced her.

He was perfect with Mama. Serious, charming, a little rueful about his long absence from England, very flattering to her as the mother of such a delightful daughter. With Step Papa he was slightly deferential, as to an older man, but they were soon deep into travellers' tales with all formality gone. During the evening they both kept smiling at her and Sophie realised they were happy, and relieved, and had no qualms that she had found the ideal match. And neither had she.

The happiness that she was doing the right thing survived the night and waking up to the luxury of the Duchess's suite and Mary's attentive care.

Cal met her as she descended the sweeping staircase, caught her hand in his and kissed it. 'You have made up your mind,' he said as he steered her towards the back of the hall. 'The breakfast room is through here.'

'Made up my mind?'

'To marry me.'

'Of course I had. I would not have come otherwise.'

The breakfast room was empty except for two footmen. Cal waved them out and opened the tall windows, letting in the cool air and birdsong and the smell of newly-scythed grass. 'Yes you would. Rather, you would have told me if you had definitely decided against, but you were unsure yesterday, weren't you?' He began to lift covers from the dishes on the buffet, then handed her a plate.

'I...' Sophie took refuge in the array of breakfast dishes, selected eggs and bacon and crisp rolls and sat down before she answered him. Cal deserved honesty. 'I did have doubts, yes. We hardly know each other.'

'But my kisses convinced you?' He had added devilled kidneys, bacon, sausage, eggs and mushrooms to his plate. He set down his food at the head of the table at right angles to her place and went back to the buffet. 'Tea, coffee or chocolate?'

'Tea please. Your kisses were persuasive but your superior bathing arrangements clinched the argument I was having with myself.' She watched him as he carried her cup over to her, saw the laughter-creases at the corners of his eyes deepen and let out the breath she had been holding. He did have a sense of humour, even about this.

When he sat and began to stir his own coffee he was serious again. 'I am relieved, both by your decision and the fact you took time to make it. It is good to know that you want me for more than my title, even if it is my bath tub that made up your mind.' No, not entirely serious, on the surface, but there was truth behind the bantering words.

'When I made my list of necessary qualities for a husband I included well-bred and well-off because I want to remain in contact with my friends and my family and with the world I know,' Sophie said carefully. 'But anyone who was received and who was in easy circumstances would have done, if I had liked them. An earl or a viscount would probably have been more comfortable and considerably less work.'

'You are telling me that my title is an encumbrance?' Cal was making good inroads into the kidneys, the sensitive nature of the conversation apparently having no effect on his appetite.

'Neutral, I would say.'

This time his smile reached his lips as well as his eyes. There was a faint tap at the door which opened to half way. 'My spies are warning me that we have about two minutes before your parents get here. After breakfast would you like me to show you over the house before our – *my* – guests start to arrive?'

'That would be interesting, thank you.'

They were discussing the rival merits of Weymouth and Brighton as seaside resorts when her parents came in, preceded by the footmen who bustled about to such effect that it hid the fact that the two of the had been alone and quite unchaperoned. Cal was certainly a considerable strategist.

The house was so large that it took all morning for them to do nothing more than walk through from room to room, and that omitted the attics, the nursery floor, the stables, the basement and cellars and the staff areas. When they finally reached the Long Gallery Sophie collapsed laughing in one of the cushioned benches in the window bays and refused to go any further.

'I am exhausted, stunned, impressed and horrified,' she announced. 'I cannot manage another step. How many miles have we walked?'

Cal shrugged. 'No idea. We could measure it out, there are large scale plans in the library.' He sat down at the other end of the seat, stooped to take hold of her ankles, swung her feet up and pulled off her shoes. 'Sit still and stop wriggling. Are you ticklish?'

'No. Yes. Cal!' He was massaging her feet, one large hand enveloping each foot, his thumbs working firmly on the aching arches. 'Ouch… Oh, that is bliss.'

It was surprisingly easy to do as he said, despite the fact that he – *a man* – had her stockinged feet in his hands, that his long fingers were weaving all kinds of patterns over and under them and occasionally trailing daring fingertips up her ankles. 'It feels as though we have done this before, sat here alone, very tranquil, very intimate… It feels familiar.'

'Just lean back, relax.' Under his hands the slender bones of her feet, the high sensitive arches, were as satisfying to caress as a fine piece of sculpture, only this statue was alive. 'It feels right.' Cal stopped the massage, swung his own legs up, fitted his feet on the bench between hers, leaned back against the folded shutter and closed his eyes.

He had recoiled from the thought of Madeleine here with her moods and her temper and her insecurities. But Sophie, this woman, this lovely, straightforward, honest, brave woman who stood up to him and spoke her mind, she was perfect.

He was going to have to tell her about his suspicions before much more time had passed. It was only fair and he knew now he could trust her discretion.

The thrumming beat of the gong reverberated even up here, through all the closed doors and the panelling. 'Luncheon is served.' He opened his eyes and found that she had closed hers, was, perhaps, quietly dozing. 'Shall I send the footmen with one of the sedan chairs?'

That brought her awake with a start. 'Sedan chairs?' Sophie swung her legs down with an elegant little twist that kept her skirts demurely tight around her calves. A very provocative little twist.

'My various elderly ancestors kept them so they could be carried about the place. I can just recall one very ancient great-aunt trailing fans and shawls and lap dogs as she was carted about by two perspiring footmen.'

'I will save that treat for my old age.' She put her shoes back on and stood up. 'We mustn't be late for luncheon or Mama will fret.' She looked round at the rows of portraits as they passed. 'But we must come back and you can teach me who everyone is and point out the characteristic Thorne chin or nose or eyebrows. Every family has something like that. Papa's had rather large ears which I am glad to say I avoided.'

He was teasing her about her ears when they reached the bottom of the stairs but stopped as two footmen strode past followed, at a more stately pace, by Renshaw.

'Carriages, Your Grace. Three, I believe. I have sent down to the kitchen to delay luncheon by half an hour and alerted the housekeeping staff.'

‘They are early and my aunt and uncle aren’t here yet.’ This was sensitive. Having Sophie, an unmarried lady, beside him to greet the guests was not according to protocol. It might shock some of the older ladies and Sophie could do without their disapproval. ‘Would your mother mind standing in for a few hours?’

‘I am sure not. I will go and find her.’

‘Lady Elmham is in the Chinese Drawing Room, Miss Wilmott. There is no need for you to exert yourself, ma’am. Perkins, present His Grace’s complements to her ladyship and explain the situation. Harris, James, delay things enough to allow Lady Elmham to reach the front door.’ Renshaw was as alert to social niceties as the most stringent chaperone.

‘There, you can fade comfortably into the background.’

Sophie sent him a grateful look and effaced herself to the back of the hall while the staff went about presenting the surface appearance of absolute calm with the minimum of frantic paddling below the surface. He had wondered how he would find things when he returned after so many years absence, but Prescott had kept things running as though the Duke had only left the day before and was expected back at any time. There were even a large proportion of staff whom he recalled from the years he had lived here and he smiled inwardly at his own pleasure at how warmly they greeted his return.

‘You need me, Calderbrook?’ It was Lady Elmham, almost as lovely as her daughter and so poised that no-one would have guessed that she had been summoned to act the hostess without warning.

‘Thank you. I wanted to have a married lady here in case any of the arrivals are the single girls without their mothers. Of course, this may well be my aunt and uncle, in which case I need not trouble you at all.’

The door was flung open at a nod from Renshaw, the footmen ran down the steps and Cal mentally squared his shoulders. He was home, he was the Duke and at any moment the curtain would go up on a play within a play. His courtship of Sophie and the acknowledgment of their betrothal created the perfect stage on which to watch how his uncle and cousin reacted to seeing him in the place they might covet enough to kill for. And if they wanted to do him harm, then where better than in a vast and rambling house, set in wide parklands and woodland and with a party of guests to provide distraction and cover. He made a mental note to have the archery butts set up.

The arrivals proved to be several bridesmaids, complete with two guardian mamas, in one coach; Lord and Lady Faversham in the second and Sir Tobias Greenwich driving himself in a curricle with another man in his mid-twenties beside him, presumably the old friend he had asked if he could bring along.

After his initial greeting Lady Elmham dealt with the female contingent, ushering the young ladies and their chaperones off to the care of Mrs Fairfax and leaving him to shake hands with Greenwich and his friend while the Favershams spoke to Renshaw about their baggage.

'This is an old acquaintance I had not seen for years, Your Grace,' Toby was explaining as they shook hands. 'He's been out of Town so long I thought this would be ideal for him to make himself known again.' He stepped aside and let the tall blond man a pace behind him step forward. 'Your Grace, Jonathan Ransome of Penzance.'

Cal shook hands, waved aside the *Your Graces* with the insistence they all call him Cal and turned to find Lady Faversham at his side.

'Where is Sophie?' she asked. 'I cannot wait to see her.'

'Just back here.' Cal turned and looked. The hall was empty.

Chapter Fourteen - Where Sophie Finds Trouble on the Doorstep

Sophie fled. Two sliding, backwards steps to take her under the curve of the stairs, three hasty steps to the baize door into the realm of the servants and a clear run down the flagged passageway with a glimmer of daylight at the end. Mercifully there were no staff to wonder what their future duchess was doing, running as though the hounds of hell were on her heels. She burst out into the semi-basement area at the side of the house nearest the stables and ran up the steps.

At the top Sophie slumped against the balustrade and dragged air into her lungs until the dancing black spots in front of her eyes went away. *Do not panic.* That was the first thing. *Get back to my room.* Once she was there she could feign indisposition and think. Plan. *Think of something.* There was the rub. How was she going to get out of this?

But first, back into the house. She walked round the outside with a wary eye on the windows. No-one was inside to see her and there was one ajar, the one that opened into the breakfast room. And she knew how to get from there to the bedroom floor using one of the minor staircases that she had seen when they looked round the house that morning.

The window was tall, with a low cill that was easy to climb over, and she was inside in a minute and hurrying towards the stairs in two. It took several false turns and a nerve-wracking retreat when she heard the voices of two of the maids approaching, but she found the door into the ducal apartments, and her own suite without anyone seeing her.

Lock the door. Every instinct urged her to turn the key, jam a chair-back under the handle. Instead she took off her shoes and gown, unlaced her stays, slipped on a wrapper and lay down on the bed after drawing the curtains. How long before they missed her? Best to make sure no alarm was caused by her unexplained absence. Sophie pulled the bell cord and waited.

'Yes, Miss Wilmott?' Mary appeared in a few minutes. 'Are you unwell, ma'am?'

'I have a migraine.' She lay back and made her voice a little faint. 'Please will you tell my mother that I am resting. I think I will be better by dinner time if I just lie quietly and try and sleep.'

'Yes, ma'am.' Mary closed the door carefully behind her.

She'd had migraines before, although they had become rarer as she got older, but Mama knew they were usually brought on by some stressful situation or worry and she would assume that was the case now. Mama also knew that they vanished with rest and quiet and would not fuss over her.

Sophie sat up in bed and fought the urge to bury her face in the pillows and pretend it was a bad dream. She couldn't blame Toby, who wouldn't recognise a love-affair going on under his nose unless he actually fell over the couple kissing, had never known about the disaster with Jonathan. When it became clear that her parents thought she could do better for herself that to marry him she had fallen in easily with Jonathan's urging to keep their feelings quiet, and afterwards what had happened was not something to confide in a male friend. Besides, she had thought Jonathan had gone from her life for good.

It was bad enough to imagine what Cal would do to the man who had seduced her into elopement and then forced himself on her, but she couldn't imagine his reaction if he discovered that Jonathan had insinuated himself into Cal's own home in order to blackmail her.

She had been worried before that Cal would call Jonathan out and kill him. That was bad enough, making Cal into a killer, creating the most appalling scandal, even if he did escape hanging. And there was always the possibility that Jonathan would kill him. Accidents happened in duels, people tripped, guns misfired, dualists cheated. And Jonathan was a very good shot and would have the choice of weapons, whilst she had no idea if Cal could hit a barn door at ten paces.

But now, surely, he would simply tear Jonathan limb from limb, and while a death in a dual might escape the full penalties of the law, hot-blooded murder would not. Although if anyone could cover it up, it would be a duke with experience in some of the wilder parts of the world…

What was she thinking? Sophie flung back the covers and began to pace the room. Murder was not an answer. It was *never* the answer to anything. She had to get herself out of this quagmire, the swamp she had got herself into because she was such a terrible judge of men. She had thought she had paid for that mistake, but apparently not.

The first thing was to write to Mr Tanner. Anonymity would have to be sacrificed. Her sitting room contained a lady's desk, set out with fine notepaper, ink and pens, sealing wax and all the accessories she could possibly want.

The situation has become urgent. Please contact me as soon as possible at Calderbrook Park, Somerset, with any information, via the shop next door to you. I have bought a cane from them, they can send me a receipt. Sophie Wilmott. Miss.

PS Please pay the shopkeeper whatever you think is appropriate and charge it to my account.

She sealed that, addressed it to Mr Tanner, then put it within a note to the owner of the shop next door, promising recompense for a delivering the enclosure and forwarding the reply under cover of a receipt for the cane she had bought.

Her mother, thank goodness, did not insist on reading all her correspondence as the mothers of many of her friends did, but she was sure to ask, out of interest, what post Sophie had received. A discreet wave of the receipt and a whisper that it was about Cal's gift, would be almost truthful and would prevent her mother asking any more questions.

She stamped firmly on a fantasy of Mr Tanner's large associates kidnapping Jonathan and handing him over to the press gang and made herself face the reality of what to do next. Sooner or later, and probably by seven at the latest, she was going to have to emerge, apologise for her indisposition and face Jonathan. He was certain to want a *tête à tête,* so that he could gloat and put on more pressure for money, so she had to be calm and collected and confident when that happened.

She would stick to what she had said to Jonathan before, that Cal knew she had lost her virginity, but she knew he would still threated to tell all and sundry just where that had happened, embroidering the tale until it became a shocking one of orgies and excess. She was prepared to face that down – she was, after all, known in Society for her blameless character – but she could guess what Cal's reaction would be. And Step Papa's. She could imagine them coming to blows over who was going to disembowel Jonathan first with Toby hot on their heels.

So, until she could find some weapon to counter his threats she was going to have to deal with the blackmailing demands for money. Jonathan could be led to believe she had very little now, that Step Papa gave her only a small allowance of pin money and insisted on having all her bills delivered to him. Then she could promise to pay him when she was married, and surely he would think her more vulnerable to continued demands when she was the duchess, because she would have so much more to lose.

Yes, that was the approach. Appear to yield and agree to pay in the future and meanwhile hope and pray that Mr Tanner came up with sufficient discreditable history to apply blackmail of her own. All while keeping this from Cal's sharp eyes and playing the part of the modest, but happy, fiancée.

No-one said being a duchess was going to be easy.

Cal came across the drawing room towards her, his hand held out, and Sophie found herself smiling back with real pleasure. *I do like this man, please let me keep him.*

'Sophie, darling.' He lowered his voice as he reached her and took her hands in his. 'Should you be out of bed?'

'It is nothing,' she murmured back, with a smile directed across the room to her mother. 'I think I must have been more nervous than I realised and I get horrible headaches when I become very tense.' A glance around the room told her that all of the guests must have arrived and the long chamber was full enough for her to be unable to see Jonathan. 'I should speak to your aunt and apologise for not being here when she arrived. I have met her in London often enough for her to know I would not deliberately neglect the courtesy.'

Lady Peter was a big woman, bony rather than fat, and surprisingly colourless for such a large physical presence. She rose when Cal brought Sophie to her, smiled wanly and kissed her on both cheeks. 'Dear girl,' she murmured. 'So happy.'

But not ecstatic, Sophie thought with an inward grimace. She supposed that Cal's marriage heralded the end of her husband and son's positions as heirs presumptive to the dukedom and no fond wife and mother would be delighted about that, however sensibly resigned they might be. It would be impossible that Cal's long absence in remote and dangerous places had not raised some faint, unacknowledged hopes in Lady Peter's breast.

But the two families would adjust to co-existence soon enough, although the production of a male heir at the earliest opportunity might not be a bad idea. The thought of which led to an involuntary glance at the man at her side which was met by a disconcertingly warm smile.

'I must drag Sophie away to greet the rest of our guests,' Cal said, his hand sliding under her elbow. 'You two can have a long talk later. What is it?' he asked as they crossed the room to a knot of guests by the long windows open onto the terrace.

'I was just thinking that the sooner you have a son, the better,' Sophie said before she caught herself. 'Oh. I didn't mean – '

But strangely Cal seemed neither to take her indiscretion as an expression of desire, nor as the insult to his aunt that it certainly was. His expression became guarded, almost dark, but all he said was, 'You are quite right about that. We must discuss it later.'

Lord Peter and his son were with the group by the window, along with several of the bridesmaids and two gentlemen Sophie knew by sight. Jane, Phyllida and Amelie all greeted her with hugs and kisses, Ralph claimed a *cousinly kiss* which darkened Cal's expression still further and she shook hands with Lord Peter, Mr Harrison and Lord James Fitzdene.

Where the devil is Jonathan? He was the last person she wanted to see, but the knowledge that he was here, that she was going to have to deal with him at any moment, was beginning to prey on her nerves.

It was fortunate that she was thinking of him, because when he said, 'Miss Wilmott, what a pleasure to see you again,' from directly behind her she did not jump or even, she thought, go pale.

Sophie turned slowly, a bright social smile on her lips. 'Mr Ransome. You abandon London society for years and now I find you popping up wherever I turn.'

'I thought you might have forgotten me,' he said with that charming smile, the one that had dazzled her into loving him.

Cal had turned to say something to Toby who seemed to have been out on the terrace with Jonathan. It was safe to hit back, because she was not going to let him think he had cowed her. 'Oh, no, Mr Ransome. I recall exactly where I last saw you that last time, and how you looked.'

He had been naked, except the stockings which bound him to the bedposts and a pink satin bow neatly tied around his flaccid penis. The venom in his eyes told her that she had just poked a viper with a stick, so she slid her hand under his arm and said, 'Do show me what you were admiring from the terrace, Mr Ransome.'

He allowed himself to be led outside, then turned at the edge of the paved area, one hip negligently propped against the balustrade. 'That was a very expensive little joke, Sophie.'

'I am sure it was,' she said, chin up. 'But I do not have money now and I will not until I marry. My stepfather is not generous with my pin money.'

'I could insist.'

'I have no jewellery I can safely sell or pawn, no way of raising money. Jonathan, if you are greedy now and push too hard I would be forced to tell the Duke the truth. When I am married…' She shrugged and waved a hand in a gesture to encompass house and land. 'He will be generous. Just be patient.'

'Very well. Much as I would like to punish you, Sophie, I would rather make you pay in money.' His eyes were full of hate and resentment and she guessed he was jealous of Cal, as well as bitterly angry with her. 'Revenge may be sweet but it pays no bills.'

He wanted both, she knew that. He wanted money and he wanted to torment her and the second desire was almost as great as the first. She repressed the shudder that was somehow more than anger, more than fear of his revelations.

'There is still a payment you could make, Sophie my sweet. One that doesn't involve any money at all. I have a large empty bed just upstairs, one that I would like you to warm up for me.'

And then she realised what was repelling her – he still wanted her sexually, he still wanted to force himself on her and take his revenge in that humiliation as well as in any other way he could think of.

'Unfortunately I will be too busy elsewhere, Jonathan, with someone else if you take my meaning, so I will have to miss the opportunity of discovering whether your technique has improved at all. It seems unlikely.'

'Sophie?' It was Cal, standing at the window. From his watchful gaze he had sensed something amiss.

'Coming!' She walked back, leaving Jonathan where he was, and murmured to Cal, 'I had forgotten what a tiresome man he was.'

'In what way?' He slowed, on the point of turning back.

'A bore. Heavy flirtation. You must have seen the sort before. Thinks he is irresistible just because of his looks. No doubt if any lady actually responded to his advances he would flee like a startled rabbit.'

Cal snorted. 'If he is bothering you, I'll have him out of here.'

'Goodness, no. He is not important. I just wanted to show off this wonderful parkland and forgot how wearying he was. Now, who else haven't I met?'

It had been something of a risk, but at least now she had established a mild dislike of Jonathan in Cal's mind and that would explain any expression he caught on her face as she looked at the man, or why she might seem to be avoiding him.

'I think you know everyone else.' Cal surveyed the room. 'Probably a lot better than I do. Extraordinary how men you thought were perfect companions, entirely in tune with your thoughts and feelings, turn out to have either not grown up at all, or have become positively middle aged in the intervening years.'

'Lord Micklethwaite?' she guessed. 'I was surprised that he had been a close friend of yours, I would have thought you had little in common. Unless you have been hiding your passion for Old Testament scholarship and forestry from me.'

'We did once share many interests, but neither of those,' Cal agreed with a snort of laughter, then sobered. 'Will you ride out with me tomorrow? I would show you the estate and there is something I must talk to you about before many more days pass.'

'That sounds ominous.' Sophie gave a little wave to Lord Peter who was watching them, his expression inscrutable. After a second he raised his hand in response.

'It is serious, but not, I hope, ominous. Ah, here is Renshaw.'

'Dinner is served, my lady.'

Sophie found herself seated on Cal's right hand at the top of the table, her mother opposite her. At the foot of the board her father was making conversation with Lady Peter in her role as hostess and Jonathan, thankfully, was on her side of the table and well towards the middle.

Provided Mr Tanner found something substantial to Jonathan's discredit she could deal with this without anyone's life being in danger and without any great scandal enveloping Cal and the dukedom.

It took Cal a while to get to sleep that night, despite a replacement bed from one of the guest chambers which was a better fit for his height. The knowledge that only three doors and two private rooms separated him from

Sophie did not make for tranquillity. He was concerned about her and that attack of nervous tension and headache. She seemed strong, both physically and mentally, but he was asking a lot of her. Marriage to a man she hardly knew, the prospect of great rank and responsibility, might not bear down on a woman of less imagination than Sophie, but she was more sensitive than she allowed him to see much of the time.

And tomorrow he was going to add to the stress by telling her about his unresolved suspicions, the reasons he had left England. He wasn't sure he could blame her if she called the match off. Would she fear she was in danger herself? He was convinced that she would not be, not until she was with child, and if this was not resolved, one way or another, by then he would take her away, show her some of the world, until it was. Cal smiled a trifle grimly, punched the pillows and turned over to try for sleep. All the more reason for celibacy until the wedding day.

He drifted off, vaguely aware at the edge of consciousness, of the chime of a distant long-case clock. *One, two...*

Something woke him, brought him up out of shallow sleep into near-consciousness, a sensation that there was someone else in the room with him. He lay still, ignoring the itch between his shoulder-blades that reminded him that his naked back was to the door, that he had no weapon to hand, that sheets had wound themselves around his legs, that someone was breathing in the room and that it was another man.

It was a moonlit night. *Roll to the edge of the bed away from the door, grab the edge of the curtains, yank them back across the window and let in the moonlight, kick off the sheets and there's a good heavy candlestick on the window ledge...*

He was braced to move when the air shifted, a faint draft touched his cheek, the door closed with a click.

It took precious seconds to kick his way free of the sheets, to get to the door, open it onto an empty passageway and to run to the door onto the main corridor. Empty.

He looked down at himself, stark naked. By the time he had gone back to his room, pulled on even a minimum of clothing, whoever it was would be long gone. It was not a comforting thought to recall that the rooms his aunt and uncle and his cousin always used were just around the corner.

Chapter Fifteen - Where Sophie Visits a Castle

'My dear, of course you want some time alone with my nephew.' Lady Peter was rather more forthcoming the next morning after breakfast when Sophie asked her if she might be excused for a ride with the Duke. 'The gentlemen seem to have plans involving the stables and the Home Farm and I was going to suggest that the ladies take a walk to the Temple Folly overlooking the lake for a picnic. But we will all quite understand if Calderbrook wants to show you around. Mind he gives you a nice steady mount though.'

Cal was sitting on the mounting block talking with an elderly groom while half a dozen horses were led around the stableyard. He stood up and raised an eyebrow as she hurried under the arch and the groom effaced himself. 'Thank you, Hooper. Problem?'

'No, I am sorry I kept you, but I had to make my apologies to your aunt.' The eyebrow was still up. 'She is your hostess, after all.'

'So she is. What nice manners you have, Miss Wilmott.' He took her hand in its tight calfskin glove, turned it and dropped a kiss on the exposed skin of her wrist. 'Do you ride as well as you drive?'

'I hope so.' Sophie perched on the step of the block and watched the circling animals. 'I like the bay gelding.'

'Not too big for you? I haven't ridden any of these, but Hooper says they all have reasonable manners except that beast.' He nodded towards a rangy chestnut that was sidling round the yard showing the whites of its eyes and keeping the lad leading it on his toes.

'So I suppose that is the one you will be riding,' she teased him.

'Not when I am out with you, no.' Cal turned, shielding her from the busy yard with his body. 'I want to take care of you, Sophie. I want to keep you safe.'

That seemed a touch melodramatic when all they were discussing was one chestnut gelding in need of a few lessons in manners. Or was it? Sophie had the uneasy feeling that Cal was talking about more than horses.

'Which then?' She pulled off her glove and touched his cheek, very smooth from his morning shave. She brought her fingers to her lips, the scent of lemons touching her senses, and his eyes darkened.

'*Sophie.*' The moment lengthened, her breathing shortened, then he smiled and said, 'The grey.'

Cal led the way out of the yard at a walk, and kept to that pace for half a mile.

'Where are we going?' She had thought he was going to show her the park, but they were heading out of it, towards the line of hills that rose to the west. 'Are we leaving your land?'

'We are going almost to the edge to where the first Thorne had his stronghold. Over there,' he waved at the far distance where the hills rose higher. 'That is where the Cheddar Gorge runs. Jocelyn de Thorne was, by the sound of it, a local robber baron and he had his own miniature gorge here, running back into the crest of the line of hills in front of us. That's where he built a castle and proceeded to expand eastward, getting control over as much good land as he could lay his hands on.'

'By marriage?'

'By marriage and by battle and by downright trickery, I strongly suspect. His son was a landowner with some power hereabouts. His grandson was rich enough and powerful enough to be made an earl, and so it has gone on.'

'You own land beyond the crest?'

'No. There are minerals on the far slope and mines here and there, but it is tough country and the Thornes never concerned themselves with it, not when there were easier pickings, rich farm land and wealthy heiresses between them and Bristol. There is a village over the crest, but the road doesn't even run this way and it is a poor place – or it was when I left.'

'And the villages on your land?'

'Brookwood is the nearest and largest. Then there's a couple of hamlets, Rundene and Herriots End. I must visit those soon because most of the property belongs to the estate and so they are my responsibility.'

'Does your uncle still act for you?'

'No.' Cal used his heels and the grey broke from a walk into a canter. By the time she caught up with him he seemed disposed to answer. 'When I left I employed Prescott as a secretary. He is, in effect, my confidential assistant. He deals with my agents, carries out my orders and I have total trust in him – he is intelligent enough to do what I would do under any circumstance, which was necessary when I was often months away by post.'

They reached the edge of the parkland and Cal held a gate for her to pass through into a mix of small fields and woodland that became scrub and moorland as they climbed. Then he turned from the open country onto a wide track through the wood and into a valley, steep and narrow. Through the trees Sophie glimpsed outcrops of rock above their heads.

'Where is the river?'

'This is dry. The rock here is limestone and water eats into it. Streams run a short distance then vanish into chasms or quite small holes, only to reappear miles away. At one time a stream must have cut this miniature gorge and then hit a fault in the rock and vanished underground. Here is the castle.'

At first she could see nothing, only an expanse of rock, then she realised that it was the ruins of a simple fortress – two turrets, a length of connecting curtain wall, broken down, covered in some place by ivy, in others providing anchorage for saplings. 'How romantic! Can we get in?'

'I doubt it is safe. It needs checking thoroughly before I would risk you in there, but I confess that it would be interesting to restore it, make this area part of the park. Come and see the Duke's Spring.' Cal swung down out the saddle and held up his hands to help her down.

It was easy to put her hands on his shoulders and slide down, his fingers firm on her waist, his body strong and steady against hers. The kiss was inevitable, prolonged, delicious torture. Sophie felt her resolve weakening, just as Cal moved back and released her.

'A moment when a cold stream would be very welcome,' he said ruefully.

'Yes,' Sophie agreed so earnestly that he laughed. 'Show me the spring.'

'It isn't a spring any longer, unfortunately. Here.' He led her to the foot of one of the towers and showed her the ragged gash in the natural stone by its side. 'Water used to gush out of here and, by a long-held superstition, only the Duke could drink from it. Then, the day after my father died, it dried up. Not so much as a trickle. You may imagine the talk hereabouts. There were rumours of everything from a curse on the ducal house to some wretch drinking from the spring causing the death. And, to reinforce the superstitious talk, a new spring appeared, just over there, two days later.'

He took her hand and helped her over some tumbled stones to a narrow path. The sound of water grew louder and Sophie stopped, sniffed. 'That's odd…' but Cal was forging ahead to where a narrow vertical crack in the rock gushed a torrent into a natural basin beneath before it vanished into another crack in the rock.

He bent, scooped water up in his palm, drank and shook off the drops, grimacing, making her dance backwards with a laugh.

'May I have a drink?'

'Certainly not. This is the Duke's Spring, remember. Anyway, like most spa waters, it doesn't taste good. I've got water in my saddlebag.'

Sophie followed Cal back through the trees, over the fallen stones to where they had left the horses and then, taking the bay's reins, down to where a flat rock made a natural seat overlooking the land below. 'This is what your ancestor saw and coveted.'

'Yes.' He unbuckled the saddlebags and began to unpack a flask, two horn beakers and a packet wrapped in waxed paper. 'Just a little something to keep us from collapse.' They shared out the bread and cheese, poured the water, which turned out to be wine and Sophie settled to admire the view.

'This is what my ancestor coveted.' Cal echoed her words, his own voice grim. 'I think the time has come to tell you why I left England. When my father died I was seven years old. A healthy, fit child. My uncle, my father's younger brother, my only adult male relative, became my guardian. The estate could not have had a better master, nor could all the parts of the ducal empire – because that it what it is – if it had all been his. Which of course it would be if I died.'

The cheese fell from Sophie's hand, rolled down the stone and vanished into the gorse below the rock. 'You don't mean… no, of course you don't…'

'I began to fall ill with vicious attacks of sickness and fever that left me exhausted. I lost weight after every bout so each subsequent one hit me harder. And then I started to have accidents when I was fit enough to get about. A stone fell from the parapet, missing me by a foot, about the distance that a shot missed me in the woods. A poacher, no doubt, and failing mortar that no-one had noticed, perhaps. An over-polished top step on the stairs – there was a broken arm that time. Or the worn girth that broke. That fall broke my leg.'

'Cal, young boys, youths, have accidents.'

'True. That is what I believed. Ralph would take tumbles too, although oddly stones never fell near him, nor did shots almost take his ear off. The doctors lamented my poor health: some weakness of the constitution, they said, some incurable illness that perhaps I would grow out of as inexplicably as I had developed it. None of them knew what it was. My aunt encouraged whatever lunacy they came up with for treatment. Lord knows how much blood they drained off me.

'I came up to London, joined in the Season when I was just twenty, found myself much better. It was almost as though the air of Calderbrook did not agree with me, I thought. Then Ralph joined me. Two days later I was attacked by footpads in an alleyway off St James's Street and left for dead. Ralph had me carted home and then the sickness came again. I had fought the footpads, done them some serious damage. I could not fight this.'

Sophie felt dizzy. She could guess where this was leading but she could not bring herself to believe it.

'I overheard the doctor in the next room talking to his assistant. They must have thought I was asleep,' Cal went on. 'They were circumspect, but what they said made me wonder and then, the more I thought, the more suspicious it all seemed. Someone was poisoning me, systematically. Someone was arranging accidents. And who could that be but my heirs? My uncle or my cousin. Or both of them.'

'And so you left?'

'It felt like running away, but I could do nothing else. I was so weak and I could prove nothing. Courageously staying put and dying didn't seem like a very sensible approach. And who would believe me? I began to make preparations, found Prescott and made arrangements for him to take over as my agent while I was away, took Jared into my confidence and found he shared my suspicions. It began as an experiment, but my health improved halfway across the Atlantic and I have never had another bout of that sickness and fever since.'

'And accidents?'

'Some.' He shrugged. 'Many. But all of them I can account for by my own recklessness, or the dangers of the situation I was in – avalanches, footpads, raging rivers, falls from horses. Once I had regained my strength and health I could have turned around, come back to England, confronted the situation.'

'But how? How do you prove their innocence?' *Or guilt.*

Cal shrugged. 'That was partly why I did not come back, I had no idea how to tackle this. And in the event I found I was enjoying myself, that I loved travel. I was healthy and young and in control of my life and I could manage everything at home at arm's length. Before long I had a wife and child. Then Madeleine died and I knew I had to come back. I couldn't drag Isobel around the world, I couldn't leave my responsibilities at a distance any longer. Seven years were almost up. I needed an heir. So I came home to see what reaction that would provoke.'

He shook his head and lobbed a crust off into the bushes, making a blackbird erupt with cries of panic and fly away down the hill. Sophie could feel the frustration coming off him in waves like the heat from a fire. 'And I am no further forward. My uncle and cousin reacted when they saw me in ways that could be perfectly innocent. My health is fine. I have suffered no accidents.' He pushed his fingers through his hair and took a deep breath. 'I have either spent years abroad having abandoned England for nothing more than a fevered imagining, or there is real danger and I am drawing you into it. I had to tell you, although I cannot believe you would be in any danger until – '

'I was known to be carrying a child?'

'Exactly.' In the silence that followed Sophie could almost hear the cogs of Cal's brain working. 'I could not go any further without telling you, but I did not feel able to say anything before – ' He stopped, sent her a sideways look.

'Before you knew you could trust me,' she stated for him. The whole situation was appalling, but beneath that was the warm glow that he could trust her with this, believe that she would support him and not laugh in his face, or reject him, or gossip.

'It is a lot to ask you to deal with. I would not blame you if you found that we were… incompatible.'

'I think we are very compatible.' Somehow she had shifted and was sitting close beside him, her arm linked though his, her head on his shoulder. Cal tipped his to meet hers and they sat, silent, sharing thoughts until her memory threw up something disconcerting that she had kept from him.

'Cal, I told you that Ralph was in love and wanted to marry a woman he knew his father would disapprove of?' Cal nodded. 'He said he would have married her long ago but that his father expected him to do his duty by the dukedom, that he was an heir and must marry well and suitably.' Cal sat up straight and swivelled to look at her. 'Ralph is of age, he is older than you. He has independent means and his own lands. There is nothing to stop him marrying where he wishes and yet his father put enough pressure on him to marry as if he was the actual heir apparent. It was his father's wish that he marry me, or someone like me. It is Lord Peter who is treating this inheritance with deadly seriousness.' Cal's face was bleak and she remembered that this was the man who had been like a father to him. The sense of betrayal must be like a stab wound. 'Your aunt is not happy to see you wed, either.'

'No,' he agreed flatly.

'Cal – could it have been her, all along? Who better than a woman to poison your food, or however it was that made you ill?'

'And the accidents?'

'Anyone with money can employ criminals to do anything, I imagine.'

'Oh, hell.' He flashed her an apologetic look for his language and she smiled back at him, both forgiving it and, she realised with a jolt, happy to be this close to him, sharing his secrets, even if they were so grim. 'I thought there were just two of them to investigate.'

'It is almost impossible to prove a negative,' Sophie mused. 'If nothing ever happens again that you cannot clearly account for, then you will always be left suspecting them. So, you are going to have to leave yourself open to attack and investigate from there while the evidence is fresh.'

'You are determined to thrust your future husband into danger I see.' He looked amused.

'You are a big, strong man with intelligence and powerful resources, no longer a sickly youth. I would say that anyone attempting to kill you now is the one in danger.'

'There was someone in my bedchamber last night, after two o'clock,' he said abruptly. 'Something woke me. By the time I had got out of bed and into the corridor they had gone.'

Sophie felt the blood leave her face, but she kept her voice as steady as his had been. 'A knife in the back?'

'Difficult to disguise as an accident. Something in the water in the carafe by the bed, or a pillow over the face, perhaps?'

'They couldn't hope to subdue you like that, you would be too strong for one man.'

'Thank you for that.' Cal's tone was light, his hands as they fisted on his bent knees gave another message.

‘So, what is the plan?’ As she spoke Sophie felt Cal’s whole body become alert, tense against hers. She followed his line of sight down the slope and saw movement amongst the trees, gone almost as soon as she noticed it.

‘Deer?’

‘No.’ Cal relaxed. ‘Jared. Watching my back whether I like it or not.’

‘He is your employee, surely what you want happens?’ She did not like the fencing master, but she welcomed the idea that he was behind Cal.

‘He is my friend first, someone who works for me when it suits him, second. I must tell him we saw him, he will be mortified.’ Cal’s grin was wicked. ‘But a plan? Can you talk to my aunt? Be less than tactful.’

‘Talk of how much you owe her for bringing you up like a son? How noble and selfless of her it is when her own son will not inherit a title or any of the lands her husband has cared for so devotedly? And then watch her reactions. I can do that. You will lock your bedchamber door tonight?’

‘Most certainly not. I will leave it open and sleep with a knife under my pillow and a pistol on the bedside table.’

‘Why not have Hunt sleep in your sitting room with the door ajar?’

‘I do not need a nursemaid. If anyone is sleeping with me, it is you, and as we have agreed, that is not going to happen. Yet.’

It would be so very easy to become distracted, to turn into his arms, tell him she really did not want to wait. And yet part of her did, part of her had a superstitious dread that if they slept together she would immediately become pregnant, a hostage to whatever malign fate was waiting for Cal.

‘As a witness, another pair of eyes, another hand on a knife.’

'A good idea, but not in my sitting room – in yours and with the door unlocked between the rooms. I find the idea of giving you a bodyguard appealing.'

'*I* do not! I do not care for the man, he makes me think of a snake about to strike, or a hawk sitting in a tree waiting for something helpless and small and furry to blunder past.'

'Yes, a perfect description. And I would trust him with my life, and yours, and Isobel's.'

'Where is she?' Sophie remembered guiltily that she had not seen the child since that initial awkward meeting in the hall. To be truthful with herself she had been glad of it. Isobel resented her, with some reason, and she had no clear idea what she could do to make things right.

'I told Nanny Jenkins to keep her to the nursery wing, to tell her that this was a grown-up party and not for little girls. I hope that is going to pique her to such an extent that she will do almost anything to be considered fit to join the adults. If she can bring herself to behave for a few days she will realise she likes you and that you are not going to take her father away from her.'

'Yes, of course.' Sophie was dubious, but Cal knew his own child, so perhaps that would work. 'What else can we do, besides ensuring that any nocturnal visitors get an unpleasant shock?'

'Anything that I am presented to eat or drink that is for me alone I will only pretend to consume and we will have it tested. As for accidents, we wait for them to happen and then analyse them.' He saw her expression and reached out to touch her cheek. 'Sophie, we have to know the truth and hiding is not going to help. You'll allow Jared into your sitting room?'

'Yes. Unless he snores.'

It was good to hear Cal's laughter, to be caught up in his arms, to feel the strong body shaking with amusement. It was good to have his mouth on hers again. And a torture.

Chapter Sixteen - Where the Duke Succumbs to the Beauties of Nature

'Sophie, let me make love to you. No,' Cal said as she made an involuntary sound halfway between plea and protest. 'Not that. But let me give you pleasure, let me touch you, learn your body. I am dying of thirst here, Sophie, have pity.'

She was not certain what he meant, or how whatever it was could assuage his thirst, give him pleasure. Surely a man needed to do what Jonathan had done, take his satisfaction by penetrating her body? But she trusted Cal and she needed him too.

'Yes,' she said against his mouth and then, when he pulled back so she could see the dark heat in his eyes, 'But where, Cal?'

'Here.' He stood, went back to the horses and unstrapped the greatcoat from behind the saddle, spreading it on the ground in the lea of their rock look-out. 'Just here. The grass is soft beneath the coat, no-one will get past Jared below and above the castle the rock rises into a cliff-face. No-one from the villages on the other side of the crest can get down here.'

'No?' Wariness was struggling with desire and desire was winning.

'It is a different world over there. Patches of industry, mines, dirty, shabby villages. I am glad our medieval forebear decided that mining was not for him: I would not like to be responsible for sending those poor devils down a lead mine.'

Reassured, she came down from the rock and joined him on the thick, lush grass. 'Cal, I am not experienced. What happened before happened quickly.' *Thank goodness.*

'You were right to part company with the man.' Cal took her by the shoulders, drew her close. 'When a man makes love to a woman, *with* a woman, it should not be rushed, unless you both want that, the excitement of urgency. He should have made love to you slowly, pleasured you, cared for you. Let me show you, Sophie.'

She placed her hands, palm down, against his chest, felt his heartbeat, steady and strong and watched his face as she slid them upwards, beneath his coat, sliding over the linen of his shirt, pausing when he felt the nubs of his nipples harden under her fingers. He let her play, her fingertips circling, then her nails scratching, while he watched her, his eyes heavy-lidded with controlled desire. When she pushed his coat from his shoulders he shrugged it off, pulled his shirt free from his breeches and dragged it over his head and let it fall.

'Oh.' She had imagined what he would look like stripped, but the muscle and the long bones and the dusting of hair on his chest were all so much more than she had imagined. He was hard, and there were scars on the skin that still carried the faint golden flush of hot tropical sun.

Cal pulled her close and the golden skin was hot as though it retained that exotic warmth and he smelt of plain soap and the lemon cologne he used after shaving and leather and fresh sweat. Sophie spread her palms on his back and let them trail down, following that fascinating masculine triangle of broad shoulders, narrow waist. She wanted to slip her fingers under the waistband of his breeches but she was becoming very aware of how aroused he was, that the evidence of that, hard against her belly, was promising something considerably… *more* than Jonathan.

'My turn.' His fingers worked on the fastenings of the short jacket she wore, his knuckles bumping between them as they worked, sending little shocks of sensation through her breasts. Then he tossed it aside, found the fastenings of her long riding skirt and sent that after the jacket. The rest of her clothing followed, but Sophie lost track of what Cal was doing. *He knows very well how to undress a woman*, she thought hazily, then pushed aside the speculation about how many women, when… She knew he was not a virgin and she was not going to start being jealous of his first wife, of whatever women he had known before. She was his future and she could only hope he would stay faithful to her.

The speculation had stopped her feeling shy, she realised. So had his speed. The soft, warm air on her body, the rider's calloused hands stroking over her skin, pulled her back to the full realisation that she was naked, that Cal was easing her down onto his greatcoat and that she had no idea what he intended.

'Will you unpin your hair?'

'I will never get it up again.' Oh, the look on his face as he watched her.

'You will be galloping riding back. Your hat will come off, pins everywhere. Easier to take it all down and plait it.'

'You have an answer for everything.' She smiled back at him as she raised her hands to the pins, then swallowed as his gaze followed the lift of her breasts as she moved. Jonathan had grabbed, painfully, when he had her naked, but Cal just looked with something like worship in his eyes and she wanted to weep for what she had lost that night, for the fact that it was not Cal who had shown her how a man was with a woman that first time.

Instead she shook down her hair and leaned towards him so he could comb his long fingers through it. 'Guinea gold,' he murmured. 'You are so beautiful, Sophie. You must hear that every day, how lovely you are, but it is more than looks. So often a beautiful face hides a selfish mind, a cold soul. It is so easy to fall for the outward beauty, to equate that with goodness, or intelligence or kindness.'

'I know.' The bitter little agreement escaped her and she bit her lip.

'Your first lover? He was a handsome man?'

'A beautiful man. To look at. I don't want to talk about him. I let myself fall for that cliché, that outer beauty is a sign of inner beauty too. I was a fool.' She looked at the man kneeling before her. 'When I look at you I see strong bones and a strong will. I see good looks but I also see the struggles that made you who you are, added steel to your spine and scars to your body. I see a handsome man, but not a beautiful one, except, I think, on the inside.'

Cal closed his eyes and she wondered whether she had embarrassed him, whether she would have embarrassed herself when he opened them again and looked at her.

When he did, he said simply, 'You have robbed me of words. Let me show you how I feel about you.'

He laid her back onto the heavy silk lining of the greatcoat and came down beside her on one elbow, the buckskin of his breeches against her hip, his left arm beneath her shoulders, his right hand finally, *finally*, touching her, down over her breasts to her belly, up again, caressing, exploring, leaving a tingling, aching trail of pleasure.

Sophie forced open her eyes and watched his face, stunned by his expression, the focus. She shivered and his gaze snapped back to her face.

'Are you all right, Sophie?'

'Oh, yes, but you…'

'Are in heaven. And purgatory.' He bent to kiss her, capturing her mouth, letting her hide by sheer closeness as his finger fretted at her nipples, pinching lightly until the hard nubs were sending shafts of aching pleasure from her breasts to her belly, to her sex. She moaned into his mouth, arched against him as his hand slid lower, down to the nest of curls, slid between her thighs, even as she instinctively pressed them together.

'Let me in, Sophie. Let me love you.'

The words were like a key, freeing her, letting her resisting muscles relax for him. Cal found the core of her, the wet, aching centre, touched her perfectly with one perfect relentless, gentle stoke after another and her world imploded.

She screamed, but Cal's mouth was there to capture the sound, his hands were there to hold her safe until she came back to herself. His voice was there, calling her back. 'Sophie, Sophie my love.'

'Cal?'

'Mmm?' He was nuzzling her ear which was good because she was not at all certain she could face him, not after that totally abandoned flood of passion, the intimacy, the shock of his words.

Sophie, my love. He didn't mean it of course, he couldn't, but the word, the concept would not leave her. *I am falling in love with him.* She should be terrified after what had happened last time, but all she felt was a rock-solid certainty that she was right to love him, that he cared for her, that he was a good man and she could trust him with her heart as well as the rest of her life. *Such a fool to reject love because of one bad man.*

'Sophie?'

'I am sorry, I was drifting.' She snuggled down against him, then raised her head and me his gaze across the bare expanse of his chest. 'I am being very selfish, don't you want me to …' Her voice trailed away. She knew some of the things that he might wish her to do, but she wasn't certain she had the words for them, or even the nerve to mention them.

'To what, Sophie?' He was smiling at her, but not

laughing at her ignorance.

'To pleasure you.' Her hand seemed to move of its own volition to the falls of his breeches.

'Do you want to or do you just think you ought to?' If she hadn't known him so well now she would have thought it merely a request for information, but now she could hear the desire behind the words and his concern to keep it from being a demand.

'Want.' That was the truth. 'Show me.' Her fingers were already busy with the fastenings and Cal lifted his hips to give the breeches a sharp tug down. Sophie kept her eyes locked with his as her hand explored, found him, curled around. His eyes closed, his lips compressed on a groan.

'Oh, so soft, like mushroom.'

Cal's lids flew up. 'Like *what?'*

'Mushroom skin, or suede. So soft, and so hard underneath.' Fascinated, she began to experiment. 'So mobile.'

'Sophie.' It sounded as though Cal's teeth were gritted. 'Did you never touch your lover like this?'

'No.' She was up on her elbow now, her hair trailing across Cal's chest. 'He just, er, entered me.'

'Bastard.' Cal fell flat on his back with a gasp. 'Sorry, him, I mean. Oh God, harder, Sophie, like this.'

He reached and covered her hand with his, tightened her tentative grasp, showed her what he needed, then jerked her against his chest, kissing her as he arched into her grip, moving with her until he bowed up, his cry hoarse against her lips and fell back.

The breeze swirled around them bringing the scent of crushed grass, musk, salt, sweat. Heaven. Sophie closed her eyes and slept.

She woke to the sound of pigeons cooing overhead, the distant sound of sheep and the awareness that she was alone on the crumpled greatcoat. 'Cal?'

He came back through the wood carrying the water

bottle and a large handkerchief, poured water over it and hunkered down beside her to wash her hands.

'You are dressed.'

'I thought it best. We can hardly stay here naked in the woods for the rest of the day, although you tempt me.' He picked up her clothes and began to shake them out and hand them to her. Stockings and garters, chemise, stays. He knelt to lace them, then found her shirt.

He knows the correct order to put things back on again as well as being an expert in taking clothes off, Sophie thought ruefully as she fastened her skirts and shook them out. 'I don't suppose you have a comb.' It was strangely reassuring that he shook his head. At least the man did not go out equipped for *al fresco* seduction.

She managed a reasonable braid with the aid of a piece of leather thong that Cal found in the saddlebag, then he tossed her up into the saddle, mounted the grey and led the way down the track away from the castle, whistling.

Sophie urged the bay gelding up alongside. 'Where has Hunt got to?'

'He will be back behind us now, covering. Look, there's the herd of fallow deer.'

Sophie followed his pointing finger and admired the herd, listened as he talked about the park and its history and thought about what it would mean to love this man and how she was going to raise a family with him unless they discovered the truth about his mysterious illnesses and the accidents that had driven him from home.

And then she looked across and saw his face, animated, engrossed, as he talked about the land and what it meant to him and she knew that duke or not, under threat or not, she was going to carry on falling in love with him and she would stand shoulder to shoulder with him to fight whatever threatened them, and the family they would have.

'There is a man I could take a thoroughly irrational dislike to with no provocation at all.' Jared lounged against the panelling of the drawing room and narrowed his eyes at the nearest group who were talking while they waited for dinner to be announced.

'Who?' Cal shifted his position so he could look down the room to the object of Hunt's attention.

'Mr Beautiful, the big blond.'

Eyebrows raised, Cal studied the men. 'What, Ransome, do you mean.' He was the only large fair-haired man close by. Jared grunted assent. 'You would call him beautiful?'

'Of course I wouldn't. But the ladies do. Heard those two who are hanging on his every word rhapsodising over him when I was coming back from the stables. *So beautiful, such a profile, oh those blue eyes,'* he mimicked in an unlikely falsetto that made Cal snort with laughter. 'And he thinks he's God's gift to the female sex too. Look at him modestly exerting all that charm. Makes me want to apply the toe of my boot to his perfect backside.'

'Jealous, Jared?' He studied Ransome with covert interest. So that was what women thought made a *beautiful* man was it? Beside him his friend snorted. Ransome shifted, his gaze over the heads of the pair of worshipful bridesmaids. What was attracting his interest? Then he saw Sophie, laughing, as she turned away from Sir Tobias, caught the predatory, almost smug, expression on Ransome's face as he looked at her and saw her expression freeze into a mask when she saw the man's attention on her.

Jared, alert at his side, turned at the hiss that escaped him. 'What is it?'

'Nothing. My imagination, merely.' Sophie, dismissing her lover as a *beautiful man.* What had she said about him? *I was mistaken in him.* From the evidence that Cal had gained that morning he labelled that man selfish and clumsy in the bedchamber and there in front of him was boundless arrogance hidden behind a handsome façade and practiced charm. He had arrived with Sir Toby who admitted he hadn't seen Ransome in years and Sophie, who had seemed completely well until the moment Ransome stepped down from the curricle, had suddenly vanished pleading a headache.

No, it was not his imagination, surely? But if he was right, then what was Ransome doing here? It wasn't by Sophie's invitation, that was certain, not with the way she was reacting to him. Cal put down his glass and, beside him, Hunt did the same.

'Who are we going to kill?'

'No-one. Stop it, this is not the back streets of Buenos Aires. Stay here, I am simply going to be the gracious host.'

Ignoring Jared's snort Cal strolled over and insinuated himself in the group around Ransome, who promptly stopped gazing earnestly into the eyes of Miss Belinda Wraythorne (sweet nature, large inheritance, unfortunate teeth) and nodded respectfully to his host.

'You've fine stables here, Calderbrook. Your uncle gave us a thorough tour and I have to confess to being green with envy. And that was just the facilities. The bloodstock is superb. Lord Peter was telling me you have your own stallion for stud purposes.' He broke off and looked apologetically at the young women. 'Forgive me, I should not mention farmyard matters before ladies.' His smile caressed Lady Penelope Beauville (pretty, lively, impoverished family, excellent connections) and she blushed and dimpled back.

Jared's desire to plant his boot on Ransome's buttocks seemed perfectly reasonable to Cal. He showed his teeth in an approximation of an agreeable smile. 'My uncle built up the bloodlines when I was in my minority and I have simply carried on from a distance.' Lord Peter was coming towards them and he turned, opening the group out in invitation.

It was the first time he had seen his uncle here in Cal's ancestral home since he had left England and it struck him unpleasantly how very much at home the older man appeared, how naturally his manner had become that of the host.

'Ransome complimented me on my stables and their occupants,' Cal said. 'I was just saying how much the strong bloodlines owed to the days when you were in control here.' He took great care with his expression, and his tone, but his uncle's gaze sharpened. No fool, Lord Peter. 'That must seem a long time ago now.'

'A very long time,' his uncle agreed, but his gaze flickered to his wife, holding court from the central sofa and then to his son, one foot on the edge of the hearth-stone, his elbow on the mantle-shelf, entirely relaxed and at home. 'We all look forward to seeing you re-established here with your wife.'

'And daughter,' Cal said, easing in the gentle reminder that he was capable of siring children and that an heir must surely follow.

'A ready-made family?' Ransome interjected. 'I had no idea you had previously been married, Calderbrook. How delightful for Soph… for Miss Wilmott to have a stepdaughter.'

Now, had that slip with Sophie's name been an accident or quite deliberate? Cal looked across to where Sophie stood, her straight back turned to them, and let his affection show in his expression. 'Sophie is going to make a wonderful mother and she has already made a great impression on Isobel.' And that was something else he must tackle before much more time passed. Isobel had spent quite long enough contemplating how much she was going to hate her new mother, hate him for remarrying and plotting how to punish them both.

The familiar sharp pang of love for the child gripped him. She was brave and intelligent and a real little fighter, combining the toughness from both parents with her mother's looks and ability to twist the unwary around her little finger. She was his and he adored her and she terrified him. How did one protect your child in this big, dangerous world full of carefully disguised sharks such as Ransome? But at the moment it was not on his daughter's behalf that he needed to load his shotgun, it was his betrothed's.

Chapter Seventeen - Where the Duke Suffers

Jonathan was talking to Cal. The fear prickled up and down Sophie's spine and she could feel her feet almost twitching with the urge to turn around, see what was happening behind her.

But the conversational tone did not change, there was the occasional ripple of amusement and no sound of fist hitting jaw. Jonathan obviously had the sense not to antagonise Cal. Gradually she felt her shoulders relax and the social chit-chat came more easily. After all, what had she to worry about? Someone might be attempting to assassinate her husband-to-be, the child who would be her stepdaughter hated her, she would have a dangerous man sleeping in her sitting room that night, she was carrying on a secret correspondence with an enquiry agent and her former lover was blackmailing her. A normal house-party at a ducal mansion, no doubt.

And now she must tackle her hostess, behaving in a manner that would be tactless and insensitive if the woman was innocent, and possibly dangerous if she was not.

Sophie took a glass of ratafia that she did not really want and made her way over to Lady Peter who was, for the moment, alone on the sofa. 'How nice, I have so much been wanting to talk with you.' She sat down, sipped her drink and waited, as was only proper, for the older woman to speak.

'You like what you see of Calderbrook Hall, Miss

Wilmott?'

'It is magnificent and yet I am sure it will be a wonderful home when it is lived in by a family again. It must owe a great deal to your direction of affairs while Lord Peter was the Duke's guardian. How difficult to manage two great houses at the same time.'

'I would not describe Pointings Manor, our own country home, as a great house.' Lady Peter's voice held no great affection. 'It is considerably smaller and older. Very easy to leave while I was needed here.'

'It must have been a sacrifice, even so. And what devotion to duty, to raise what must, in effect, have been another son, when all the time your own, the elder, would not be the heir of all this.' Her gesture took in the drawing room, the house, the entire ducal estate.

'When one marries a younger son, one marries his sense of duty to the family.'

'Of course. And then for the Duke to be abroad in such dangerous and far-flung places! Again, duty must have come to your aid and impelled you to raise Mr Thorne so that, if the worst happened – ' *That could have been more tactfully put, Sophie!* '– your own son could rise to the occasion as the heir. I must say how much I admire you for that.'

The silence that followed that crashingly tactless observation was so prolonged that Sophie risked a sideways glance at her hostess. Lady Peter was biting her lower lip, a demonstration of emotion that seemed extreme for such a rigorously controlled woman.

'However ambitious a mother is for her son it is also her duty to raise him in the expectation that he makes his own way in the world within the sphere in which he finds himself,' she said with dignity. 'For Ralph to have succeeded as duke would require a tragedy to have happened and I am certain he never had any thought of such an eventuality.'

But he had, or, his father had. And beside her Lady

Peter was looking at her husband, her expression unreadable. Lord Peter? Ambitious for himself and Ralph, or only for his son? A man who would sacrifice his own honour and duty to see his son a duke? She did not believe for a moment now that the woman at her side had tried to poison her nephew by marriage, and she rather thought that Lady Peter's initial chilliness towards herself was due to suspicion that no woman was good enough for Cal. But something disturbed her inner peace, something made her suspicious of her husband's intent, even though Sophie doubted she had ever articulated those fears to herself.

'Dinner is served, my lady.'

Lady Peter pulled herself up as though startled out of thoughts that were a long way away, but she rose to her feet and supervised the ordering of her guests with calm authority. She had apparently decided on some informality for this second dinner and the long table had been split into three and another round table added to the vast dining room. The pairings to go into dinner had been changed, with less attention to the rank of guests and more to introducing those who had been separated the night before.

Sophie found herself with Toby to her left and Lord Faversham, Christobel's husband on her right, at one of the rectangular tables. Lady Beauville, the mother of Penelope, one of the bridesmaids, was shown to her seat by Mr Wraythorne, Belinda's father, and finally they were joined by Jonathan Ransome escorting Mrs Pickering, who, Sophie gathered, was a bosom friend of Lady Peter's.

Jonathan checked the place cards and seated himself halfway down the table, within easy earshot of Sophie and in her direct line of sight as she sat at the foot of the board with Mr Wraythorne at the head.

Under her firm direction the conversation turned to how the guests had spent the day. Toby was delighted by the opportunity to purchase one of the litter of pointer puppies that the head gamekeeper had shown the men and that discussion turned naturally to the horses in the stables and then to Lord Faversham's assessment of the countryside around for hunting.

Mrs Pickering then entertained them for ten minutes with a plant-by-plant description of her newly-designed parterre and Sophie relaxed when Lord Faversham's previously unknown passion for gardening was revealed and the two of them drew everyone into a discussion on whether the London parks were better left as they were or should be landscaped with more flower beds.

She had begun to relax so much that when the gardening discussion flagged she was taken unawares by Jonathan.

'And how did you spend the day, Miss Wilmott?' he asked with his most charming smile.

'Exploring the further reaches of the park with the Duke,' she responded with a smile equally as calculated as his. 'We looked at the ruins of the ancient medieval castle up in the hills and I learned much about the history of the area.'

'Fascinating,' he said warmly. 'You must be becoming so attached to this place. What a wonderful future for you.'

'Indeed.' She imbued the agreement with just the slightest edge of reproof at his very personal comment and turned to look at the man at the other end of the table. 'Mr Wraythorne, Belinda tells me you are thinking of spending some time at Weymouth later this year. Is it a resort you know well?'

Please let Mr Tanner have found something, please let him write and the letter be there tomorrow.

The sounds from beyond her door were muffled, but something in their urgency woke her. She stared into darkness, then she saw the line of light under the door to the sitting room. The room had been in darkness when she retired and the door was unlocked, as agreed, but there had been no indication that Jared Hunt was inside on the couch, her silent, unwelcome bodyguard.

The sounds came again as Sophie slid out of bed, found her wrapper by touch and pulled it on as she made her way towards the line of light. Caution made her hesitate, her ear to the panels before she opened the door, but it seemed to her that the stir of movement was further away, perhaps in Cal's unused sitting room. When she slipped inside there was no-one in sight, but she had a clear view through two rooms to Cal's bedchamber which was lit by several candles.

'Cal?' She picked up her trailing skirts and ran, heedless of bare feet, unbound hair and half-tied robe.

He was lying on his bed, his skin grey, his eyes shut, and did not stir as she erupted into the room. Hunt, a bowl in his hands, spun round as she entered. 'Stay there.'

'Why?' Sophie demanded, ignoring the order. Then Cal's very stillness halted her. 'Oh my God, he isn't – '

'No. But he's been poisoned.' Hunt opened the dressing room door and thrust the bowl inside. 'He's got rid of everything he's eaten today, I should think, and I finally got some water down him.'

When she touched Cal's forehead it was dry, the skin tight and hot, and he moved his head restlessly as though the light pressure of her fingers caused him pain. Sophie tiptoed over to Hunt. 'Should we call the doctor?'

'To what end? They had no idea before, and these are the same symptoms. Bleeding him will do no good.'

'My instinct would be to try and cool him down and get him to drink as much as possible,' Sophie said.

'I agree.' The dark man just stood there looking at her.

'Then let us do that.'

'You had best go back to your room, Miss Wilmott.' He looked at Cal. 'He is not wearing anything.'

‘Oh for goodness sake, Mr Hunt! I am about to marry the man. I think I can cope with the sight of his bare flesh, under the circumstances. Help me with the bedclothes. We will need towels, but I don’t want to involve the servants, do you?’

‘No.’ He began to strip the covers off Cal who suddenly groaned and curled up.

‘He looks to be in such pain.’

‘He told me it was agony in the past. Tearing cramps in his guts, shooting pains in his limbs, a blinding headache.’

I will weep for him later, she resolved, as she lifted the last of the bedclothes away. It was difficult to believe that such a big, strong, fit man could be laid so low. *He needs me to be strong now. And when I discover who has done this, I will kill them.*

‘Have you any idea what the poison is?’

‘I wondered about arsenic.’ Hunt came back from the dressing room with an armful of towels and began to lay them around Cal’s body. ‘But the symptoms aren’t quite right.’

‘And how is it administered?’ She put the rest of the towels in place. ‘Does it hurt him to be touched?’

‘I don’t think so,’ Hunt said, frowning in thought. ‘As for how he took it, I’m puzzled. He has been careful not to eat or drink anything that other people haven’t shared.’

‘The drinks before dinner?’ Sophie eased down on the bed beside Cal and began to massage his back until the bent spine eased straight and he lay back with a sigh. ‘There were crowded groups, someone could have dropped something into a glass.’

‘Ralph Thorne didn’t go near him, I was watching.’

‘But his uncle did,’ Sophie remembered. ‘Can you bring wet towels and we’ll try and cool him down.’

‘Sophie?’ Cal turned his head on the pillow, eyes closed, one hand reaching for her.

'I am here, so is Mr Hunt. No-one else.' She took the glass that Hunt handed her and slipped her arm under Cal's head. 'Can you drink this? We are going to cool you down, but you need water.'

He lurched up, got his elbows under him and sat up.

'Lie down!'

'No. Pillows.'

'You are the most stubborn man.' Frightened for him, Sophie packed pillows at his back, then offered the water again. This time he drank, swallowed, waited through what looked like a savage cramp of pain and reached for the glass again.

Hunt came back with dripping towels and began to drape them over Cal's hot body, making him gasp. The fencing master ignored the protests. 'Why aren't you lying down?'

'Not giving in to it,' Cal said through gritted teeth. 'Need to find out who. Sophie, go to bed.'

'Now I *do* believe you are ill,' she snapped. 'You lie there, looking like death, and you expect me to go off to bed and leave you? What a nice restful sleep that would be, full of pleasant dreams, I'm sure.'

'Sorry, Sophie my love.' Cal produced the ghost of a smile.

'Then stop talking nonsense and drink this,' she said briskly, ignoring the stab of pleasure the endearment gave her.

'Bossy woman,' he murmured. But he took the glass and managed to hold it himself.

By the time the clocks were striking four Sophie was beginning to feel optimistic. They had removed the wet towels, Cal was under the blankets again, dozing between mouthfuls of water and then, half an hour later, he was doubled up in pain again, had lost all the water they had got into him and was the colour of dirty snow. But at least his temperature stayed down, she thought, as Cal took the glass in both shaking hands and doggedly began to drink again.

When the clocks struck seven Sophie was ready to sleep on her feet, Hunt was looking drawn and Cal was reviving. 'You both need to go down to breakfast. Watch my uncle and cousin. If one or both of them thinks they have poisoned me they will betray it somehow. But don't say I have been ill.'

'But – ' Sophie broke off as the door opened and Michael Flynn came in balancing a tray with a cup on it.

The valet stopped dead, put down the tray and closed the door sharply behind him. 'Why didn't you call me?'

'We managed,' Cal said. 'I need you now, fresh. Jared, Sophie, get ready for breakfast.'

Sophie looked at Hunt who shrugged. 'He is right. If there's anyone out there braced for Flynn to come running down yelling that Cal's dead, we need to be there to see.'

She didn't want to leave him, but Flynn, she knew, was trustworthy. She dragged herself back to her room, rang for Mary and concocted a story of a troubled night racked with nightmares to account for her shadowed eyes and barely-suppressed yawns. 'I really must avoid eating cheese in the evenings,' she said as the maid helped her into a sprig muslin morning dress and threaded a ribbon through her hair.

Jared was already at the breakfast table and Sophie took a seat on the other side and toyed with toast as the other guests arrived, sat down and began to eat and talk. Lady Peter swept in and sat down beside Sophie to drink her chocolate and her husband sat opposite. Ralph found a chair free and Jared shifted his position slightly so he was looking at him. All three of the Thornes appeared entirely normal, well-rested, relaxed – or as relaxed as Lady Peter ever allowed herself to be – and perfectly innocent of anything except, perhaps, one too many brandies the night before on Ralph's part.

Her parents came in, her mother giving her a sharp glance and a frown that left Sophie in no doubt that she looked positively haggard. Fortunately Mama was too far away to comment.

Time to give things a prod. 'I wonder where Calderbrook has got to,' Sophie said. 'He is usually amongst the first of us down.'

The be-ringed hand next to her continued to butter a roll without a tremor. When she glanced at Hunt he raised his eyebrows and gave a slight shrug. The Thorne family either had nerves of steel or they were all innocent.

And then the door opened and Cal walked in.

Chapter Eighteen - Where the Duke Draws a Blade

Sophie released the handle of her coffee cup and it rattled into the saucer, splashing the cloth around with droplets of brown liquid.

Cal looked like a man who had spent all night awake and seriously ill. His skin was pale and tight, his eyes shadowed, his walk careful. Yet no-one seemed to notice anything amiss as he sat and gestured to a footman for coffee. Conversations broke off as people said *Good morning* and Cal replied briefly. Perhaps they assumed he was simply badly hung-over.

'The post has arrived, Your Grace,' Renshaw informed Cal. 'Your correspondence has been delivered to your study.'

'Please distribute our guests' letters.' Cal glanced round. 'We are informal here, please, feel free.'

The letter sat beside her plate, ignored, while she sipped at her fresh cup of coffee and tried to watch Cal without appearing anxious and drawing attention to him. Jared Hunt's mouth was a tight line that she supposed was frustration and Cal was making no pretence at eating, nor, she was glad to see, drinking the strong black coffee.

'It is drizzling this morning,' Lady Peter observed. 'I suggest, ladies, that we take our sewing to the Long Gallery. Perhaps some of you might care to play for us on the piano there.'

Sophie made sounds that she hoped signified interest and agreement, all the time aware of her mother's gaze on her face and of Cal, apparently staying upright in his chair by sheer force of will alone.

She caught his eye and mouthed, *'Go to bed,'* at him and felt herself blush as he raised one eyebrow and sent her a look that suggested she might like to join him. Perhaps he was not about to die, after all.

'Sophie.' She jumped, her nerves raw, and found her mother standing beside her chair.

'Mama?'

'What have you been doing? You look dreadful. Are you sickening for something?'

'I had a very disturbed night, Mama, and hardly any sleep. I really cannot account for it.' Which was true enough, she had no idea what had made Cal so ill.

'And Calderbrook looks decidedly under the weather as well.'

'So does Mr Thorne,' Sophie murmured. 'And Mr Hunt doesn't look quite his normal self either. Perhaps they were drinking rather heavily last night.'

'I do hope not. I do not like to think of such nice young men drinking to excess.'

'No, Mama.'

'Who is your correspondent, dear?'

'Correspondent? Oh, I have a letter. I hadn't noticed.' Mama did not move. Although she would not insist on reading her daughter's letters, she would certainly expect to be told who was writing.

Sophie picked up an unused knife, slit the seal and partly unfolded the first sheet to show the stick-maker's letterhead. Why couldn't she have opened it earlier, before her mother came to stand right beside her? 'It is from the stick-maker.' She lowered her voice. 'I bought a cane from him as a present for Cal and he has sent his account.'

'To this address?'

And why did Mama have to be so intelligent? 'I stupidly forgot to give him our London address, but I told him I was coming here and who the cane was for so he could engrave Cal's initials on the silver band.'

'I see. He is most urgent for his money, I must say.'

Sophie shrugged. 'I was a new customer, I suppose he is a little cautious. It is not a large shop.'

Out of the corner of her eye she could see Hunt engaging the other men in an earnest discussion of the rival merits of billiards, a visit to the gun room, reading the newspapers in the library or braving the drizzle for a walk. Inevitably the billiard table and the gun room won out and the men began to leave the table and straggle out.

Only Sophie seemed to notice Hunt stop beside Cal, partly shielding him from the room so that he could get unsteadily to his feet and pause to regain his balance. 'I want to see those new Manton's of yours,' Hunt said as they left the room, tucking his hand companionably under his elbow as they strolled out. It was beautifully done.

'I think I will go and lie down, Mama. If I can get a few hours' sleep I will feel so much better. Otherwise I will be poor company later today.'

'That might be sensible, dear. Would you like me to come and read to you while you drop off?'

'Thank you, no. Perhaps you could explain to Lady Peter, give her my apologies?'

Sophie closed the door of her bedchamber behind her and leaned against it with a sigh of relief, then went through the linking rooms to Cal's bedchamber. Flynn emerged from the dressing room. 'Are you alone, Miss Wilmott?'

'Yes. Tell me, how is he, honestly?'

'Sick as a horse,' the valet said frankly. 'But Hunt says he wasn't near so bad as he was the times before he left home.'

Sophie noted the informal way he spoke of the fencing master and wondered just how he addressed Cal when they were alone. She suspected the three had formed a close friendship during their travels. 'He's not a sickly youth now,' she said. 'He is strong and fit. That might make a difference.'

'True, ma'am.' Flynn moved to straighten the brushes on the dressing table. 'Even so, they both think that this time he had a smaller dose of whatever it was. I've been testing everything in here – cologne, tooth powder, shaving soap, the water in the carafe beside the bed, although I filled that myself last evening.'

'How have you tested things?'

'Tried them myself. Drank the water, shaved with the soap, used the tooth powder, splashed on the cologne. Feel as fit as a flea, but then, it might take all day.'

'That is very loyal of you to do that. For goodness sake, tell us if you feel at all unwell.'

The valet shrugged. 'He saved my life, him and Jared. And he didn't mind who or what I was. Gave me a job, turned my life around. I owe Cal… I owe His Grace a lot.'

That answered the question of just how close the three men were. The duke, the fencing master and the valet were on familiar-name terms and apparently willing to risk their necks for each other. She felt some of the anxiety for Cal retreat, just a little. There was nothing she could do at the moment, best to see what Mr Tanner had to report.

The note was on very thin paper sealed with a glued wafer, not wax, so that it could not be felt within the folds of the thick paper the shopkeeper used for his bills. She spread it flat and read.

Madam, the Subject has attempted blackmail before, having seduced the daughter of the vicar of a parish some ten miles from his Cornish home. However, the attempt at extortion was unsuccessful as the girl told her father who is one of the school of parsons as at home on the hunting field as he is in the chancel. He took to the Subject with his riding crop and then went into the pulpit to denounce him for an unnatural act which I hesitate to describe in a letter to a lady, but which involved sheep.

When the Subject attempted to counter this with the truth no-one believed him, or rather, I should say, no-one would admit it, as the young lady is much-loved thereabouts. However, the local people are exceedingly proud of their vicar for his robust actions and my agent was able to put two and two together easily enough after a number of sessions in the local inns.

I am continuing to investigate as he may well have been involved in discreditable dealings elsewhere. My agent is attempting to discover where he has been between now and his last stay in the Capital.

I remain, Madam, your obedient servant to command,

Josiah Tanner.

Sheep? *Sheep?* How outrageous of the vicar, and how clever. He had accused Jonathan of a perversion so embarrassing, and by its nature so secret, that any amount of fury and bluster could be put down to guilt. Would make him seem more guilty, in fact.

But was it enough to silence him now? Perhaps he had recovered his equilibrium and poise and could laugh it off, say it was all a joke by some drunken friends. Cornwall was a long way off and if he kept his head he might carry it off. Best, perhaps, to wait and see if Mr Tanner's agent turned over any more rocks to reveal nasty secrets beneath them. She itched to go and confront Jonathan, throw this outrageous rumour in his face, but if he called her bluff she would be without weapons, he would be on his guard and sheer spite might make him even more dangerous. He appeared to be enjoying himself at the house party, beyond any satisfaction to be gained by tormenting her, so she thought she was safe enough for the moment.

The letter fitted easily behind the mirror in her dressing case, the bill for the cane, she left lying on the desk. The deceit felt uncomfortable, like too-tight shoes.

That was another score to lay at Jonathan's feet, he had made a dissembler out of her. The reflection that stared back at her from the dressing table mirror was no comfort, she looked like a woman who had spent most to the night awake and terrified. An hour's nap would be a good idea and at least made her excuse to Mama a truthful one, which was a depressingly deceitful thought in itself.

Sophie woke at eleven, according to the clock on the mantle shelf, and lay muzzily wondering why she felt so apprehensive. *Cal.* She was at his bed chamber door, hair still mussed, gown wrinkled, before she could pause to think. But the room was empty, the bed covers uncreased. He should have been resting, she fretted.

When she reached the hall, hair hastily tamed, skirts shaken out, there was no sign of life except for the ever-present footman by the front door.

'Good morning.' She wracked her memory. 'James. Where is His Grace?'

He beamed, then got his face under control before the butler caught him. 'In the gunroom, Miss Wilmott. Shall I show you the way?'

'No, just explain. I must learn to get my bearings.'

'Through that door then, Miss, and along the passage, left at the end, down the six steps, right…'

'…six steps, right, third door into another passage – that must be it.' She could hear voices and, worryingly, the clash of steel. Sophie ran.

He was sweating like a pig, his stomach muscles felt like the devil was winching them through a mangle and everything ached, but the exercise was getting the remains of the poison out of his system and whoever had put it there should now be most thoroughly convinced that they had failed.

His cousin and uncle were in the room along with all of the male guests, several of whom were holding foils ready for a bout with Jared. They had pushed the long table back to the side, leaving ample room for a pair of fencers, and making makeshift seating for the audience who were not leaning against the walls and gun cupboards.

The fencing master had casually thrown down a challenge when Cal had taken him on one side and suggested that it might be a good idea if he demonstrated that he was alive and kicking. Jared had promptly wagered an elegant new foil he had brought with him that no-one could disarm him.

'What do the losers pay?' Ransome had asked.

'Nothing. I like to fight.' Jared had shown his teeth in a smile that showed Cal that his friend still didn't take to the other man, even though, naturally, he had said nothing about Sophie's secret or his own deep suspicions.

'I'll start,' he offered. Best to get this demonstration over while he could still stand up. But although it hurt like the blazes, although he felt weak, he found he could fight and find the strength from somewhere. He'd toughened up with all those years of travel, all the dangers and the adventures and the relentless need to keep fit to look after his little household. Jared was being careful, being more than careful – he was making Cal look good – but even so, he could feel pleased with himself. *There.* A sudden opening, a lunge, Jared's expected feint, recovery, and Cal slipped through with a cut that would have sent a lesser man's blade flying.

Only this was not a lesser man. Jared kept hold of his foil, twisted, met Cal's eyes and Cal, reading the message, let his own grip weaken. His foil was flicked away and the blunt end of Jared's blade touched his throat.

As a ripple of applause went round the room Cal threw up his hands, palm out, in the signal for surrender and headed for a chair, collapsing in it with a show of exhaustion that needed no playacting. 'You're too good,

Hunt.'

'You are not bad yourself, Your Grace.' Jared had hardly broken a sweat. 'But then I did teach you.' Amidst laughter he turned to the other men. 'Who is next?'

'I'll try.' Jonathan Ransome picked up a foil and sauntered into the centre of the room as a movement by the door drew Cal's gaze.

Sophie? She was white to the lips, but she slipped in, behind the row of men who were all watching the new contest begin, and knelt by the side of his chair unobserved.

'What are you doing?' she demanded in a furious whisper. 'You should be lying down, not exerting yourself, let alone *fighting.'*

'Making a point,' he whispered back, enjoying the sensation of moving his lips so close to her ear, feeling her curls tickle his nose, inhaling the light, spicy perfume she wore. 'And the exercise has done me good, sweated the rest of the poison out.'

'I was looking for you, and then I heard the clash of the foils – I was anxious.'

'Thought Jared would spit me, did you?' He kept his hand on her shoulder as she knelt by his chair. She shouldn't be here, not in this room full of men, and he was not going to draw attention to her by standing up and giving her his chair. In a moment he was going to have to get her out of the room, but he enjoyed the feel of her warm skin under his hand.

'I don't know,' she muttered resentfully, even as she arched her neck to give him better access. 'You men seem to duel at the slightest provocation. Who is he fighting now? Oh.'

'Don't you like Ransome?'

Sophie shrugged. 'He is too full of himself.'

'Very handsome, or so I am told.'

She made a complicated sound, a cross between a snort and a huff. 'I really don't notice him.'

And that is a lie. His hand went still on her shoulder. Sophie did not lie to him, he would have sworn. But that was untrue. Her body was stiff now and last night she had deliberately ignored Ransome although he had reacted to her. All the suspicions of the night before flooded back. 'Sophie…' No, this was neither the time nor the place.

Jared was focused on Ransome who was a showy fencer, but good, Cal admitted grudgingly. There was a intensity about him, backed up by solid skills, that would make him very dangerous indeed. Just as he thought it there was a flurry of movement, Jared lunged and Ransome's feet went from under him, landing him on the floor with a thud.

'That was luck on my side.' Jared extended his hand. 'You turned your heel on that uneven slab.'

Not a good loser, Cal thought, seeing the fury in the man's eyes, the artificiality of his smile as he waved away Jared's hand and got himself to his feet. Sophie had joined in the applause with a will. He was going to get to the bottom of this. But not yet.

'You had better slip out again,' he murmured in her ear. 'I'm leaving too, to see Isobel, you go first.'

She got to her feet and tiptoed out and Cal got to his feet, collecting the attention of the guests who had been in the middle of a technical discussion of Jared's last move. 'I need to go and check up on a few things. If you'll excuse me gentlemen. Ring if you want refreshment.'

He pulled on his coat and caught up with Sophie around the first corner. She turned at the sound of his feet on the flagstones, then flung her arms around his neck and kissed him, full on the mouth. Cal let the impetus carry him back to the wall, propped his shoulders against the panelling and enjoyed the sensation of being fiercely kissed by a furious woman.

'I could *hit* you,' she stormed at him when he came up for air. 'You should be in bed resting and what do you do? You start a *fight*. And you were magnificent and I thought it was *exciting* and I am *furious* with myself and with you.'

'Magnificent? Jared disarmed me.'

'He is a professional, and besides, you let him get the better of you right at the end. I have never seen men fence before and you – ' She broke off, biting her lip. 'I found your… muscles quite distracting.'

How ridiculously flattering. Cal got his grin under control, bent his head and kissed Sophie very thoroughly to make certain she was as excited and distracted as could be before he let her go. 'I really must go and see Isobel now.'

'I will come.'

'Jared made an exhibition out of Ransome just now,' he observed, giving her an opening if she chose to use it.

'Yes,' she agreed indifferently.

'I can't say I take to the man. I would have thought Sir Toby would have better judgement. Ransome's shallow.'

'Toby hasn't seen him for years, I expect he forgot what he's like.'

'Did you know him before?'

'Yes, I met him when he was last in Town.' Her voice was completely colourless.

Confide in me, for Heaven's sake, woman! She had told him nothing about her lover that he could take violent exception to on her behalf. If he was right and Ransome was the man then he had to ignore it unless she asked him to send him away or the man offered her some insult or unwanted intimacy. But he could wish she would talk to him. The nagging thought that now she had caught her duke she would then stop being honest with him was disturbing. Sophie's openness with him was something he found he valued deeply.

Chapter Nineteen - Where Sophie Works Magic

Sophie fetched her embroidery before she went with Cal up to the nursery. She had an idea about how to handle Isobel and it would be a useful accessory.

'Do you expect tantrums?' she asked as Cal paused at the door.

'Probably.' When she took a breath to speak, then closed her lips firmly on the words he looked down at her with a smile. 'Thank you for not telling me to go and rest.'

He pushed open the door onto a scene that made her heart sink. Nanny Jenkins, hands on hips, was confronting Isobel, who had taken up the same pose.

'I don't *like* this house. I don't *like* my lessons. I want to go out.'

'You will go outside when your father says you may and not before.'

'I'm a lady now that Papa's a duke. You have to do as I say.'

'A lady has manners and a lady knows her duty,' the little Welsh woman said. 'Your father has put me in charge of you. It is your duty to become an educated, well-informed and well-mannered young lady.'

'That is boring.'

'I expect you are too young, really, to have Mrs Jenkins to look after you instead of a nursery maid.' Sophie stepped into the room. 'Your papa obviously has great confidence in how grown-up and intelligent you are, but he must be mistaken. Good morning, Mrs Jenkins. May I join you?'

Mrs Jenkins bobbed a curtsy, Sophie smiled and took a seat in the window, shook out her embroidery and sat back.

'Good morning, Miss Wilmott. Good morning, Your Grace.'

'Papa!'

'Mrs Jenkins. Isobel. I have come to see how your lessons are coming along.' Cal bent and picked the child up, kissed her cheek and set her back down again.

Isobel tossed her ringlets. 'I am working very hard. I don't like this house.'

'You do not know this house. But if Mrs Jenkins thinks you have been good this morning then after luncheon you may go outside and explore. With two footmen, Mrs Jenkins. I do not see why you should have to chase after the child and fish her out of the lake.'

'Thank you, Your Grace. We had been studying deportment. As we have a visitor, Isobel, I would like you to go and greet Miss Wilmott and make polite conversation while your papa and I sit down quietly over here.' From the way she was looking at Cal Sophie could tell she recognised that he was unwell.

Isobel, lower lip thrust out, marched over to Sophie who laid her embroidery on the seat beside her. 'Good morning, Miss Wilmott. Welcome to the nursery. I hope you are having a pleasant stay.'

'Good morning, Lady Isobel. Thank you, I am having a delightful time.'

Isobel turned with a smirk and marched back towards Mrs Jenkins who simply waved her away. 'Conversation, Isobel.'

Sophie reached over and pulled up a small chair so that it was facing her. 'I have embroidery to work on. Do you sew, Lady Isobel?'

'No.'

Silence fell. Sophie, who had faced down more daunting social situations in her time, placidly made a row of French knots and waited.

'Why do you sew? Why not buy what you want?'

'It is interesting to create exactly what I would like and satisfying when I have made it. This is a present for my mother, a cover for her wash stand.'

'I don't have a mother.' *And you are not going to be one*, the fierce brown stare promised.

'You have a father though. You could embroider his initials on a handkerchief, then he would think of you every time he looked at it.' Sophie took a large plain square of fine linen from her bag where she had put it with just this in mind, smoothed it out on the seat beside her and picked up her embroidery again.

'I don't know anyone who does that. Nanny Jenkins knits.'

'You know me.' Sophie glanced over the dark head to where Cal was stretched out on the battered chaise longue, hands folded on his flat stomach, eyes closed. Beside him Mrs Jenkins placidly knitted something grey and lacy.

'You don't like me.' Isobel scuffed one toe into the rug.

'Why do you say that? I don't know you.'

'I was rude to you. Nanny Jenkins says people don't like people who are rude to them.'

'It makes it hard, I agree. But it helps if you know why someone is rude. You thought I was going to try and take your mama's place and that your papa wouldn't love you as much if he married me.' Sophie outlined a rose with steady stiches, her eyes on the work.

'How did you know that?' When she looked up Isobel was staring, mouth open.

'Because my mama married again after my father died, so I know how easy it is to worry and to feel jealous. But I got to know my new Step Papa and I love him very much now and Mama still loves me just as much as ever and now I have Step Papa as well. He can never take the place of my real papa, he's a different sort of papa. I would be a different sort of mama for you.'

'Oh.' A lot of silent thinking went on while Sophie rethreaded her needle with deeper pink. 'Must I call you Mama?'

'Not if you do not want to. We could think of a name together.'

'Will you show me how to make a handkerchief for Papa?'

'Of course I will.'

Cal woke to the smell of chalk and lavender. He lay listening to the clicking sounds close to his ear and, further away, the murmur of feminine voices, one soft and low, one higher-pitched and threatening to escape from a whisper.

He was in the nursery, he realised, not troubling to open his eyes. He felt warm, relaxed and considerably better than he had when he had yielded to Mrs Jenkins's urging to lie down and rest himself.

He wondered vaguely what magic Sophie had created to enchant Isobel and then let himself drift towards sleep again. Time enough to get up and flex his muscles as he rather suspected he was going to have to do if Ransome continued to make Sophie so uneasy. No-one was going to distress the woman he…

Sophie saw Cal stretch and begin to sit up and whisked the linen square with its shaky pencil outline of a letter C into her sewing bag. 'Don't tell Papa, then it will be a surprise present.'

'You'll come back, show me how to sew it? Please?'

'Of course.' She raised her voice from a whisper. 'The warning gong has rung for luncheon, Your Grace.'

'Have I been asleep and neglecting three ladies?'

Cal stood and scrubbed one hand over his face. 'What a dreadful example in bad manners to show my daughter. I must go down and change, I came here direct from the fencing bout.'

'We have entertained ourselves very well, but I would be glad of your escort to my room.' Sophie made her farewells, laying a finger on her lips in warning to Isobel who was obviously bursting with her secret, and let Cal take her arm on the stairs. His colour was back to normal and only the dark shadows beneath his eyes betrayed that he had been wracked with pain and sickness for most of the night.

'You are an enchantress,' he said. 'What did you do to tame the child?'

'I remembered one of our grooms showing me how to handle a colt who was so wild that no-one could get a halter on him. Jim would sit on the fence, polishing some leather, paying the animal not the slightest attention. It became unbearably curious and came closer and closer until it was butting him with its nose for attention. Then he would put out a hand, still not looking at it, and pet it. Within a few days he could do anything with it.

'Isobel worries that I will try and replace her mother and that you will love her less if you… if you have someone else in your life. I told her that I have a stepfather and understand. And now we have a secret to keep from you and she adores that.'

'What secret?' He sounded so suspicious that she laughed up at him.

'It is a *secret*. Cal, you look much better, I am so relieved.'

He drew her close to him and rested his cheek on the top of her head. 'I knew, during the night when it was really bad, that you were there. I should have had the strength to send you away and not inflict that on you.'

'Of course,' Sophie said, rubbing her cheek against his shirt front. 'And I should have realised how much better I would have felt if I had just gone back to bed and to sleep and left you there. Why, I would not have worried in the slightest.'

'Wicked woman.' He did not release her.

'Does it concern you, hurt your pride, that I saw you when you were ill?' she asked.

'Hmm.' That, she supposed, was agreement.

'We are going to be married, Cal. I need to know you, to understand you. I know now that when everything is stripped away and you are in pain, you are still brave and still fighting.' The hand that had been stroking her back went very still. 'I want us to be honest with each other.'

'Yes, let us be that.' He released her and began to walk briskly along the corridor towards his rooms. 'Now we must hurry if I am to wash and change and not be late for luncheon. And I must send a note to Prescott. I will need him here if things become… complicated.'

What had she said? Perhaps she had simply embarrassed him with what he saw as an excess of sensibility. Or perhaps he instinctively knew that she was keeping something from him.

Sophie let herself into her sitting room from the inner passageway and put down her sewing bag. The clock chimed, a thin silvery note, and she turned to the bedchamber door. She would be late for luncheon. There was no need to ring for Mary, her gown was in perfect order, so was her hair, she saw with a glance in the mirror. All she needed to do was wash her hands.

Her hand was on the dressing room door when she felt the prickle of awareness down her spine that warned her she was not alone. She turned and there, lounging on the bed in unconscious imitation of Cal on the nursery chaise, was Jonathan.

'Get out of here. Now.'

'We need to talk, Sophie dear.'

'Not here and not now. Everyone will be going in to

luncheon.'

'All the better for a quick, private talk, don't you think.' He stood up and walked towards her. Sophie stood her ground, chin up, but he kept coming until they were toe to toe. 'I am not enjoying myself much here, Sophie. I do not feel very welcome, the way you look at me, the way your duke looks at me. And his tame fencing master. I've been patient, but I want money. Now.'

'I told you – I do not have any.'

'Ask your duke, he'll give you what you want. Take him to bed and please him. You lied to me, didn't you Sophie? Made me think you were sharing his bed. But you aren't are you? I checked.'

'That was you in Cal's room the first night.' The relief that it was not someone with a knife or a phial of poison must have shown in her voice, for Jonathan looked at her strangely.

'I won't be patient much longer, Sophie. I want five hundred pounds by tomorrow night or I will start telling tales.'

'And I will tell the duke and he will kill you. He is at least as good as you with a rapier, you saw him this morning.'

'I don't think you will, Sophie.' He moved, forcing her back against the dressing table. 'Look what you have to lose, all this wealth, all this status. You will be a good girl and do as I tell you. And, just for old times' sake, I think I'll take a kiss on account.'

She reached behind her, searching for the hairbrush, swung at him as his right hand closed over her breast, then twisted as his other hand came up to grab for the heavy silver-backed brush. It flew away, crashed into the glass of a watercolour by the door, shattering it. Sophie's recoil sent her across the dressing table scattering bottles and boxes to crash to the floor.

'You stupid bitch.' Jonathan hauled her to her feet and she came up fighting, kicking and scratching as he dragged her towards the bed.

The sound of the sitting room door crashing open seemed part of the struggle until there was a roar of rage and Jonathan was dragged off her. Sophie reeled back and fell onto the bed as Cal hit Jonathan across the room.

'Sophie, are you hurt?' He moved to stand between her and the fallen man.

'I don't think so. Bruised, perhaps.' She kept the tremor out of her voice with an effort. Cal looked incandescent, if he guessed how shaken she was she could not imagine what he would do next.

'Good. Then I do not need to disembowel this scum before I kill him.'

Jonathan shambled to his feet. 'You wouldn't commit murder.'

'I wouldn't bet on it if I were you,' Jared Hunt drawled and she realised he had followed Cal into the room, Flynn at his heels. 'He might not, I would.'

'You want to protect her now, but wait until I tell you what she is. I took Little Miss Virtue's – '

'Virginity, yes, I know.' Cal sounded bored, if anything. Sophie stared at the broad back, the slowly clenching and unclenching fists, wishing she could see his face. How had he known it was Jonathan? 'Dreadful judgement on Miss Wilmott's part, taking something like you as a lover, but she was young and innocent and we all make mistakes. Yours, Ransome, was coming within a hundred miles of her again.'

'I'll wager she didn't tell what else happened that night, who else had her.' Jonathan dragged the back of his hand across his bleeding mouth.

'No-one did,' Cal said with total assurance. 'But Sophie humiliated you, which is why you haven't been back to London since. What was it? Did she threaten to tell everyone how pathetic your bedroom skills are?'

Cal appeared to be possessed of some kind of black magic arts. Sophie brushed aside Flynn who was attempting to roll back her cuffs to check her wrists for bruises and got off the bed.

'I thought we were eloping,' she said, seating herself elegantly in the nearest chair before her knees gave way. 'It was the night of Lady Houghley's masquerade ball and I knew I would not be missed for hours. He took me to some squalid ale house just across the Thames where he was obviously known, given the number of drunken oafs who greeted him. He dragged me up to a repellent bedroom and said that if I didn't let him do what he wanted then he would invite all his friends in too. So I did. He was getting drunk by then, and afterwards he drank more and passed out.

'I tied him to the bedposts with his cravat and my stockings and took a pink silk ribbon from my chemise and tied it in a pretty bow around his – ' She waved a hand, searching for the right word.

'Prick?' Flynn suggested.

'Exactly. Prick. It was about the size of a bodkin by then so that is exactly the right word.' Cal gave a snort of laughter and Jonathan went scarlet. 'Then I crept downstairs and discovered that I was close to the river. A waterman took me across, then I found a hackney carriage and I was back at the ball just before the unmasking. No-one ever knew I was missing.' She risked a glance at Cal's profile and found he was smiling, albeit grimly. 'Jonathan vanished from London and I didn't see him again until before we came here. He is trying to blackmail me.'

'Is he now?' Cal linked his fingers and cracked his knuckles ominously. 'So he is a liar, a rapist and an extortionist.'

'You can't challenge him,' Hunt observed. 'He is not a gentleman.'

'No. Pity.'

'I am not the first,' Sophie said. Her legs had stopped shaking so she got up and fetched Tanner's letter from the broken wreckage of her dressing case and handed it to Cal. 'I had him investigated.'

His gaze flickered from the letter heading to her face, then back down to the letter. 'He has a taste for sheep, it would appear.'

'That's not true! That bloody parson – '

'But everything else is accurate, isn't it? Come now, Ransome, you may as well admit it. I might be squeamish about facing you on a field of honour, but I have no objection to beating a confession out of you.'

'All right, I admit it. All of it.'

'Even the sheep?' Flynn asked and got a murderous glare in response.

'But you can't say anything, not and keep her name out of it.' He jerked his head at Sophie and Cal growled, deep in his chest.

'Is that American friend of yours still docked in Bristol, Jared?'

'Oh yes, he'll be there for a week or so getting stocked up for his voyage to the East Indies. Are you thinking what I think you are? Hand over this fine, hardworking crew member to him?'

'You can't do that!' Jonathan made a dive for the door. Cal caught him by the collar and lifted him, gasping and struggling.

'Do you the world of good. Captain Lucas runs a tight ship, lots of invigorating work and the lash for shirkers. Very colourful area, you'll enjoy it. Head-hunters, an entire text book of tropical diseases, typhoons, pirates. Big rough, *very* frustrated sailors who will welcome a beautiful young shipmate with open arms.' He dumped Jonathan on the floor and left him scrabbling at his neckcloth in an effort to breathe. 'Flynn, take him and lock him in his room and tell the servants that he is unwell and must not be disturbed. I'd tie him to the bed if I were you. Oh, and take a loaded pistol with you. Jared – can you get him to Bristol tomorrow, early? You'd best take

Flynn along. Ask Wilkins in the stables to sort you out a carriage and some grooms who'll keep their mouths shut.'

Cal waited until Flynn and Hunt dragged the struggling and protesting Jonathan through the door then closed it behind them. 'Aren't you going to beg for mercy for him? He was your first lover, after all.'

So, he was angry with her. Sophie thought she could hardly blame him. 'No. he is a menace to women, condemned out of his own mouth. If this came to court he would go to prison for years, as it is, he has a chance. If he works hard for that captain he might be able to start a new life in the East.'

'But you couldn't trust me with this, could you, Sophie? You took a chance on telling me half the story, that you were not a virgin, and you judged rightly that it made no difference to me. But you kept the rest from me, you lied to me on Ludgate Hill, you had no faith that you could let me help and protect you. I wasn't looking for love in this match, you know that. But I *was* hoping for honesty.'

Chapter Twenty - Where Sophie Keeps Her Pearls On

So Jonathan has won after all. I love this man who doesn't want my love and I could not trust him when trust was what he needed. But she had to try.

'I thought that if I told you, you would kill him in a duel. You are the Lost Duke, with gossip swirling around you from that long absence. Probably you would not be hanged for killing a man in a duel, but how could I be certain? And then, when I discovered that someone was trying to kill you, how did I know they would not take advantage of such a situation, fabricate evidence, perhaps, to condemn you?'

'In other words, you were protecting me?' Cal enquired, looking every inch the duke, from the scorn in his voice to the rigid lines of his face.

'It was my error in the first place, my lack of judgment. It was for me to deal with.'

'Sophie, you are betrothed to me. I protect what is mine. If I cannot do that, I am less of a man than I should be.'

'I have wounded your pride, for which I apologise.' Her tone was not conciliatory, but she was as angry as he was now. *Male pride be damned. Why should* I *fight to save this marriage?* 'I assume you wish to call off the engagement? I will explain to all and sundry that I found myself over-faced by the splendour of this place, unable to meet the high standards expected of the wife of a duke. You will receive much sympathy, I am sure.'

‘I had not thought you a coward, Sophie. Nor cruel – what will Isobel think? She has lost her mother, now you do not feel you can take on that role.’

‘I could be very happy raising Isobel as my daughter. But spending my life married to you? I think not.’

‘You will marry me, Sophie. You have got too close, you know too many secrets. Besides, I want you, and we dukes, we get what we want, do we not?’

‘It would appear so. How do you intend to force me?’

‘Who said anything about force? You told me that you would regret lying with me before our wedding day. Well, you have been lying *to* me, Sophie, so I think you will lie *with* me now, regrets or not. You are no lightskirt, you expect to marry the men you sleep with.’

‘You intend to force me?’

‘No, Sophie. I intend to seduce you tonight. Not now, we have kept our guests waiting quite long enough for their luncheon, don’t you think?’ He went to the window and threw it open, then jerked the bell-pull, waiting in silence until Mary appeared. ‘A cat got in through the window with a bird that it caught. It has created chaos and Miss Wilmott was hurt falling over chasing it out. Clean it up, please – and mind the broken glass. Come along, Miss Wilmott.’

‘You – ’ She wrenched her arm away the moment they were out of the door. ‘You will *not* seduce me. I will not allow you to.’

Cal merely smiled.

The tale of the cat and the sparrow explained both the delay and Sophie’s ruffled appearance to the entire satisfaction of the group gathering around the luncheon table. Two young ladies declared themselves terrified of birds in the house, Lady Peter expressed her displeasure at a stable cat being allowed anywhere near the mansion and

Sophie's mother shook her head over the thought of her daughter chasing animals around her bedchamber in such a harum-scarum manner. 'You should have rung for a footman, Sophie,' she chided.

'Oh, and Ransome will not be joining us,' Cal said as Jared came in, face expressionless as he straightened his cuffs and took his place with a word of apology. 'He did not appear to be feeling very well. He seemed abstracted to me and certainly luncheon was the last thing on his mind.'

Sophie was close enough to overhear her mother murmur to Lady Peter, 'No loss to the company, in my opinion. I always thought there was something not quite right about that young man.'

I wish you had said that to me, Mama. Although I was probably too in love with being in love to have paid any attention.

'Too handsome for his own good,' Lady Peter observed. 'Gives them an inflated opinion of their own charms.' She frowned down the table at two of the bridesmaids who were lamenting the absence of *that nice Mr Ransome.* Despite everything Sophie was amused to see their eyes turn towards Toby, happily unaware that he was about to become the object of their flirtations.

For Sophie the afternoon dragged into evening on leaden feet, although all the guests appeared to be enjoying themselves, from the flirtatious bridesmaids to the gentlemen who had ridden out when the drizzle eased. Cal was the perfect host, teasing the younger ladies, charming the older ones and finding entertainment for every gentleman whether they wanted to read in the library or borrow a hack.

She chatted, strolled on the terrace and spent an hour with Isobel helping her with her embroidery. Whenever she went downstairs Cal appeared as though by alchemy and she was conscious of his heavy-lidded, sensual gaze upon her. She responded by smiling sweetly whenever their eyes met and tried to hide the quiver of anticipation as the hands of the clocks crawled round their dials.

That furious refusal to marry him had been nothing but shock and reaction, she knew it perfectly well and she suspected that Cal did too. She loved him, she was certain of that now. Loved him, was in love with him, desired him. Rejecting him out of pique because he was angry with her, did not appreciate her motives, would hurt only her and would punish him simply because he had felt deceived and lied to.

She felt uneasy too about her motives for refusing to make love fully before their wedding day. The suspicion that she had not fully committed herself to this marriage kept nagging at her. She had no virginity to lose, and she had been as intimate with Cal as it was possible to be, without that final act of joining, so had she insisted on holding back until the wedding night in a pretence that the fiasco with Jonathan had never happened? It felt like hypocrisy to have insisted on denying them both, as though respectability and doing the "right thing" were more important than their feelings for each other.

Restless, Sophie abandoned the small drawing room, leaving the older ladies to a hushed discussion of the latest crim.con. case and the younger ones to a thorough dissection of the latest issues of *La Belle Assemblée,* and went in search of the housekeeper.

She found Mrs Fairfax in the Chinese Drawing Room, arranging great bowls of red and white roses. 'I was hoping you might have time to talk to me about the management of the house,' she explained. 'Not detail yet, of course, but to give me some idea of what is involved for the mistress of something this large, and with an experienced housekeeper such as yourself on the staff.' It was a declaration, a commitment, that she knew she had been avoiding making.

The housekeeper beamed. 'Of course, Miss Wilmott.

I would be only too happy, if you do not mind me putting the finishing touches to these.' She snipped a few stems, adjusted some fern fronds and stood back. 'What do you think?'

'They are a very striking colour combination.'

'One of our Calderbrook traditions.' Mrs Fairfax swept the trimmings into the basket that had held the roses. 'It is such a joy to have the Duke back in residence and to observe them all again. These are for the red rose of Lancaster and the white rose of York that were combined into the Tudor Rose to mark the end of the Wars of the Roses. The first Earl of Calderbrook was ennobled by King Henry VII and the family always displays red and white roses in tribute to the Tudors whenever they are in bloom.'

'What other traditions are there?' Sophie rescued the flower snips and the unwanted fern fronds and followed Mrs Fairfax out into the hall.

'There's the garland of ivy from the old castle that decorates the coat of arms up there.' The housekeeper pointed to where an ancient and battered shield hung high on the wall, wrapped in fresh green strands of ivy. 'The venison roast from the park herd on the first Sunday of every month, the fetching of water from the Duke's Spring, the raising of the flag whenever the Duke is in residence and the annual Duke's Bounty which is a great celebration on the anniversary of the creation of the Dukedom on the first day of September, 1662.'

She opened the door hidden under the curve of the staircase. 'Those are the main traditions. If you'd like to come down, Miss Wilmott, I will show you below stairs. Of course, there are other things that are special to this house, like the spice cakes Chef makes for the Duke, the great scale on which members of the family are weighed annually, the strewing herbs I stuff the Duke's pillow with to promote sleep…'

Mrs Fairfax bustled through the labyrinth, invading

Chef's domains, the butler's territory, all with a courteous greeting and the news that the new mistress was with her. Sophie grew dizzy with names and posts, the intricacies of the pastry room and the confectionery cupboard, the boot boy's lair and the coal hole, the silver vault and the wine cellar and had to be revived with cowslip wine in the housekeeper's own sitting room.

'I am very impressed, Mrs Fairfax, as I expected I would be, considering how well the house is kept above stairs and how efficiently everything runs.'

The older woman beamed and demurred, praised Lady Peter's oversight of the house and murmured about the pleasure everyone had at the return of the Duke. 'And to know that we will be welcoming a new Duchess so soon, now that really puts the cream on top of the cake!'

Sophie was slightly tipsy on the effects of two glasses of powerful cowslip wine and the head-full of information when she finally climbed the stairs with the sound of the dressing gong still reverberating around the hall.

'Where have you been?' Toby enquired, falling into step with her half way up the flight.

'Indulging in a surfeit of domesticity.'

He wrinkled his nose. 'Sounds dull.'

'Actually it was surprisingly soothing.' It had certainly helped her to decide what to do about Cal's threats of seduction that night. She would meet fire with fire and discover whether they could heal the breach that had opened up between them.

Sophie allowed Mary to undress her, then, when she had bathed, she dismissed the maid.

'But your hair, Miss. Don't you want me to take it down and brush it for you?'

'I will see to that, Mary. It will be soothing.'

Soothing was not exactly what she had in mind, inflammatory was more the effect she was looking for, but she could hardly tell Mary that.

'Yes, Miss.' The maid helped her into her nightgown and robe and cleared away the evening dress, locked up the pearls Sophie had worn and took herself off with a bob. 'Good night, Miss.'

Sophie promptly took out the gown and put it on again. She had chosen it because she could manage the fastenings by herself and it did not rely on tight lacing for its fit, and after a few wriggles she was dressed. She opened the jewel case and put on her pearl necklace, locked her door, blew out the candles and tiptoed through to Cal's sitting room where she curled up in a chair near the door to the bedroom and settled down to wait.

She had counted on him not lingering over the brandy or the billiard table, not with the promise of seduction on his mind, and she was rewarded with the glimmer of light under the door and the sound of male voices after only half an hour.

'…looking seedy,' Flynn said. 'I told him to stop fishing for sympathy. There's nothing wrong with him except for a right hook to the face.'

'He's a sorry specimen indeed.'

'Not fit to be around young ladies, that's for sure…' The valet's voice faded, cupboard doors closed, there was the sound of splashing water, voices further away. They would be in the dressing room. After perhaps ten minutes Flynn must have come back into the bedchamber. 'Miss Sophie's got backbone, standing up to Ransome the way she did.'

'She has that,' Cal agreed. 'That will be all, Michael, thank you. I'll let you get back to your seedy prisoner. Hunt will be up to relieve you shortly.'

Sophie heard the bedchamber door close, then the sharp click of the key in the lock. She stood up, shook out her skirts, took a deep breath and opened the connecting door.

Cal turned the key in the lock as the whisper of a draught brushed cooler air around his bare ankles beneath the hem of his robe. Someone had come into his room behind him, opened a window or a door. He moved casually to the chest next to the door and slid his hand under the pile of shirts that lay on top of it. When he turned he was holding one of a pair of duelling pistols. Its mate was under his pillow.

'Are you accurate with that?' Sophie asked. She was fully dressed, her hair still up in its intricate formal arrangement, and her voice was perfectly steady. *Oh yes, Sophie has backbone.*

'Deadly.' He eased back the hammer and laid it back on the chest with a silent prayer of thanks that he hadn't simply spun round and fired.

'It was Jonathan in your room that night, I think,' she said, closing the door and coming further into the room. 'He tried to blackmail me into sleeping with him and I said I spent every night with you. He must have been checking.'

'One less assassin to worry about. Sophie, what are you doing in here?'

'Waiting to be seduced.' She wandered over to the dressing table and began to examine the silver-backed brushes arrayed on it.

Cal felt the remains of his anger with her vanish like a soap bubble in the sunlight. He could not stay cross with Sophie because she simply knocked his feet out from under him with disarming frankness every time. But he was not going to let her get away with it so easily.

'It doesn't work like that. You stay in your bed chamber and I come and exercise my wicked wiles on you.'

'I had no idea there were rules,' she said earnestly. 'How complicated.' She was laughing at him, the little witch.

'What did your maid say? I expected to find you in

bed in your prettiest nightgown.' Cal prowled a little closer, waiting to see if she backed away. He had no intention of frightening her, although the likelihood of anything scaring Sophie was beginning to look unlikely.

She didn't retreat, simply drifted away from the dressing table and over to the bookshelves. 'I told her I would do my own hair and so on. I did not like the idea of sitting in bed passively waiting.' She reached up and took a book down. 'What do you read in bed? Oh, philosophy?'

'Helps me sleep.' He watched her replace the book, then trail her fingertips along the spines. Every bump on his own backbone tingled at the sight. Then she ran two fingers up and down a handsomely-embossed specimen and he had to close his eyes. *Damn it, who is supposed to be seducing who here?*

'Are you still angry with me?' She turned from the bookcase and looked at him, not teasing now, her face serious and a little frown line between her brows.

'No. I think I understand why you did what you did. Are you still determined not to marry me?'

'No. I think I understand why you reacted as you did.' She smiled suddenly, a vivid, happy smile that compelled him smile back. 'I am glad we can talk about it.' She twisted the little pearl ring she always wore, suddenly, disarmingly, uncertain. 'Does this mean that you will not be seducing me?'

'That was anger and frustration talking. I would never force something like that on you, Sophie.'

'I know. But it is disappointing. I was rather looking forward to being seduced.'

'Before our wedding night?' he asked, every carefully-controlled sensual instinct shaking off the shackles and coming to attention.

'I thought about it and I think I was being foolish, pretending something I thought I *ought* to want when, actually, what I want is you, Cal.'

'Here? Now?' He wouldn't move, not until he was certain, because once he touched her he was not at all sure he could stop.

'Mmm.' Sophie agreed. She raised her hands and did something at the nape of her neck, then pulled her sash free. With a little wriggle her evening gown slid from her shoulders and she stood there, lit by the six-branched candlestick on the dresser, quite naked except for her pearls.

Chapter Twenty One - Where Death Follows Love

'Exactly who is doing the seducing here?' By some miracle he could still speak. Sophie naked in the sunlight on the hillside had been beautiful, but they had been entangled together and, so exposed in the open, they had been conscious of a certain urgency and tension. And besides, he had been focused on reassuring her, giving her pleasure. His memories of Sophie had been softness and glimpses of curves and tangled curls, gasps of pleasure and her sweet taste. Now the whole woman stood before him, blushing a little, it was true, but powerfully seductive, naturally sensual in the shimmer of candle light. And his.

She kept her gaze on his face as she lifted her hands again and began to unpin her hair, one glorious golden curl at a time. He was dreaming of course. No woman, other than the most skilled courtesan, could feed his fantasies with such innocent, frank, delicate sensuality.

And then she lost her nerve and fumbled the pins and the blush became rosy and her hands dropped into the age-old gesture, one hand over the feminine triangle of curls, the other arm across her breasts. She was no longer some erotic goddess but Sophie, and that was so much more. Sophie, shy and curious, sensual and still innocent, Sophie full of the courage to come and show him what she needed.

'Ah, Sophie.' He moved to take her in his arms and she burrowed against the silk of his robe, her nose, which was endearingly cold, pressed against his bare sternum through the gap in the lapels. 'I am glad you changed your mind.'

'About this?'

'About marrying me. And this.' He bent and picked her up, a satisfying weight in his arms. She settled against his chest with a wriggle and a little sigh. 'Don't get comfortable there.' He dropped her onto the coverlet and she squeaked as her bare bottom met the cool dark blue satin, then lay like a Venus in a sea-pool, watching him as he threw off his robe.

The frank admiration with which Sophie looked at him should have exalted him. Instead it was terrifying. What if he could not live up to what she thought she saw in him? What if he disappointed her, or hurt her through some clumsiness? His body had no doubts and he saw her eyes widen as she looked down from his face. And suddenly Cal had no doubts either. He wasn't a god and she was not a goddess. They were two mortals who cared about each other and who were about to make love. Nothing real was ever perfect and Sophie was real and so was he.

'What are you thinking about?'

'The nature of reality and the importance of imperfection. Your reality, my imperfections.'

'Philosophy. I do hope that doesn't mean you are about to go to sleep.' Her smile was utterly wicked.

'Oh no.' And then he was on the bed beside her and he could caress her soft, cool curves with hands that remembered each dip and swell and now could linger, arouse, tease her into forgetting her shyness. He spent long minutes on her breasts, licking and sucking and tormenting the eager nipples into hard peaks, wondering if he could make her come by this alone, she seemed so responsive.

But her hips were restless, lifting a little, nudging against the impatient thrust of his erection in a way that threatened a total loss of control if he stayed where he was. It was still too soon, he thought, for all her passionate response, and she was far too new to this to rush her.

Cal slid down the bed, parted her thighs and began to make love to Sophie's hidden secrets. She gave a little cry when he slid a finger, then another inside her, but it was surprise, not pain, and she began to move against the heel of his hand, her breath coming in little gasps. When he kissed her there, his tongue searching for the hard pearl of her arousal, she cried out, then came apart almost instantly and he nearly lost control himself as the scent and the taste of her flooded his senses.

'Sophie?'

There was a weight on her and she felt boneless and blissful and when she opened her eyes Cal was above her, supported on his elbows, his hips fitting perfectly between her spread thighs.

'Oh. Cal.'

'Who did you think it was?' His voice was teasing but his eyes were dark and heavy with desire.

'I mean, *Oh, Cal!'* Somehow it was possible to joke, just a little.

'Look at me, Sophie.' Her eyelids were drifting down but she managed to drag them open to hold his gaze as he shifted a little until she felt him pressing against her. It had hurt when Jonathan had done that, urgent and fast, and there was a little quiver of anxiety as Cal entered her.

And then it was all right, and *all right* became incredible and intimate and tender and fierce and the world became the sensation of Cal within her, Cal above her, until the now-familiar tightness began to ravel to impossible, almost painful heights and then shattered and she cried out Cal's name as she broke and heard him shout hers and everything swirled down into soft velvet darkness and the security of his arms.

Someone was hammering on a big drum and shouting, which was unfair because she was so sleepy and comfortable and warm.

'Stay there,' a voice… Cal… said sharply, then there was cool air on her body for a moment as the covers lifted and Sophie was wide awake.

She was in Cal's bed and there was the very faintest dawn light through the gap in the curtains and the drum beat settled down to someone knocking on the door and the shouting became Hunt's voice, low and urgent.

Cal was pulling on his robe as he strode to open the door and Sophie dived under the covers as it all came back. She was naked, in Cal's bed, and they had made love last night and it had been perfect and now…

'He's dead,' Jared Hunt said as the door closed.

'Who?' Cal demanded sharply.

'Ransome.' That was Flynn. 'He was complaining last night. Stomach ache, head ache. I thought he was bluffing, trying to get my guard down. I gave him plenty of water because he said he was thirsty, but not hungry. Then he still kept moaning, so I gave him laudanum to help him sleep. That quietened him down, but he was still restless when I locked him in and left him. When I went in just now he was quiet, so I went to look and he was cold and dead. He'd been sick. Very sick.'

'And he ate nothing?' Cal asked.

'Nothing,' Flynn said. 'He hadn't even got some pills or sweetmeats in his pockets because I checked him over when I put him in the room in case he'd got a knife. It looks like whatever you were ill with.'

Sophie wriggled up from under the covers, clutching them to her chest. 'Where did the laudanum come from? And the water?'

All three men turned to look at her. Flynn promptly developed an interest in the fireplace and Hunt raised one eyebrow and shifted so he was at an angle to her.

'Cal's… His Grace's dressing room, both of them,' Flynn said. 'We haven't needed the laudanum since Hunt broke his toe in Calcutta. The water was from the big carafe the maid brought up yesterday afternoon.'

'I did not drink from the carafe in my room before I was ill,' Cal said slowly. 'I don't think I drank anything but coffee, ale, wine and brandy that day. Oh, and a cup of tea after dinner when we joined the ladies.'

'But you drank water from the carafe *after* you became sick,' Flynn said. 'A lot of it. You emptied it. And you aren't dead, in fact you recovered fairly quickly.'

'But it would be the easiest way to poison someone.' Sophie almost let the covers slip as she wriggled into a more comfortable sitting position.

'Gentlemen, my sitting room.' Cal ushered them out and followed on their heels. 'I'll be back in a moment,' he said over his shoulder.

Sophie wrapped her arms around her bent legs and shivered. *Jonathan dead. Jonathan… poisoned?* She had feared him and disliked him, but once, however misguidedly, she had loved him and no-one deserved to die alone and in distress.

The water from Cal's bedchamber. If he had drunk it last night, would he be dead now? She burrowed down into the bed again, down into the still-warm hollow Cal's body had left. He had thrust most of his pillows aside, some to the floor, some pushed up against the headboard. As she disturbed them the sweet hay-scent of ladies' bedstraw drifted to her nostrils. Bedstraw and thyme and some herb she did not recognise. This must be the sleep-pillow that Mrs Fairfax had spoken of, part of the traditions the household were adopting now their duke was back in residence.

Traditions…

'Here are your nightgown and robe and slippers.' Cal was standing right by the bed. 'What is it?' He dropped the clothing and sat beside her. 'Sophie? I know it is a shock, a dreadful thing to happen, however much of a swine he was, but – '

'No.' She scrambled out of bed, pulled on her clothes and bent to jam her feet into the slippers. 'Cal, there is this.' She thrust the pillow into his hands. 'And ivy from the castle tower around the coat of arms in the hall and your flag flying over this house. Traditions.'

He stared at her and she could almost see the thoughts chasing through his brain, the calculation and memories. 'The Duke's Spring. It has to be. Come on.' He almost pulled her into the sitting room. Flynn and Hunt stood, but Cal waved them back down to their seats. 'Jared, do you remember the Duke's Spring?' Hunt nodded. 'Michael, who brought the water for the carafe? Did they say anything particular about it?'

'No.' Flynn frowned in thought. 'Come to think of it, I didn't notice it being brought up, or I would have checked it out, had a sip or two. Could have been the maid who brought the pillow with all the herbs in. She said something about how good it was to have all the old traditions again, but she was in here when I arrived. She might have had both the carafe and the pillow. I had the stuffing out of that and made sure it was safe, but its all ordinary herbs.' He shifted uncomfortably. 'I slipped up, didn't I? I shouldn't have missed the water. I was too busy thinking about Ransome.'

Cal shrugged. 'We all had other things on our minds.'

'I'll get hold of the girl, find out who gave it to her to bring up.'

'I can answer that, I think.' They all turned to stare at Sophie as though the chair she was curled up in had spoken. 'Mrs Fairfax.'

'Mrs Fairfax? Never. I've known her since I was a small child.'

'The Duke is back, so the housekeeper orders water

from the spring for you, and you only. They will have been in turmoil, getting ready for the house party. They probably only spared someone to get the water yesterday. Flynn, it's a spring up by the old castle, there is this superstition that only the Duke drinks from it.'

'Which makes it a safe thing to target once it is in the house.' The valet nodded in comprehension. 'There should be no risk of anyone else drinking it.'

'I'm not sure it is that.' Cal frowned. 'I am beginning to see a pattern. But leave it now – and no-one touch water left in this suite until we are certain. Michael, check Ransome's rooms, leave no traces that you were in there at all last night. We all get back to bed and we wait for the alarm to be raised when the maids take in the morning tea trays. No, on second thoughts, you had best be passing and offer to take it in for the girl on that corridor, tell her he's got a bit of a reputation and you don't want her chased round the bed. We can spare her finding a body.'

The two men left, looking grim, and Cal opened the door into Sophie's sitting room. 'You had best get back to your own bed before your maid arrives.'

'Cal.' She caught at the lapels of his robe on the threshold. 'That was murder. We cannot keep it secret and cover it up.'

'If it was murder, then the nearest Justice of the Peace is my uncle, which is a slight problem. If it wasn't, then I have an idea that at least needs investigating.'

'Mr Tanner, the agent who investigated Jonathan for me, he will know all about his home and what relatives are still there. I'll write to him and ask.'

'And have the man know that your blackmailer has conveniently, and mysteriously, died? Tanner may be a good man, but I prefer not to give hostages to fortune. Some research in the library ought to locate likely Cornish Ransomes if there is nothing in his luggage. Sir Toby introduced him to me as "of Penzance". We'll have him buried here temporarily until we know what his family's wishes are.'

He gave her a swift kiss. 'Sophie, my love, this isn't how I expect to wake up with you the first morning we had been together. Are you all right alone?'

'Of course.' *Sophie, my love. Oh, Cal.* 'You go, I will be fine.' He was already off elsewhere in his head, planning and calculating, she was certain. She went to her room, remembered where she had left her evening dress and hairpins the night before, ran back to Cal's bed chamber, scooped everything up and fled before she was tempted to stay and fuss over him. Or kiss him.

She put away her pearls and the gown, piled her hairpins on the dressing table and got into bed because that seemed the best way to make it look slept in. Tossing and turning came quite easily, she found. Her body ached pleasurably in unexpected places, nothing like the soreness after Jonathan had lain with her. She had worried, a little, that it might spoil things with Cal, that she would be haunted by the image of the other man, of the misery of that experience. But Cal's lovemaking was so different that it seemed something else entirely.

Learning to make love with Cal was going to be wonderful. She burrowed into the pillows, hugging one to her, but its softness was no substitute for Cal's hard body.

Body. Somewhere under this roof Jonathan was lying cold and stark after suffering all that Cal had the other night, only worse, because this had killed him and he had been alone. He hadn't even been able to get to the bell and ring for help, it seemed. No-one deserved that.

Mary came in an hour later, subdued and pale. 'Oh, Miss Wilmott, it's awful. That Mr Ransome took ill and died in the night.'

'Oh no.' She sat up, rubbing her eyes. 'Mary, how dreadful. What was it? Food poisoning? Perhaps other people are sick.'

'I don't think so, ma'am. Mrs Fairfax has sent all the

maids round to check though. And we ate all the left-overs in the servants' hall last night and we're all fine. Chef's in a right taking though. They've sent for Doctor Paulson from the village.'

There was no need to act now. Sophie washed and dressed hastily, decided on a sombre grey and lilac muslin morning dress to wear, then went to find her mother. She met her at the door, one hand raised to knock. 'Come in, Mama. Is it not it dreadful? I was just coming to see you.'

'His Grace said Mr Ransome was unwell last night, it must have been this coming on. So sudden. Perhaps it was heart failure or a seizure, though he was a young man and seemed fit enough.'

The guests assembled downstairs, subdued and tending to huddle in small groups, speculating. Sophie, lingering outside Cal's study, overheard the doctor talking to Lord Peter and Cal and realised that Hunt and Flynn must have removed all the evidence of vomiting. The doctor, elderly and over-awed by his surroundings appeared to have taken a rapid look at the body, announced there was no evidence of self-harm or injury and suggested a brain seizure.

She moved away from the study door when she heard movement inside and went back to the drawing room where Lord Peter, in the role of Justice, announced that he was satisfied with the doctor's verdict and would release the body for temporary burial in the parish churchyard pending his family's wishes being known.

'It is too warm to keep him hanging about for days, even in the wine cellar,' he said, with an unfortunate lack of sensitivity and Lady Beauville gave a low moan as she slid to the floor in a faint.

By luncheon, which everyone picked at, spirits had revived enough for there to be universal agreement that the house party would go on. 'It is very sad, but it is not as though he was related to anyone here,' Lady Peter pronounced. 'Naturally, the gentlemen will attend the funeral.'

Cal drew Sophie aside after the meal. 'Will you join us in the library? There is something I want to talk through.'

Hunt and Flynn were already there, with several maps spread out on the big table. Sophie could see that some were estate maps, others were rougher, older plans. 'Is this about the Duke's Spring?' she asked as they made room for her to sit down.

'Yes.' Cal nodded. 'I started to become ill after my father died and the obvious inference was that it was because I was now the Duke and someone wanted to do away with me. No-one had been sick with those symptoms before, certainly not my father who used to drink the spring water regularly. He was superstitious about it.'

'But his spring dried up,' Hunt said.

'Exactly. The local people saw that as an omen of bad fortune, linked to his death, but then, two days later, the new spring appeared. That confirmed all the tales – the spring died with the old Duke and was created again with the new one – you can imagine the sort of thing.'

'And you drank the water and became ill?'

'No, that is why I never made the connection. I avoided drinking the stuff because I had tried it in my father's day from the original spring – secretly of course – and didn't like the taste. Typical spa water. You know the sort of thing, full of iron. Of course, all the old retainers muttered about not keeping up the traditions.'

'But somehow you were given it?'

'Yes. But how, I don't know.' He shrugged. 'Yes, I do, of course. They would add it to things, I am sure, because that was the traditional thing, the right thing. I was a foolish youth, ignoring the old ways that my father had observed so that would have been corrected. I doubt I would notice the taste in chocolate or broth, for example. No-one meant to do any damage, it was just a harmless but important tradition to them.'

'So, the old water was safe, the new spring not?'

'That seems the only explanation because, you see, I took a mouthful of it when you and I were there, Sophie. And that night I was taken ill. I drank it right from the source.'

'So no-one is trying to murder you?' The relief was indescribable.

Cal stared at her, his face bleak. 'Oh, hell. What have I done?'

Chapter Twenty Two - Where The Duke Breaks A Heart

'Nothing. You have done nothing.' What was the matter with Cal?

'Nothing? I have believed either my uncle or my cousin capable of murder. I have shared that slander with four other people. I left this country and my duties and responsibilities for years because of it. And you say I have done *nothing*?'

'You acted to save your life on the information you had. And it *did* save your life. You were getting weaker and weaker. None of your caring relatives recognised what was happening or troubled to investigate. Sooner or later your well-meaning household would have dosed you with enough of that water to kill you. And what about the accidents?' Sophie wanted to shake him. Cal torn by doubt and wracked by guilt was not the man she knew, the man she loved.

'If I eliminate the times when I was sick from the water, or weak and probably clumsy as a result, then what is left is no doubt the same tally of mishaps and injuries that befall any adolescent boy.'

'But the circumstantial evidence pointed to foul play. It might still be, for all we know. Perhaps they *did* know about the water and let nature take its course. *I* don't know – and I like your aunt and uncle and I contemplated marrying your cousin, for heaven's sake.'

'We still have to prove it *is* the spring water,' Hunt pointed out.

'Which means tracing the source.' Cal was focused again, to Sophie's vast relief. 'It must lie on the other side of the ridge in a stream that goes underground there and did so only after my father's death. And, equally, the source of the old spring must be there, blocked up at the same time.' He scrubbed his hand over his face. 'How to prove which water runs where?' He snapped his fingers. 'Bluing from the laundry. Sophie, can you go and ask Mrs Fairfax for all the bluing in the house?'

'And what will I tell her I want it for?'

'An experiment in land drainage,' Cal offered, already bent over the maps again.

Sophie returned with the information that for once the admirable Mrs Fairfax was having trouble concealing her irritation with the queer starts of the Quality and was, even as she spoke, scribbling a frantic order for new supplies before laundry day arrived. She found the men had drawn lines over the older map that showed the hills beyond the old castle and Flynn had a sheet of paper and was making copies of two sections of the land nearest the crest, drawing in waterways in blue ink.

'We need more than one colour as a marker,' Cal muttered.

'The yellow ochre they are using to paint the farm buildings?' Hunt suggested. 'I noticed yesterday they have just started and there are a lot of buildings. The stuff is pretty concentrated.'

'We know it takes two days from source to the spring because of the delay when the old spring died and the new one began.' Cal sat back and studied the sketch plans. 'I will take blue, you take yellow and we'll each dose all the possible swallow-holes in our section, then put a watch on the spring. Once we've got the area narrowed down we can repeat it until there is only one source possible.' He turned to look at Sophie. 'Do you want to come with me?'

'Of course.'

‘I will just go and talk to Isobel for a few minutes. She’ll sense something is wrong, however careful everyone is around her.’

‘I will ask the ladies to include her in their activities today, shall I?’ Sophie suggested. ‘That will give them something to think about other than Jonathan and they are all sensible enough not to start gossiping in front of her. I won’t be long.’

Sophie changed into her riding habit and begged the female guests help with Isobel, explaining that Cal was very much occupied and that she felt she must support him. If they were left with the impression that he was making arrangements for the funeral and contacting Jonathan’s family, then so much the better. Prescott was, he told her, already working on the arrangements.

They rode out, heading in the direction of the old castle, then split a mile from it, Flynn and Hunt cantering northwards, she and Cal taking a winding lane that led from the park boundary up into the hills, following the contour until they had worked their way around to the north-facing slopes.

Almost immediately she noticed the difference. ‘I can smell coal smoke.’

Cal nodded, gesturing to the track they were now following, mired in mud and churned by wagon wheels. ‘Small scattered industries all over the area.’

They dipped down into little dry valleys that Cal marked on his map, occasionally dismounting to check the size of trees growing at their bottom, or to look for water-weathering on the stones. Gradually the sound of industry, of hammer on metal, grew louder and the smells worsened and they climbed another valley that, by Sophie’s calculation rose on one side to the crest of the hill above the castle.

Plumes of black smoke hung above the trees and they passed deep scores in the rocks, some raw and new, others overgrown. ‘Rakes,’ Cal said. ‘They are where seams of minerals come to the surface – silver, although there's not much of that, zinc, lead, some iron. They mine coal over to the east.' As he spoke an empty wagon appeared, coal dust coating its side and base. The driver stared at them but did not stop.

'I hear water,' Sophie said and the sound became louder as they rode on.

'Look.' Cal urged his horse up the bank beside them. 'This is a dam, diverting the flow that way – see, that is where the stream used to go.' He pointed down to where a dry ditch went under the road and vanished. 'That must have run into a swallow-hole over there and would have come out somewhere near the castle.' He dismounted, knelt and dipped his hand in the water, took a cautious sip and spat. 'This tastes as the old spring's water used to, of some mineral or other. But it is pure, there is no smell and it is quite clear.'

He remounted and they rode on, the diverted stream bubbling and chuckling beside them now, and were suddenly in a village. Sophie gasped at the shock of emerging from the greenery of the woodland into mud, dirt and industry. The low cottages huddled around mired lanes and smoke and noise filled the air from the workshops all around.

Children ran out as they approached, most of them, Sophie saw with distress, dressed in rags and barefoot. All of them appeared to have been distracted from some kind of labour, judging by the shouts from the workshops that sent them scurrying back inside.

Cal reined in at the edge of a rough plank bridge. It had been made across the stream where it crossed the largest lane in a sea of mud before emptying into a circular basin, half choked with rocks. More were being dumped in as they watched and some men were agitating them with long poles and brushes.

'That's a buddle,' Cal shouted to her above the din. 'For cleaning ore before it is smelted.'

Men started to come out of the workshops, sweaty, filthy and, to Sophie's eyes, hostile.

'Stay behind me.' Cal nudged his horse into a walk and crossed the bridge. For once Sophie did not feel inclined to dispute his orders. The last thing they needed at the moment was a fight breaking out because Cal took exception to the way the men looked at her.

'You wanting someone?' the biggest man asked.

'Just riding past. That's a good flow of water you've got there. Had to divert the stream, I see.'

'Aye, many years back. And what's it to you?' The man narrowed bloodshot eyes. 'We've got rights for mining all over this hill.'

'I don't doubt it. Good day to you.' Cal let the horse move off at a walk and she trotted up to ride beside him. The hostile gaze of the villagers felt like a physical pressure on her back. The stream emerged from the buddle and ran on, discoloured and sinister now. The horses splashed through liquid running down from some sheds to join the brook and Sophie gagged at the smell.

'Cess pits and a pig sty, I imagine.' Cal urged the horse into a trot until they were clear of the stench and round the corner out of sight of the village. 'If this is our stream, the source of the spring, then it's a wonder I was not dead after one mouthful. Look, it goes off down there.'

He dismounted, tossed the reins to Sophie and pushed his way through the bushes, emerging a few minutes later, hat in hand, with leaves in his hair and a long smear of mud down his sleeve. 'I think that this is it.' He took the packets of bluing from the saddlebag and went into the bushes again. When he came back he wiped his powder-dusted hands on the grass, leaving long blue streaks. 'I do not fancy washing it off in that water.' He looked faintly nauseous.

'I am not surprised.' Sophie found she was shivering with reaction. 'That filth – and I suppose there is stuff in the ore that is poisonous as well.'

'I imagine so. Certainly the fumes from lead are, and I have no idea what else gets washed off. I imagine that it has built up deposits all the way through the underground system over the years and that it is stronger now than it was in the beginning. No wonder it killed Ransome.'

'But not you.'

'I have picked up some pretty exotic things in my travels, been as sick as a dog in a lot of places, so have Flynn and Hunt. I think it toughens the system up. And I only had that one mouthful this time. Ransome was feeling pretty rough, I imagine, and must have downed most of the carafe before he realised how foul it tasted.'

'Now what do we do?'

'Meet the others who should be coming along this track from the opposite direction, go home and sort out a team of watchers for the spring. If it doesn't flow blue in two days, then we've got the wrong stream, but the diversion is too much of a coincidence if that's the case.'

They rode on in silence, Sophie in a muddle of relief, lingering horror over Jonathan's death and growing concern for Cal who seemed lost in some dark daydream, his shoulders rigid, his face grim.

Finally, as they rode through a glade so utterly different from the grim little village that it seemed like another world, she could bear it no longer. 'What is it? Why aren't you relieved?'

'I am,' he said bleakly. 'Relieved and feeling damnably guilty. How the hell can I apologise enough to my uncle and to Ralph without telling them what I believed for so long? And I can't tell them and yet I cannot let go of the feeling that I should confess the whole damnable mess.'

'Of course you must not tell them,' Sophie said crisply. 'You hurt them enough by leaving, you can't salve your own conscience by confessing what you suspected – they would never recover from it. What you thought was understandable, given all the evidence and the fact that you were in no position to investigate further. You can feel regret that you were forced into the position of suspecting them, but wallowing in guilt is self-indulgent. And confessing would make *everyone* unhappy.'

'Ouch. You can hit hard when you want to, Sophie. Have you been talking to Jared?'

'To Hunt? No, why should I? I am not at all sure I like the man, although I believe he is utterly loyal to you.'

'He thinks I am too prone to feeling guilty. I was stupid enough, in my cups, to wallow – as you so painfully put it – over my feelings for Madeleine and got a rollicking from him on the subject of misplaced guilt.'

'What – Cal, what were your feelings for her if they made you feel so guilty?'

'I could not love her. I tried, although I did not know what I was supposed to feel, what she expected of me. But she loved me. I thought at first she had trapped me because she wanted an English gentleman, thought I would take her to London, that I had grand connections and lots of money. And there might have been that at first – her father was certainly mercenary enough. But she managed to fall in love with me.

'You were right, that first night when I overheard you up in the gallery with Sir Toby. Love is an illusion, a snare. It is never equal, never balanced. It leads to jealousies and misery and misunderstanding. Look what we have, Sophie – desire and friendship. That's strong, that will last, a good basis for a marriage.' He dropped his hands and let the horse walk on, then reined back when Sophie didn't follow.

'You do not think love might grow, after marriage?'

'Why would you want it? What does it add? Heartache when it ends, that is all.'

Sophie felt ill again. Out of her own mouth she had condemned this marriage. 'Cal, what was your parents' marriage like? Were they in love?'

'How did you guess?'

Sophie shrugged. 'That was not the norm for aristocratic marriages in those days, even less than it is now.'

'They caused a scandal. She was betrothed to someone else, my father saw her, fell in love with her, fought a duel with the discarded lover who shot himself a week later. It ruined my mother's reputation, almost made my father an outcast, but they seemed oblivious to all that because they had each other. No-one else mattered.'

And not you, from the bitterness in your voice, she guessed, her heart aching for the child on the outside of that intensity.

'When she died he was a broken man.'

And so you promised yourself you would never do anything so foolish as to fall in love. Then you marry a woman who loves you and you see how unhappy that made her... so you add guilt to a mixture of emotions as toxic as that spring water. And I love you.

'I am so sorry,' she managed to say.

Cal shrugged. 'It was tragic for them, a lesson for me. When I heard you that evening at the ball I could hardly believe my good fortune. You are beautiful, intelligent – and we are totally in accord on what makes a good marriage.' He leaned across from the saddle and dropped a kiss on her lips.

He did not appear to find it strange that she was silent as they rode on. Perhaps he assumed she had been shaken by what they had found, or was tired after the horrors of the morning or was happily digesting the good news that he felt himself incapable of love and saw it as a positive handicap to a marriage.

'There they are.' Cal raised a hand in greeting as Hunt and Flynn appeared around a bend in the road.

The others turned back as their route had been the shorter, and Sophie sat and thought while Cal told them about the mining village and the diverted stream and the polluted water.

She came to awareness of her surroundings when they began to discuss plans for the watch on the spring.

'We cannot cover it with the three of us, or even four, with the addition of Prescott. Not for two days and nights without being missed,' Hunt said.

'We will tell Hooper. I would trust him with any secret. He's been the stable master here for years, and he is grandfather to Ben, my tiger.'

They dismounted and when the grooms took the horses away Cal led the way into one of the empty loose boxes in a corner, gesturing for Hooper to follow them.

It took some explaining, working round why Cal had been suspicious of the water in the first place, but the old head groom was nodding intelligently, putting in a question here and there. 'So you think that's what killed Mr Ransome then, Your Grace? I did wonder if there hadn't been some foul play, that he'd brought some danger with him from London. He was not a young man I took to.'

'Foul play?' Flynn said. 'Not directed at Mr Ransome, that's for sure. It has been going on for years. He drank water meant for the Duke…'

Sophie wasn't certain, but she thought Hunt kicked Flynn who flinched, then went red and closed his mouth with a snap.

Outside something banged closed and they all went quiet. 'Looks most likely it was an accident,' Cal said smoothly when there were no more sounds. 'But we need it proved, hence the dye. The water will need watching. Easy enough by day, by night we will need lanterns on it and the watchers will need to stay awake, so best make it short shifts of two men. Who can you trust amongst your staff not to gossip?'

'All of 'em, Your Grace. I'd vouch for the lot of 'em. A bad business this, poisoned water. *You* could have been killed if he hadn't drunk it by mistake. Leave it to me and I'll tell the lads we want to find out where the water goes – they'll understand we can't knowingly let it pop up somewhere else, kill livestock, mayhap, or some stranger taking a drink. And they'll see they can't speak of it in case one of the neighbours thinks it's a good idea to blame every dead sheep on our water.'

'Good man, Hooper. We had best start with a pair up there now, just in case, and keep them changing over every three hours. They will need lanterns…'

Sophie wandered out of the box, too restless to listen to detail. Cal had shown her the stables quickly on their first whirlwind tour and she had promised herself a leisurely stroll around the spacious quadrangle with its big stone water trough in the centre. She had visited less elegantly designed houses before now.

The second stall held a big grey hunter who turned and came to snuffle at her hand when she held it out. 'You *are* handsome,' she told him. He was also rather warm and his saddle was casually dumped on the door of the stall. Her foot tangled with the bridle which must have slid off to the ridged blocks of the floor.

Sophie picked it up, noting the dirty bit. Someone had come in and untacked the horse in haste. She craned to look and saw he had at least got water in his bucket and hay in the net. Perhaps the stable lad had been called away and would be back in a moment.

The sound of men leaving the other loose box drew her back. Hooper went across the yard with his rolling horseman's gait and called a group of grooms to him. Flynn and Hunt headed back to the house and Cal stood looking round. When he saw her his smile transformed his face, chasing away the bleak look that was beginning to haunt her. 'There you are. Lord, Sophie, I think you are the only thing keeping me sane here. All these emotions swirling inside me and then there's you. No emotion, no drama, just clear, frank common sense and friendship.'

She slipped her hand into the crook of his elbow and gave his arm a little squeeze. *I could give you so much emotion you would not know what had hit you,* she thought grimly. *I love you, you wretched man, and you can't see it and I dare not tell you, because what if you are appalled, what if you have to pretend out of pity? What if we have to start lying to each other? I do not think I can do this any more,* she thought.

Chapter Twenty Three - Where The Duke Makes a Confession

I must tell him I want to end the engagement. It is the only honourable thing to do, I cannot keep pretending this is all about desire and friendship and a suitable *marriage for both of us.*

'Cal,' Sophie said when they were inside the house, standing at the foot of the great sweep of staircase. 'What are you going to do? Talk to Lord Peter?' The whole household needed to be warned about the water sooner or later, but she supposed, knowing him, that his conscience would drive him to seek out his uncle at once.

'Now? I do not think I can bear to face him, not yet, not with this… revelation about just how wrong I have been about him all these years. I need time, Sophie, time to do it right. Time to decide whether to tell him what I had suspected. Or not.' He looked down at his hands, still smeared with blue dye, crushed grass and earth. 'I need to wash and change. And think. I will see you at dinner.'

She watched him climb the stairs, aching for him, and turned away. The peace of the rose garden beckoned. Perhaps sitting there in the scented peace would help her clear her mind.

Ten minutes later Sophie got to her feet, squared her shoulders and walked back to the house. She had never lied to Cal and she was not going to start now. She would tell him that she could not marry him and she would tell him why. She would beg him, on his honour, not to lie to her about his own feelings and make him see how impossible it would be for them to marry now. How miserable it would make them both. How she was going to explain to Isobel she wasn't sure, but, hurt as the child might be, it was better than her growing up at the heart of an unhappy marriage.

The climb upstairs seemed mountainous, the corridor to the Duke's wing, endless, like a passageway in a nightmare where, however fast you ran, you never got anywhere. Then the handle to his bedchamber door was under her hand and she opened it without knocking and went in, closed it behind her without taking her eyes from the man in the middle of the room.

Cal, stripped to the waist, stood quite still facing her and she felt dizzy for a moment, remembering the feel of that body under her hands, its weight over her, the heat of his desire. She had to speak now, otherwise she would be in his arms, kissing him, and she would lose her nerve and never do what was right.

He looked grim, as though she had already told him. His eyes darkened as he looked at her, then, when he spoke, his voice was harsh. 'Sophie, leave at once. You know you should not be in here. *Go.*'

That was certainly enough to knock any erotic thoughts from her head. His severity made it easier. 'Cal, I came to tell you that I cannot marry you – ' Then she realised that his attention was not really on her at all, but on something over her shoulder, and she turned, slowly, sick with apprehension.

'Oh, *Ralph.* You startled me…'

Ralph Thorne was white to the lips but his hand holding the long-barrelled pistol was quite steady, pointing squarely at Cal's chest. 'Can't you ever behave conventionally, Sophie?' he demanded, sounding ludicrously like an irritable chaperon.

Strangely, she felt no desire to laugh. 'Ralph, what are you doing in here, with that? Put it down before someone gets hurt.'

'That, I believe, is the intention,' Cal said. 'My cousin is here to protect his father. It seems he overheard something.'

He was wearing riding clothes and she realised what had happened. 'In the stables – that was your grey in the next box, wasn't it? Or were you somewhere in the hall when we came in?'

'Both,' Ralph said tightly. 'I cannot live with this any longer, with the suspicion. I heard you say the water that Ransome drank was poisoned, that it was meant for you. And then in the hall…' His face was ashen.

'Hell.' Cal made as though to scrub his hand over his face, then let it drop when Ralph jerked the pistol. 'I haven't time for this now – Sophie, why can't you marry me?'

She had forgotten all about that. *Incredible how looking at the sinister gleam of a gun barrel is enough to drive the most important things out of one's head.* 'I – '

'Never mind your damned love life. What do you intend to do about Father?' Ralph shifted the pistol and Sophie realised that there were things more mesmerising than a gun barrel – the little black eye in its end, for one.

'You have suspected him of trying to murder me all along, haven't you?' Cal said with the air of a man who has finally had a puzzle solved. From the corner of her eye, when she could drag her fascinated gaze from the pistol, she was aware of Cal shifting his weight in subtle increments. She hoped to Heaven that he was not about to try something heroic, like throwing himself in front of the gun.

'And he suspects you,' he went on. 'I couldn't make out the looks I kept intercepting between you, but that is it, isn't it?'

'Why did you have to come back?' Ralph demanded. 'I thought you were safe out there, away from us.'

'Because it was my duty to come back. Because I am the duke and because I could not live with suspecting two people I loved like a father and a brother of trying to kill me. I needed to become Duke of Calderbrook, I needed to find a wife and I needed, above all, to solve this mystery and get some peace.' He moved away from Sophie slightly and the gun barrel followed him.

Sophie let her own weight shift, opening the gap just a little wider. Ralph was a very good shot, she had heard of him winning wagers at target shooting before now. If they could keep him off-balance, surely Flynn would come soon? 'We thought it might be either of you, or both,' she said.

'But it wasn't,' Cal added, bringing Ralph's head round to him again. 'It was accident, pure and simple. A stream diverted and made foul by industry and a village's waste, a youth made clumsy because he was weakened by the poisoned water and all the accidents that befall adolescent boys. That was all. No villains, Ralph, no blame.'

'You are not thinking, Ralph.' The gun barrel swung round to Sophie again. 'This achieves nothing. You heard Cal, he does not believe it was foul play by anyone. It would break your father's heart if you shoot Cal. You would hang and for nothing. It would kill Lord Peter – '

The door opened and Flynn strode in, half-obscured behind a pile of folded shirts. Ralph started, his hand jerked, even as Cal launched himself sideways, crashing into Sophie, bringing her down to the ground as the gunshot roared in her ears along with Flynn's yell and the impact of their landing.

Someone was sobbing, 'Oh, God, oh, God,' over and over, Flynn was swearing, then there was the sound of knuckles hitting flesh and a thud. Her heart was beating like a hammer and she couldn't see and Cal's weight was pinning her down. His dead weight.

'Cal? Your Grace?' The weight shifted and rolled

off her and there was Flynn, white-faced, blood all down his shirt, blood on his knuckles. 'Miss Wilmott…'

'Never mind me. You are hurt.' She scrambled to her knees. 'The blood.'

'Not mine.' Flynn grabbed one of the shirts and wadded it against Cal's right shoulder. 'Get Hunt. Hell, he's bleeding like a stuck pig.'

Sophie staggered to her feet. Cal was shot. Cal was bleeding because he had dived to take the bullet meant for her. Beyond, Ralph sprawled unconscious, the mark of Flynn's knuckles red on his chin. She wrenched the door open and ran, then forced herself to a sedate walk as she reached the head of the stairs. Renshaw was, thankfully, walking across the hall below.

'Renshaw, do you know where Mr Hunt is?'

'Yes, Miss Wilmott, he has just gone to the study and is speaking with Mr Prescott, I believe.'

'Will you tell them both to go to His Grace's bedchamber *immediately*.' She managed a smile. 'Thank you, Renshaw.'

Back in Cal's room Ralph was sitting up against the wall, his head in his hands and Flynn was arguing with Cal.

'Stay where you are, damn it! Lie still.'

'The bullet went right through, I think.' Cal's voice was strained, but he was coherent. 'I can feel wetness under my back, I think you need to plug both holes.'

Flynn swore again as he grabbed for another shirt.

Sophie knelt beside them. 'Let me press this one against his shoulder, then tip him up to rest against me and you can deal with the back.' It would hurt him. He might be dying. She was not going to cry. She was *not*. There would be time for that later.

'I'll bleed all over you.' The words came out on a gasp as Flynn hauled him up and Sophie put her free arm around him.

'That is a major consideration, of course. I should

have thought of that in advance, but you are also bleeding on the carpet, which is probably more valuable than my gown.'

'Are you… humouring me?'

'Yes,' she admitted. 'Hunt and Prescott will be here in a minute and you can bleed all over them.'

'Good.' His voice trailed away, then strengthened. 'Why won't you marry me, Sophie?'

'I…I can't talk about that now. Flynn is here.'

'He's not listening.'

'No, I'm not,' Flynn muttered.

'Humour… me some more.' Cal's voice was fading again.

Perhaps if she could seize his attention it might keep him conscious. 'Because I love you.' But he was slumped unconscious now.

Flynn made a sound that he bit off, then the door swung open and Hunt and Prescott were there and took Cal out of her arms. Sophie found herself sitting on the floor, covered in blood, confronting Ralph, who was quietly sobbing.

'Stop it,' she snapped. 'Pull yourself together and do something useful.'

'Send for the doctor,' Hunt said from the bedside.

'Accident,' Cal said, his voice slurred. 'Showing me the gun, it went off. Accident.'

'He tried to kill you. You or Miss Wilmott,' Flynn interjected, indignant.

'Accident,' Cal repeated. 'All of you, listen to me. Sophie… go with Ralph, call the doctor, make sure he doesn't say anything stupid. He's in shock.'

'Come on.' She stood up, sized Ralph by the arm and tugged. 'Get up, try and be *some* use.'

Their appearance, Ralph shaking, she blood-covered, galvanised the household. A groom was sent galloping for the doctor, Mrs Fairfax went running for bandages and smelling salts, Renshaw sent footmen to help Hunt and the other men while he fetched the brandy.

Sophie had a sudden awful thought and ran down to the kitchen. 'Where is the water from the Duke's Spring?'

'Here, Miss. Shall I send some up?'

'No!' She poured the contents of the jug down the sink. 'Wash that thoroughly. Scour it. Is there more?'

'Yes, Miss…'

'Pour it all away, do you hear me? It is poisoned, polluted with mine waste. Boil some water from the pump and bring it upstairs.'

Leaving a tumult of questions behind her she ran upstairs to find Lord Peter shaking Ralph by the shoulders by while a group of guests huddled round. 'What has happened? What have you done?'

'Shot… Cal.'

There were shrieks but Sophie saw Lord Peter's face, saw the look of horror. But he was not surprised. *He thought it was Ralph, all this time. And Ralph thought it was him.*

She elbowed her way through to the two Thornes. 'It was an accident. They were looking at a gun, I was there.' She thought Lord Peter might faint. 'Ralph, stop thinking about yourself and look after your father.' She almost shook with the need to point at him, scream that it was all his fault, but that was not what Cal wanted. 'Please, everyone, there is nothing you can do, just go downstairs –'

'Sophie.' Her stepfather was at her side. 'You are covered in blood.'

'I am fine. It is all Cal's blood. Excuse me.'

'Come away, dear, let your mother take you to your room.'

'No. Thank you, Step Papa. I must be with him.' She walked away from them then and no-one followed her.

At his bedchamber door she stood, holding the handle, willing herself to open it. He had been bleeding so. What if Hunt couldn't… *No. Courage.* She put up her chin, opened the door and four heads turned at the sound and Cal… Cal smiled at her.

'The doctor has been sent for. They are boiling water and – oh, there you are Mrs Fairfax, Renshaw. I have told them in the kitchen to throw away all of the water from the Duke's Spring. It is polluted and dangerous, that is what killed Ransome.'

'Mr Ransome? Oh my.' Mrs Fairfax put down the roll of bandages she was carrying and hurried out.

'You have stopped the bleeding?'

Hunt looked up from tying a knot in bandages on Cal's shoulder. 'For the moment. It looks like a fairly clean wound, right through the shoulder. Provided there are no bone chips or blood vessels nicked and weakened, everything should be fine. The doctor will have to probe, of course, to make sure. I've sent for Harknett, not that old fool from the village. Might take longer but he's a better man, I hear.'

'Thank you, Jared. I feel *so* much better now.' Cal's chuckle was faint.

The fencing master grimaced. 'I thought you'd want the truth without the bark on it.'

'But perhaps Miss Wilmott prefers a less unvarnished version?'

'No. I do not.' Sophie found her legs, possibly, would have preferred a less graphic description of what Cal still had to endure. In fact her vision was beginning to narrow alarmingly. She sat down before she fell down. 'You will not let him bleed Cal. He has lost quite enough blood already.'

There were murmurs of agreement then Cal said, 'Out, all of you, I need to talk to Sophie.'

They went without an argument. Perhaps, she thought drearily, they heard the grim note in Cal's voice. She had let him down and now he had to contend with that on top of Ralph's breakdown and a bullet wound.

'Sophie, I am sorry. I have broken our agreement

and you sensed it. You seem to have come to know me very quickly, I should have guessed I couldn't hide it from you.'

'Hide what?'

'How I feel about you.' Cal shifted against the pillows. 'I wish I could touch you, and I am glad I cannot. This would be impossible with you any closer.'

Sophie sank back in her chair. 'Cal, I don't understand. I think you must be feverish.'

'I promised you the marriage you wanted, to the kind of man you were looking for. A marriage without any pretence of love to cloud things, no messy emotions. You'd had all that from Ransome. He told you he loved you, he taught you that you can't trust a man that says that.' When she did not reply he said simply, 'I couldn't help it. I have fallen in love with you, Sophie.'

'But only his afternoon you told me you hadn't loved Madeleine, that you didn't know how to love…'

'No, I did not love her, I did not know *how* to love her. But I do love you. I cannot explain what this is that I feel in any other way. And you've sensed it and that is why you can't marry me. I understand that. I am damned if I know how to persuade you to risk it again. I could say that we are friends, that we are lovers, that I will not impose my feelings on you or pressure you to feel things, say things, that you do not mean, but I am not good at begging, Sophie. I don't think I am very convincing and, even if I were, how can I try and force you into this?'

'Is that all?' she managed to ask, clenching her fingers around the arms of the chair so she did not throw herself into his arms. *He loves me.*

'Yes. Pathetic, isn't it? I would die for you, Sophie.'

'I know, because you almost did, just now. And it is not pathetic, it is brave and honest of you and you trusted me to listen to you and understand. Cal, I am sorry, but…'

Of course she was sorry. Sophie was sweet and kind

and they were friends. Of course she would be sorry he had got them both into this mess. The pain in his shoulder was almost intolerable and yet focussing on enduring it was the only thing that was stopping him gabbling, making an utter, embarrassing fool of himself.

'I am sorry, but I have gone back on our agreement too.'

She was smiling at him and for a moment he could make no sense of her words, what they meant. 'But you… Sophie, are you saying that *you* are in love with *me*?' He was feverish, hallucinating, fantasising what he wanted so badly. 'And that is why you will not marry me?'

'Yes. I didn't think it would be fair to tell you and I could not bear to live with you and *not* tell you. But, if you love me and I love you, then it all becomes perfectly simple.' She stood and came to the bedside, perched carefully beside him so as not to dip the bed. 'If, that is, you can bear to be so utterly unfashionable as to love your wife.'

'Your parents manage it without getting into the mess that mine did.' His fingers found hers and twined into them. 'We will have to be careful and not set a bad example to impressionable young people.'

'There is that,' she agreed, solemnly. 'Cal, does your shoulder hurt very much?'

'It certainly feels as though someone has propelled a lump of lead through a considerable thickness of flesh and blood, yes. It would take a lot of the pain away of you kissed me.'

'The doctor would tell me not to get you over-excited.' She stood up, clearly trying to work out how to kiss a prone man without putting any pressure on his body.

'The doctor is not here.'

'True.' Sophie bent over, put her hands either side of Cal's head on the headboard and bent to kiss him. It was agony on the back, an equal agony not to be able to touch him, but so sweet, so different, to feel his lips under hers and not above. She tasted blood where he must have bitten his lip and eased back, returning when he grumbled in protest.

When the knock on the door came she jumped so much she almost lost her grip and collapsed on top of him. She managed to get herself upright just as Flynn's head appeared round the door. 'Doctor Harknett is here.'

Hunt brought him in, a tall, thin, serious-looking man who inspired confidence with his very lack of bedside manner. 'Yes, well, we will need to have a thorough look.'

Sophie felt the room begin to close in again.

'The young lady will be leaving.' It was not a question.

'She will,' Cal said with a look that was a caress. 'That bloodstained gown is making me feel positively faint.'

Hunt snorted, the doctor raised one eyebrow, Flynn went to open the door into Cal's sitting room for her.

'I will go and change,' Sophie said with dignity, swept out, closed the door with a firm click of the lock and then eased it open half an inch. She sat down in a chair as close to the door as possible and waited. Cal had taken that bullet for her. She could not take his pain away, but she owed it to him to share it.

There was some conversation, a grunt, silence, a gasp that brought the hairs up on the nape of her neck, several words that she was grateful she did not know the meaning of and then the doctor said, quite clearly, 'Brace yourself, Your Grace. Mr Hunt, if you can just hold him –'

Chapter Twenty Four – Where the Duke and Duchess Vanish

The carpet, when she came to herself and sat up, was really quite soft and deep. Sophie climbed shakily back into the chair and listened.

'Rest now, Your Grace. That is quite clean, there is no danger of any more bleeding once it settles down. There will be some fever in the next twenty four hours, but that will be due to blood loss. You know what to look for in the way of infection, I assume? Excellent. I will call again tomorrow. Drink a lot of water, no alcohol.'

Sophie tiptoed back to her bed chamber and tugged the bell pull. Cal was going to be all right. Cal loved her. *Cal loves me.*

Mary came in, closely followed by her mother. They exclaimed at the state of her gown, helped her undress and her mother insisted on wrapping her in a blanket while Mary ran a hot bath.

'You will be in shock. What a dreadful, dreadful thing to happen. Why, dear Cal might have been *killed.*'

'I know. But the doctor sounds very optimistic that he will recover quickly. How is Ralph?'

'Almost prostrate and his father is as bad. Lady Peter is beside herself.'

'Perhaps you could go and tell her that the doctor says the wound is clean, there is small risk of infection and Cal only needs rest to heal. It might calm her.'

'You are very thoughtful, my dear.' Her mother gave her a hug and stood up. 'If it had been me and someone had shot darling Lucas I would find it hard to forgive. I will go and put her mind at rest now.'

Sophie climbed gratefully into the steaming water and lay back, trying to imagine the strain the two men had been under for years, each convinced that the other was plotting to commit murder. There were going to be some hard conversations in the Thorne household.

She sat up suddenly, slopping water in all directions. *Isobel.* Had she heard anything? Had they told her that her father was wounded? 'Mary? Please go and ask Nanny Jenkins to bring Lady Isobel down to me. Make sure she avoids any fuss – I do not want her alarmed.'

Mary ushered them in just as Sophie was tying the sash of her robe. 'Hello, Miss Sophie.' The child looked around with interest. 'I've never been in here before.'

'It is my room. Isobel, come and listen to me.' She sat down and stood the child between her knees, her hands on her shoulders, and looked her in the eye. 'Do you trust me to tell you the truth, Isobel?'

'Yes. We're friends and you are going to marry Papa.'

'There was an accident. Papa was shot in the shoulder. He is going to be perfectly all right, but he is feeling very sore and sorry for himself just now.'

Isobel's eyes widened, then, alarmingly, filled with tears. 'He's dead, like Mama!'

'No. Isobel, he is not. You can come and see him, but you must be quiet and not bounce on the bed because his shoulder hurts a lot.'

'Truly he will be all right?' One fat tear escaped.

'Truly. Shall we go and see if he is awake?'

'All right. How was it an accident?'

'Cousin Ralph shot a pistol and hit Papa by mistake. He is very upset and sorry, so you must not be horrid to him about it because it he didn't mean it. Now, wait here and I will just check.' She looked round the door and saw that the gruesome rug had been rolled up and taken away.

Cal's eyes were closed but he opened them when he heard the door.

'Are you up to having a visitor?'

'Yes. Isobel. Come here, darling.' The look he sent Sophie was full of doubt but she nodded reassurance.

'Miss Sophie says Cousin Ralph shot you by accident and I mustn't shout at him because he's very sorry and I mustn't bounce on the bed because your shoulder hurts and you're not going to die like Mama.'

'All quite true. Come and give me a kiss without any bounces.'

Sophie found her eyes were mysteriously blurred. She sniffed, blinked and held out her hand. 'Come along now, Isobel. We mustn't tire Papa out.'

'What are you going to call Miss Sophie when she is married to me?' Cal enquired, emerging from a vigorous kiss on the nose.

'Mama Sophie, of course. Will you be all better tomorrow, Papa?'

'It might take a day or two before Papa is allowed to get up.' Sophie took her hand and led her towards the door. 'But we will visit and you may come to my room so we can work on the secret,' she whispered. She delivered the child to her nurse with a kiss and went back to Cal.

'How are you?'

'Weak as a kitten. Lord, Sophie, I never thought all this would put you in any danger.'

'Neither did I. We could not have foreseen this. Cal, I saw Lord Peter's face – he has been as suspicious of Ralph as Ralph was of him. Neither wanted you dead but both thought the other did. I have sent a message to Lady Peter that should reassure her that it was an accident, but the poor woman will have her hands full with the pair of them wallowing in a morass of guilt and relief and awkwardness.'

'I had better talk to them.'

'Not until the day after tomorrow at the earliest. The

doctor said you will be feverish tomorrow.'

'Why aren't you at dinner? That is a very fetching dressing gown.' For a man in his condition the look in his eyes was positively lively.

'I have missed dinner. I thought I would have it up here and spoon broth into you in a suitably wifely manner. Unless you would prefer Flynn to do it?'

'No, he looks appalling in muslin and lace and his wifely manner leaves a lot to be desired. Besides, I love you and I don't want to let you out of my sight.'

Flynn produced a table, a laden dinner tray and Chef's best beef broth. He propped Cal up on a pile of pillows and then tactfully took himself off.

'This is thoroughly undignified,' Cal grumbled between spoonsful of broth.

'Look on it as practice for when you are ninety nine and doddering.'

'I don't feel like doddering. I feel like making love to you. It would work if I just lay here and you straddled me and we – '

'Will do no such thing. I am going to eat my dinner, put the tray out, lock the door and come to bed with you. And I will stay on one side of the bed and you will stay just where you are, and if you are so lively that you can even contemplate making love then we can talk instead.'

'Are you going to be a domineering wife, Sophie my darling?'

'Dreadfully,' she said fondly and bent to kiss him.

As predicted, Cal was feverish the next day but to Sophie's alarm the following morning she found him sitting on the edge of the bed, swearing under his breath as Flynn got a shirt arranged over his bandaged arm.

'Go back to bed this moment!'

'Sophie, I am the Duke of Calderbrook. I have a houseful of guests, a pair of relatives who are, doubtless, in a state of mental turmoil and a beautiful fiancée to make love to.'

'*Cal.*' But when she looked round Flynn had removed himself. 'The guests are being perfectly well looked after by Mama and Step Papa who have firmly told Lady Peter to forget everything except her menfolk. If you want to talk to them I will tell them to come up to your sitting room, but if you think you are going to start prowling around this house – '

'Sophie, my love, come here.'

She did, all unawares, and was seized by a strong left hand, pulled down to the bed and very thoroughly kissed.

'Do I appear to be at death's door?' Cal demanded when he finally let her up for air.

'No.' Sophie considered fanning herself and decided it would make him too cocky. 'But if you want to do that again today you will do as I ask and stay in your sitting room.'

His eyes developed the sensual, heavy look that sent shivers down her spine. 'My sweet, I am entirely yours to command. When today, exactly?'

His uncle and cousin went in to see him, looking like aristocrats on their way to the guillotine and emerged an hour later looking shaken but relieved. Lady Peter, who had been on the receiving end of nerve-wracking confessions, wept all over Sophie, which was an alarming experience and Isobel ran her ragged with constant chatter and demands to be taught to create French knots in the two hours they spent together, despite being assured that they would make a very knobbly handkerchief.

'I am exhausted.' Sophie collapsed on the sofa in Cal's sitting room. 'I would like to take to my bed for a week and you *certainly* should.'

He felt as though someone had put him through the mangle in the washhouse, not that he would have admitted it under torture. But the steak that Flynn had smuggled past Sophie's watchful eye was making up for a day on broth and he could, he considered, do almost anything provided he did it flat on his back.

'I can arrange that.' He picked up the folded parchment on the table at his elbow. 'Marriage licence. We do not have a chaplain in the household, but the vicar has been round and we can get married in four days time, here in the chapel. I thought that was long enough to let Chef whip up a feast, Mrs Fairfax polish the place from attics to cellars and the gardeners to decimate the flower beds.'

'Four days? Cal I haven't a thing to wear. And stop looking like that.'

'A man may dream. And do not tell me your mother let you come down here without a trunk full of new gowns.'

'Yes, but… We were not going to get married yet.'

'That was when we were not in love. Now we are.' Which was such an unlikely miracle that he kept thinking he was dreaming. 'Do you really want to wait?'

'No.' When she smiled at him like that he wondered how he stayed in his seat, when all he wanted was to haul her into his arms and kiss her senseless. 'No, I do not. And we have an entire houseful of guests already. All my bridesmaids are here too. Who will be your best man? Hunt, I suppose.'

'No. I talked to him about it this morning. I have asked Ralph.'

'Ralph? But he…' She broke off and he watched her face, enjoying the thinking going on behind those lovely blue eyes. 'You could not send a clearer signal to the world that it was an accident and to the Thornes that you trust them both.'

'Exactly. And Sophie, I want you to sleep in your own bed until then. I find that marrying the woman I love has made a romantic out of me.'

All girls dream of their perfect wedding day. Sophie realised that she had stopped dreaming after she had escaped from Jonathan, that night in London. Now she had no need to dream, because this was reality and the fantasy man had a face. Cal's face.

The chapel was smaller than a church, with no long nave and chancel to traverse, so she could see his expression from the moment that she stepped through the door on Step Papa's arm.

Cal was pale and unsmiling, but Sophie did not make the mistake of believing that he was not happy. She knew him too well now to mistake that look for anything but intense feeling.

Half way between the packed rows of pews she stopped, took hold of her veil and threw it back because she did not want to look at him through a haze of silk gauze. Then he smiled and held out his hand and for all she knew later she ran those last few steps to his side.

The ceremony passed as though they were in a glass bubble of sharply-focused colour and sound and beyond the glass was simply a blur. Other people were there, people she loved – her mother and stepfather, little Isobel, Toby – and she felt their love surrounding her and Cal, but they were not real, not as he was. Not real like her hand in his or his ring on her finger.

When the vicar said, 'You may now kiss the bride,' it all flooded back and she went into Cal's arms amid the scent of roses and the hum of happy voices and the sound of her mother sobbing joyfully into her handkerchief.

'You look beautiful,' Cal said as they went back down the aisle, his hand firm over hers on his arm.

'Mama sent for my wedding dress.' She looked down at the shimmering pale blue silk, the fluttering silver ribbons that she had chosen because they matched Cal's eyes, the bouquet of Love-in-the Mist, the flowers Cal said matched hers.

'That is exquisite, of course. But you would have

been beautiful in a sheet, walking towards me, your veil back, your eyes telling me how much you loved me.'

The wedding breakfast lasted all afternoon until finally all the usual toasts had been exhausted.

Cal stood up. 'Before my bride and I depart on our wedding trip, I wanted to say a few words,' he began. Sophie shut her mouth with a snap and tried to look as though she knew what he was talking about. Wedding trip? What wedding trip? She thought there would be dancing tonight and a buffet and eventually they would be able to escape up to their suite. Which would all have been lovely, although she had wanted so much to be alone with him now, immediately.

'Toasts have been drunk and good wishes given, but I want to end with thanks to some people without whom I would not be standing here today with my lovely Duchess at my side. In the years before my majority my aunt and uncle and my cousin Ralph were the parents I had lost and the brother I never had. They worked selflessly for the good of my estate without thought for themselves and I owe them a debt I cannot repay.'

Sophie looked across the long table to where Lord Peter was unashamedly mopping his eyes, his wife had her face buried in her napkin and Ralph was white with emotion.

'The Thornes!' Cal raised his glass and the toast echoed around the room. 'And then there are Jared Hunt and Michael Flynn and George Prescott who stood at my back throughout my sometimes perilous voyage of self-discovery around the globe. I give you, Good friends!'

Sophie found that she was in tears by this point. Cal sat down and handed her a spotless pocket handkerchief. 'What wedding trip?' she whispered under cover of drying her eyes.

'Trust me.'

The guests followed them down the steps to the

waiting carriage, another behind it loaded with trunks.

'Don't stay away for seven years this time,' Lord Peter said, shaking Cal's hand before he bent to kiss her cheek. Cal scooped up Isobel, kissed her and handed her to his uncle to hold, a gesture of total trust.

Sophie waved until the bend in the driveway took the house out of sight. 'Cal, where are we going? I haven't made any preparations – who packed all those trunks?'

'Wait and see,' he said. 'And let me kiss you in the meantime, Your Grace.'

She was somewhat rumpled and her bonnet was off when the carriage came to a halt. Time flew when she was in Cal's arms, but not, surely, this fast? And how had Flynn got here to be letting down the steps and helping her out? And… surely this was the back of Calderbrook House?

'Quickly.' Cal took her arm and hurried her into a small door she had never noticed before. They went up a bare little service stairway and halted on the threshold of another door where Cal, ignoring his wounded shoulder, swept her into his arms and carried her thorough.

'Cal, this is your bedchamber,' Sophie said as he set her on her feet.

'I know.' His grin was infectious, wicked and triumphant. 'The outer door to this wing is locked, no-one but Flynn and Chef know we are here. Flynn will bring us food and then vanish again. I thought we ought to be able to maintain the deception for at least four days while the carriage and the luggage coach full of empty trunks go off to one of the distant farms on the estate. If you pine for fresh air the stairs out there go right up to the leads. What do you think?'

'I think that you are a genius,' she said and meant it.

'I believe that, having carried my bride over the threshold, the next part of the matrimonial tradition is that I take her to bed. Does that please Your Grace?'

'It does.' She had missed him so much, even though it had only been a few days. Sophie restrained her desire to rip off her clothes and then his clothes and let Cal set the pace, undressing her slowly, as if she was a fragile gift-wrapped present, his fingers and lips caressing each inch of skin as he uncovered it.

When all she had on were her stockings and garters and pearls she turned to him, stripping away his elegant wedding clothes with as much tender care, easing away his coat and shirt from his tightly-strapped wounded shoulder. He was healing well, motivated he had told her, by the desire to make love to her day and night. Now he was naked his aroused body was clearly ready to oblige.

'There are so many things I want to do, so many ways I want to make love to you,' Cal said as he lifted her onto the bed and followed her down. 'But this first time as man and wife I simply want to do this.' He slid into her in one smooth stroke and then paused, looking down at her. 'I want to make love to you very slowly, watching you, convincing myself that this is real, that you are truly mine.'

It was exquisite and slow and they moved together, wordless, looking into each other's eyes, saying all they needed to with their bodies while the cool air bathed them in the scent of mown grass and the sound of evening birdsong and, distantly, the music from where the people they loved were celebrating their marriage.

'Come with me, Sophie,' Cal whispered when the tension had built to the point of exquisite torture. 'Come with me, my love, my darling, my heart.'

And she did as they flew free, came home, became one. Converts to love at last.

THE END

About the Author

Louise Allen lives on the North Norfolk coast close to the 18th century seaside town of Cromer. She is a passionate collector of late Georgian and Regency ephemera and prints and is the author of over fifty historical romances and non-fiction works, mainly set in the Georgian and Regency period. She also blogs about Georgian life at http://janeaustenslondon.com/

Full details of all her books, including extracts and buy-links, can be found at www.louiseallenregency.com

Danger & Desire - Coming Next

The Swordmaster's Mistress

Who was he? Jared Hunt has been living a lie since he was seventeen years old, making his way as a teacher of swordsmanship and the friend and bodyguard of the Duke of Calderbrook. But Calderbrook's life is no longer in danger and Jared's sword is for hire again.

An elderly husband hires him to protect his young and beautiful wife against an unknown enemy, but it not the wife who is in immediate danger and Jared finds himself defending a widow who threatens his heart and the secrets he has kept for so long, even as he fights to unmask the enemy who threatens her.

66871046R00161

Made in the USA
Charleston, SC
30 January 2017